Matthew Jones: The Boy Who Changed Things

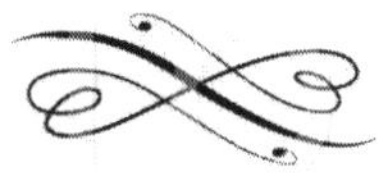

Kelly Lewis

Acknowledgements

Those of you who know me will know that I like nothing more than a challenge. After running the marathon, learning how to pole dance, completing Tough Mudder, a Spartan run and a duathlon *and* solving the Rubik's Cube, I decided I would write a book, for no reason other than it seemed like a good idea at the time. I never imagined, that nearly five years later, I would actually be putting it *out there* for people (other than my family and friends) to read.

And I have lots of people to thank for helping me along the way. Firstly, my husband, Barry, for putting up with hours of one-sided conversations, when I was so involved in my story that I sometimes forgot he was there.

To my children, Millie and Alfie, who read and listened to Matthew's adventures as I wrote them.

To Mum and Dad, for proofreading and spellchecking.

To Sarah Smith and Steve Hollands for all their constructive criticism.

And To Tara Panesar, a student at the school in which I work, for an amazing front cover. I couldn't have asked for more from a professional artist.

So, what now? Well, I'm half way through writing Matthew's second adventure: Some Things Never Change, and have planned the third and final story which currently remains nameless. Hopefully, if all goes to plan, I'll be ready to do this again sometime next year. We'll just have to wait and see…

1

Sometimes things change so slowly that you don't notice them: like your hair growing, your parents getting older, or yourself getting taller. It's not until you get your hair cut, or look at an old photograph, or mark off your height on a wall chart each birthday that you notice a difference. That's how it was in 2128. Things changed so slowly that no one really worried — even though they knew what was coming.

Tick . . . tick . . . tick . . . The second hand hammered out its message: Time's passing when you should be asleep. Tick . . . tick . . . tick . . . He lay on the sweat soaked sheets, his heavy eyelids twitching in the sunlight that streamed through the crack in the curtains and onto his face. Tick . . . tick . . . tick . . . Squinting through one eye, he glanced at the clock. *It can't be time to get up already*. The alarm rang out to prove him wrong. This annoyed him nearly as much as his brother's persistent snoring. He silenced the clock with a single slap and then gazed up at the broken ceiling fan. The heat in the room magnified the smell of sweat and socks that hung in the air.

Outside, the rain had stopped some time during the night, but thunder still rumbled in the distance. It was quarter to seven and already thirty-five degrees outside, despite being only the second week in January. If he didn't get up soon, he'd miss the bus. Matthew lay still for a few precious seconds longer, listening to the muffled noise that came from under Steve's duvet. Then, against his better judgement, he kicked back the sheets, swung his legs over the side of the bed and forced himself up.

As he pushed open the bathroom door, Matthew came face to face with his reflection in the cabinet mirror. His dark, shaggy fringe covered his eyes and the rest of his hair sprouted at wild angles, refusing to be tamed by the broken plastic comb — Matthew's mother used to cut his hair herself, but recently she hadn't been around much — He turned on the tap and let it run cold before splashing his tanned face.

Matthew's stomach rumbled, echoing the thunder. He hadn't eaten since yesterday's school dinner, which hadn't been nearly enough to nourish a growing twelve year old. He trudged down the stairs, wearing only his thin cotton pyjama shorts and a vest that was two sizes too small. Flicking on the light switch, Matthew stepped into the kitchen. A pile of old newspapers covered the table, and the work top groaned under the weight of the peelings, packagings and dirty crockery. He found the bread bin, but only the crusts remained. He hated the crusts, so he reached for a box of cereal from the cupboard above his head and poured a heaped bowlful. A milk carton stood empty next to a sink, overflowing with dirty dishes, which included his mother's empty breakfast things — So she'd been the one to polish off the last of the bread and the milk — Typical.

Matthew sat by the window and looked out across the street as he ate. The postman whistled merrily to himself as he kicked off his bike stand and jumped into the saddle of his shiny Royal Mail bicycle, which he then free-wheeled to the end of the street. Matthew swallowed the last of the dry cornflakes and watched as the first few students from school drifted by.

A calendar pinned to a cork board caught Matthew's eye. January's picture of snowdrops under a barren tree reminded him of what winter used to be like — should be like.

Eighteen months had passed since the biggest news story of his lifetime broke on TV.

The end of the world as they knew it.

The end of life on Earth edged nearer and, as a result of the most recent war in the Eastern Territories, the changes in climate began to spiral out of control.

Initially people had panicked. Some came up with crazy plans on how to survive, though many refused to believe a problem existed. Everyone had been warned to be ready, but for now all they could do was wait. As the weeks turned into months, the changes crept up on them until everyone believed. The time *was* coming, and people rallied in a way that only ever happens in times of tragedy. Funny how disaster can bring people together in a way that no happy event can, but incredibly, life plodded on as usual.

Matthew wondered, as he did most mornings, if it would happen today.

Ten minutes later, dressed in the bottle green shirt and itchy shorts that were compulsory at Newdale High School, he slammed the front door, hoping it would annoy Steve. Steve hadn't been to school since an incident involving fireworks and the school guinea pig last Wednesday. Mr Robertson, the head teacher, said it had been the final straw. Matthew didn't see how letting him lie in bed till lunchtime was a suitable punishment for a fifteen year old. Surely extra homework, or even manual labour, would be more of a deterrent. Still, head teachers were funny things.

The bus drove past the end of the road and Matthew knew that he could just make it if he ran, but he decided *not* to run. What was the point?

The thirty minute walk gave him time to think. He dragged his second hand school shoes against the sticky tar that used to be pavement. Every day the temperature rose. Soon it would be unbearable. Why were they still being made to go to school? It was only a matter of time until the government made a decision. His class had been through the drill a hundred times already. Every day, at the beginning of assembly, they heard the same speech. Matthew checked his watch as he neared the school. Mr Harper would probably be droning on about it by now. Matthew knew it by heart. He could almost hear his teacher's voice:

On the day of the evacuation you will be given a time and a place to meet. You must then go straight home and await your turn. Make sure you arrive at the meeting point in good time. There, you will receive a pack and further instructions. Move quickly and calmly. These are difficult times and it is important we pull together. Follow all directions to the letter. Everyone needs to stick to the plan if it is to work, so please, trust that we have your best interests at heart. We will survive this.

What plan? Matthew wondered as he kicked a stone across the road and watched it disappear into the grass on the other side. He turned the corner and a three storey building loomed up ominously before him. Ivy covered most of the red brick, but it had recently been hacked away from around the main entrance so that the sign above the door could clearly be seen. It read: Newdale High School.

He'd be in trouble for being this late, but he didn't care. A bee lazily crawled across the pavement before him. It seemed that even the insects couldn't be bothered. He sighed, straightened his tie and strolled up to the main entrance of the school.

Mrs Webber, the receptionist, sat at her desk inside a small room at the front of the school. She wore a bright yellow, paisley blouse and an equally sickly smile. Matthew hovered in the doorway. A cheap, plastic clock on the wall behind the receptionist told him he was too late to pretend he'd been in assembly, even if he could get around Mrs Webber. He sighed and stepped forward, deciding he may as well come clean. As luck would have it, the phone rang before Mrs Webber noticed him, distracting her long enough to allow Matthew to sneak past unseen.

He mooched down the long, drab corridor that led towards his classroom. Inside, his class would be well into their production lesson by now. Matthew approached a steel grey door and peered through the window. He could see rows of children working hard, heads down, answering questions from a worksheet. Gently, Matthew pushed the door open and stepped inside. A few students looked up briefly at the sound of the door closing, their zombified faces glistening in the heat, but most continued with their work.

Mr Harper, who sat hunched over his desk, looked at his watch. He was a tall, wisp of a man with thick, bushy eyebrows and perfectly combed hair that was the same colour grey as most of the school. He pointed towards Matthew's usual seat.

'See me at the end, Jones,' he said quietly. Matthew noticed the teacher continued to stare at him long after he'd reached his seat and wasn't fooled by the gentle tone with which he spoke. He turned over his paper and tried to focus on question one.

Draw a diagram to show how you would build an electrical generator using the following materials...

Matthew tried to think back to the lesson weeks ago when his class had created a ridiculous looking machine using an old bicycle wheel, some strong magnets and a car battery, but for the life of him he couldn't remember how the components were joined together. He made a mental note to look it up when he got home, then spent the next forty five minutes drawing, rubbing out and guessing answers.

At ten thirty, a bell shattered the silence. Matthew put down his pen, relieved that he had managed to answer most of the questions.

Rowland Neilson, who sat next to Matthew, turned around in his seat to face the smaller boy. Rowland was a spoilt brat from a well-to-do family that lived on the other side of town. His light brown hair had been bleached by the sun and, like everyone else in the class, his beautifully bronzed skin was damp with sweat. It was unlikely that Rowland had ever missed a meal in his life. His uniform, whilst brand new, looked uncomfortably stretched across his chubby frame and he wore a ridiculous homemade earring, a symbol of the gang to which he belonged.

Rowland looked at Matthew with menacing eyes and shook his head slowly.

'You're dead, Matilda,' he said. Then he drew his forefinger slowly across his own neck.

Matthew ignored his taunts. He'd learned long ago that it was best not to react when the other boys called him Matilda and made silly threats. He bundled his books into his bag and followed his classmates towards the door. He almost made it.

'I thought I told you to see me at the end.' Mr Harper moved to block the doorway, separating only Matthew and Rowland, who still lingered by his desk, from the rest of the class.

'Sorry,' Matthew mumbled, 'I forgot.'

'And you boy,' Mr Harper said, turning towards Rowland, 'Hurry up or you'll be late for your next class.'

'Of course, Sir,' Rowland hurried forward towards Mr Harper, 'only, there's something I wanted to talk to you about.'

'I'm rather busy at the moment, Neilson; come and see me at break.'

'It's important. I have to tell you before you mark the test. It's Matthew. I'm not certain, but I think he cheated.'

Matthew waited quietly by the door to be dismissed. Mr Harper liked to drag out the wait, make the kids sweat a bit before finding out their punishment. The best way to get through it, Matthew decided, was to zone out during the 'rant' and say *Sorry sir, it won't happen again* at the end. It came as a complete surprise when he realised Rowland was accusing him of cheating.

'Sir . . . I never—' Matthew tried to protest, but Rowland hadn't finished yet.

'I've noticed,' the bully continued, 'he's been struggling to keep up. I didn't want to say anything sir, I know it's not really his fault. It's been hard since his dad ran out on him, but I was worried that when you marked the books, you might notice and think I'd—'

'As interesting as this little story is, Neilson, I have better things to do. Give me your book! You too, Jones!'

Matthew dug his book out of his bag and handed it to Mr Harper, who snatched both boys' books. His eyes scanned the columns of answers in each before snapping them shut.

'Thank you Neilson, you can go.'

Rowland scuttled off smirking. Matthew stood silently, looking at his feet.

'Cheating, Jones, is something I won't tolerate in my classroom.'

'But, I didn't—'

'Revision, Jones, that's what it's all about. How well you do in your end of topic test depends on how much effort you put into your revision.'

Matthew hadn't even realised it had been a test, not that it made any difference, he hadn't cheated.

'Rowland must have copied my work sir,' he said, clenching his fists.

Mr Harper refused to consider the possibility. He seemed to grow an extra six inches. His eyebrows lowered until they met in the middle and he growled under his breath.

'How dare you?' he hissed. 'As if cheating isn't enough. Blaming Rowland for your inadequacies, that's the lowest of the low.'

As he spoke, Mr Harper picked up Matthew's book, and pulled at the pages on which Matthew had been writing, ripping them out slowly and deliberately.

'It will be noted, in your end of term report, that you have failed unit three, therefore you have failed the whole year and will have to re-sit Basic Production Skills next year.' He scrunched Matthew's work into a ball then held it at arm's length and dropped it into the bin by his desk. 'If we're still here next year,' he added under his breath.

Mr Harper paced thoughtfully. 'Then, there's the small matter of your punishment for cheating,' he continued eventually. 'You will spend your lunch hour picking up litter from the field. After lunch, you will join the girls who, for their production assignment, will be sewing pillow cases. Perhaps that will suit you better.' He tapped his right temple twice, 'Less taxing on the brain!'

'Yes, Sir. Thank you, Sir. I won't do it again.'

***

Three lessons and fifty minutes of litter picking later, Matthew sat under a large oak tree in the playground to eat his lunch. The actual sewing wouldn't be too bad, he thought. It was the humiliation of having to work with the girls in front of the rest of the class that worried him. Rowland would be impossible when he found out. He'd already got half the class calling him Matilda.

Matthew let his eyes wander across the playground to where dozens of children sat, or lay, under the hedge which lined the yard. A few boys took turns to kick a ball at a goal painted onto the back of a storage shed, but most relaxed in the shade of the building.

The cheese sandwich was stale and difficult to chew, so Matthew took a swig from his almost empty water bottle. He lifted his chin to drain the last few drops and noticed a girl from the year above him looking in his direction. She smiled shyly and then looked away, as if she were afraid that someone would notice. The girl was alone. Behind her, a group of three older girls made a show of turning their backs on her as she passed them, but she didn't seem to notice. Curiosity made him want to find out more about the girl and for a moment he considered following her; maybe because it was so unusual for someone to notice him, and this girl had actually smiled at him; maybe because he'd spent every lunch time for as long as he could remember alone and the thought of talking to her brought a brief smile to his lips; maybe he sensed something interesting about the girl. Either way, although he wanted to, he wouldn't follow her.

He couldn't. Of course he couldn't. How would he start the conversation?

Hi, I'm Matthew . . . you looked at me a minute ago. Do you fancy having lunch with me tomorrow?

Not exactly Mr Smooth. Matthew scolded himself for getting carried away as he watched her slowly disappear from view. He wondered what he'd done to deserve this loneliness. Why did everyone hate him so much? Why did his mother ignore him? What made his father leave when he was still so young? How did someone as cruel as Rowland become so popular? He put his lunch things into his bag and leaned back onto the rough bark of the tree.

That's when the bell rang, the bell that signalled the beginning of the end.

2

The bell rang continuously for the next fifteen minutes while the whole school assembled in front of the main building.

Mr Robertson hobbled the short distance from his office and, with a little help, climbed onto a small wooden platform, in front of a hastily assembled microphone.

'Settle down please.' He tapped the wooden podium, 'Can I have your attention?'

The boisterous chatter became hushed murmurings and eventually a deathly silence descended.

The headmaster lowered the microphone then continued, 'The day we have all been preparing for has finally arrived. I received a message only an hour ago from the governor himself, and I'm very sorry to have to tell you that our time here on Earth is up. We all hoped for better news, but alas, last minute miracles only happen in films. It has been an honour and a privilege to lead such a wonderful school. I wish you all well and hope to see some of you again under happier circumstances.' His voice wavered and his hand trembled on the microphone, causing a sudden high pitched whistle.

Numerous conversations erupted simultaneously. Mr Robertson raised his hand to regain silence.

'There is only one thing left to do before we say our goodbyes,' he continued. 'It is my duty now to divide you into three groups. This will be done randomly but fairly. Each of you in turn will approach the box which, in a moment, will be placed on the table to my left.

As the headmaster spoke, the school caretaker carried a large black box out onto the playground. The front rows of students shuffled back to allow its passage past the stage. However, the narrow pathway still proved difficult to navigate under the weight of the box, which caused the already struggling man to swerve suddenly towards a solid looking oak table. Two boys in the front row stepped forwards to help when the old man lost his balance. They steadied the box and helped heave it into position.

'You will each, in turn,' continued the headmaster, 'place your hand into the box and draw out a token: red, blue or green. It has been decided that the safest and quickest way to evacuate will be to do so in three stages. Those who receive a green token will proceed with the drill immediately and go to the nearest meeting point, which for us will be Newdale Church, by 2pm. Those who draw blue will go to the same meeting point, but not until 6pm. Those who receive a red token will have to wait a little longer. A time will be arranged once the greens and blues have been evacuated. This could take some time so please be patient. But first, of course, you are all to go straight home. Make sure all your family are there and check that they all know, not only where they are going, but when. Anyone who's been missed out, for whatever reason, will automatically join the third group, so there's no need to panic! There will be a reminder broadcast on all radio channels throughout the afternoon in case you forget anything. You alone are responsible for getting to your meeting point on time. Once there, you will be given instructions and directed to the appropriate departure point. You will only be allowed to enter a departure area within the allotted time given for the colour of your token. If it is not your turn to evacuate, you must stay at home. Failure to follow this rule will result in you being left behind. Permanently!'

The headmaster stepped down from the microphone and watched as one by one the children filed past the box. Each in turn reached in and pulled out a token. The only sound came from hundreds of shuffling feet. Matthew strained to see what was happening at the front. A tall boy with curly hair stepped up and drew . . . a red token. Another boy, shorter, with red hair and freckles received . . . a red token. Then a girl jumped up daintily and pulled out . . . a red token. Another boy . . . red. And another . . . red. A pretty girl with a long pony tail . . . red. By the time his turn came, it was clear that there were more red tokens than green or blue. A *lot* more red tokens.

Matthew approached the table cautiously. He slipped his hand slowly into the slit at the top of the box and reached down until he felt the cold tokens beneath his fingers. The headmaster smiled encouragingly as he dragged his hand through the metal pieces and let his fingers close on just one. Butterflies fluttered in his stomach. He withdrew his hand and gasped in surprise when he realised the shiny, circular token he held was green.

Before he had time to think, a group of teachers ushered him towards the swirling crowd and in seconds the jostling rabble swallowed him. He looked back and just made out the girl from the playground, rolling one of her long braids backwards and forwards between her fingers. He watched her step up to the box and pull out, like so many before her, a red token. It worried him, though he didn't know why. He didn't even know the girl and he had no idea what the red token meant for her. It troubled him, though. The reds were the largest group and yet they hadn't been given a meeting time. *Why?* They've been planning for ages and everything else has been organised so well. Now, with his token in his hand, Matthew ran home without stopping.

A musty smell filled his nostrils as Matthew entered the kitchen. The damp patch in the corner grew bigger every day. Last week, Matthew noticed, it had looked like the head of a werewolf. Now, the patch had grown to resemble a three wheeled vehicle of some kind. At least, he thought to himself, they wouldn't need to pay the plumber any more.

His mother sat at the table, which surprised him. She didn't usually make an appearance until long after dark — and these days it didn't get dark until late. Her hand gripped the tea cup tightly, threatening to break the fragile china. In the opposite chair sat Steve, his head resting on the table. Neither acknowledged Matthew's presence. The chair scraped across the lino as Matthew's mother got up. Her grubby pink slippers shuffled to the window, where she stood with her back to the room. A long, floral dress hung from her slim figure, and greasy brown hair fell limply to her shoulders, hiding her face from the boys.

Matthew felt uneasy. Not sure what to say, he sat quietly next to his brother and, for the first time since leaving the school yard, relaxed his grip on the token, allowing it to slip between his fingers.

The token clattered to the table, startling Mrs Jones. She turned, revealing her pale, drawn, expressionless face. Her eyes fixed on the token and her lips moved, though no sound came out. She leapt forward and almost spilled her tea as she darted across the room and seized the green disc.

'Oh my god! Oh my god!' She repeated the words over and over, barely pausing for breath. Then she sat in an old armchair and closed her eyes. 'We're saved!'

'Everyone's going to be saved Mum. They've made plans. This just means I'm in the first lot.'

'Don't be such a fool Matthew!'

'That's what Mr Robertson said. It's easier if we go in groups. What did they say at the shop?'

'And what about me?' Steve lifted his head from the table and glared at his mother. 'I haven't got a token at all. At least you have this red one.' He turned a token over in his hand. 'What am I supposed to do?'

'This,' Mrs Jones plucked the red token from Steve's hand and held it between thumb and finger, 'is worthless. Its only purpose is to keep us quiet. I heard Mr Jenkins in the post office say, that he'd overheard Councillor Geoffrey say, that if he hadn't already got places booked for his family, then he'd be praying every minute of every day for his daughter to bring home a green or blue token. He said it's only the first two groups that stand any chance at all. And as for not having a token Steve, I shouldn't worry about that any more. They're bound to keep families together and we,' She lifted the green token into the air like a trophy and grinned. 'have this!'

'But Mr Robertson said everyone—'

'And what's he supposed to say? Sorry, we can only save a few. There'd be riots. Do try to use your common sense Matthew. Think . . . how many people at that school of yours got a green token eh? Because at Jasper's there was one green, and one blue one. Guess how many reds. Go on . . . guess.'

Matthew shrugged his shoulders.'

'Forty-seven,' Mrs Jones threw the red token across the room, where it bounced off the toaster and landed on a pile of dirty dishes. 'Forty-seven red tokens to every one green and blue. What does that tell you?'

'I don't know. Surely there's been enough time to sort something out. We've known for . . .' But before he could finish the sentence, the truth hit him, and like a blow to the stomach, it knocked the wind right out of him.

There were a lot more reds.

They had a plan alright, but Matthew doubted there would be three stages of evacuation.

'You'll have to hurry.' His mother's shrill voice cut into his thoughts. 'You need to get to the meeting point outside the church and pick up your pack. It's about time this family had a bit of luck. Go on then! What are you waiting for?'

Matthew barely had enough time to pick up his token before she shoved him out of the front door.

'I wish I could come with you. We'll wait here until you get back. I'll see you soon, honey. Hurry, Matthew!'

Matthew ran down the front path in a daze. That was the most his mother had spoken to him in months and he didn't remember her ever calling him honey. He reached the church, still not understanding, out of breath, and surprised to see so many people there.

The church stood on the outskirts of the town. From the front, it had a certain charm. Clematis covered the porch and wild flowers grew in the hedgerow. In fact, the whole scene wouldn't have been out of place on a picture postcard. From the rear, however, it was a different story. The corner of the building had been damaged by a bomb during the Great British War and had never been repaired. The glass from the largest window had been replaced, but not with its original coloured design. It was very much a building of two halves, much like Newdale itself.

***

Newdale was a small town that used to be in Wales, before all the fighting and when Wales still existed, of course. The town had had several names over the last century but, considering its history of hostility and unrest, it remained much the same. It had become Newdale in 2113, fifteen years ago, and things had gradually settled down since then. Buildings were patched up and people's lives put back together.

Matthew had been to Newdale church only a handful of times before. The last time was about three years ago for the church fete. He remembered it well because it had been his mother's birthday — The first birthday in the family since his father had left — and he'd won a box of chocolates. Excited at the thought of surprising her with them, he'd run all the way home, stopping only at the shop to buy her a card to go with them. By the time he reached the house, he was so pleased with himself that he burst into the kitchen unaware that his mother was on the phone. She glared at him as he stood there smiling, chocolates in hand. Then she snatched them, pushed him out of the room and slammed the door. That was a long time ago now. They didn't celebrate birthdays any more.

***

The churchyard swarmed with life. Father Thomas stood outside the church, greeting people as they arrived. A group of residents from the opposite block of flats gathered outside the gate, chatting noisily and several pockets of children wearing different coloured uniforms huddled in their groups, waiting for instructions. Matthew followed the gravel path and watched Father Thomas conversing with four policemen and a handful of locals. In the furthest corner, surrounded by crumbling headstones, he counted eleven children wearing itchy green, all aged between eleven and sixteen. They were gathered before a table covered in silver rucksacks. Behind the table, Mr Harper twitched nervously, his attention fixed firmly on two armed guards in full riot gear, who hovered in the background.

Matthew quickly joined the other children, trying to avoid his teacher's gaze. He listened to the others whispering and tried to work out what was going on.

'There were twenty green tokens and twenty blue tokens in the box,' said one short blond girl to anyone who'd listen.

'What do you think will happen to the ones who got a red?' another girl asked her. 'They haven't been given a time.'

Matthew never heard the answer. He weaved his way to a space on the far side of the group.

***

Mr Harper stared at Matthew and shook his head disapprovingly. He wondered why a lazy, stupid, good for nothing boy like Jones had been picked out rather than his own beautiful, sweet, Jessie — his only child. He'd even tried to fix the lottery to ensure her safety but Mr Robertson took his job seriously and never let the tokens out of his sight, nor left his office unlocked in the weeks leading up to the inevitable. His heart had sunk the instant he saw the red token in her hand and he knew that, short of a miracle, nothing could be done to change her fate.

One by one the other chosen children joined the group, tokens in hands, until there were nineteen of them gathered around the rucksack table. They sat on the grass between the graves whispering and peering around expectantly. The final boy arrived, carrying a small leather bag in one hand and a green token in the other.

'Rowland, you're late!' Mr Harper snapped before turning to face the others. He scanned the small group, pausing momentarily to glare at Matthew.

'Quiet now! Listen up because I'm only going to say this once.'

3

A gentle breeze pushed away the last of the clouds, leaving the churchyard bathed in sunlight. Matthew's shirt felt damp, but his breathing had returned to normal after the mile long run from his home. He leaned back, resting on the edge of a gravestone and stretched his legs out in front of him. The shadow cast from a lofty yew tree stretched across the lawn providing a little protection from the intense heat of the day.

Mr Harper called for silence, and then removed a large sheet of paper from an envelope.

'As you all know,' he paused to scan the document in his hand, 'our homes here on Earth have been under threat for some time now. Every effort has been made to reverse the side effects from the war on the Eastern Territories, but it seems that the temperature will continue to rise and we may have only as little as three months before it will be impossible to survive here.'

There were gasps and shocked looks between the children. One of the smaller girls began to cry. Mr Harper silenced her with an unsympathetic glare.

'You chosen few have nothing to fear. Arrangements have been made for a number of western citizens to be relocated. We are fortunate to live in an area, not only where the topography lends itself naturally to the radical evacuation planned for us, but also very near to the United Kingdom Space Agency building where all this has been put together. Tomorrow, people will arrive from all over the country to be a part of this historical moment. We, in comparison, only have a short walk to reach our destination. You all knew there were plans being made. You all knew this day would come. People of importance have already been moved to a place of safety. The prince, the government, scientists, doctors, mathematicians, producers and many other skilled workers will be travelling with us. The problem is we have limited space so we decided that the lottery, in which you all took part, would be held to select twenty children from each high school in the country. We need young people. Young people are the future but, we couldn't take all of you. Each of you is privileged, remember that. You will survive this.'

Rowland pushed his way to the front. 'Where are we going sir?'

Mr Harper pulled up the sleeve of his suit jacket to check the time.

'Everything you need to know is written on one of these.' He picked up a pile of pocket sized green cards from a table and held them high above his head. 'Time, place and directions. When we meet tomorrow you'll be taken somewhere safe. I can't say any more; you never know who's listening in. We wouldn't want everyone turning up tomorrow, could get chaotic, so read it when you get home.

'Each of you may choose one other person to take with you,' he continued as he handed out the cards. 'It could be a parent, sibling or friend. Or whoever offers you the most.' he added cynically and under his breath. 'Some of you may have parents that have already been selected. This will make your task easier. You can take whoever you want, but choose carefully and remember . . . few people are lucky enough to be in your position.' He closed his eyes and exhaled sharply. A pained expression crossed his face for a second. Then, snapping out of it he continued, 'You only have twenty four hours to decide. Now I'm going check your token, so please have it out ready, and I'll give each of you a pack.'

The children rummaged for their tokens. Mr Harper studied them carefully before handing out the silver rucksacks, one to each child.

The packs ware small and made from a shiny silver material which hung loosely from leather straps. They didn't appear to contain much. Matthew had expected them to be full of useful equipment and food rations like he'd seen on a survival programme once.

A boy next to Matthew gave him a nudge, breaking his train of thought, then leaned close and whispered, 'Who you gonna take?'

'Dunno.' Matthew replied truthfully.

'I'm Pete.' He held out his hand. 'Pete Kettle.'

Matthew stared at it for a few seconds, wondering if this boy really didn't recognise him from school. Not only was Pete's twin brother, Arthur Kettle, in Matthew's class, he was in the gang that made Matthew's life hell, one of the boys who called him Matilda and shoved him around. Surely Arthur would have bragged to his brother about some of the things the gang had done to Matthew, then again, Pete's smile seemed genuine.

Matthew blinked, took the boy's hand and said 'I'm Matthew.'

Pete smiled then turned his attention back to Mr Harper, who had finished handing out the packs.

Matthew noticed how Pete's wavy auburn hair glistened in the sun. The boy had a splash of freckles around his small turned up nose, and an innocence in his eye that Matthew found comforting. He turned his attention back to his teacher, who took out a second set of instructions from the envelope.

The cloth of the rucksack felt soft, but strong in Matthew's hands. He pulled at one of the nylon ties that secured it and looked inside.

'If you look inside your pack,' began Mr Harper, 'you will find two security tags. I suggest that you secure one of them around your ankle now. Once on, it cannot be removed until you have reached your destination. Lose your tag and you lose your place.'

Matthew, Pete and eighteen others pulled out tags and began to secure them around their ankles.

Mr Harper returned to stand by the table.

'Give the second tag to your chosen companion. You may fill your pack with whatever you want to take with you from home. You may take only what you can fit inside. Then you and your chosen partner should proceed to the location on the green card. Do not reveal this location to anyone else and that includes friends and family. We don't want thousands of people getting in the way, so say your goodbyes at home. Don't worry about them either. Those who have a blue token will be following us later, and those with a red,' he paused, 'Arrangements will be made for them in the next twenty four hours. After we have gone, someone will give them instructions. Tell them not to panic. They won't be privileged like you. They won't be living quite as well as us but most of them will survive. We will look after them.'

Towards the back of the group, Rowland still struggled to fix his tag around his ankle. Mr Harper pushed his way through the group and crouched down to help the boy. Then, the twenty children, complete with shiny metal anklets, were dismissed with instructions to bring their companions to the departure point by 1pm the following day along with their packed rucksacks.

***

Matthew found his mother and his brother in the kitchen, both on their feet this time and desperate for news.

'Well?' his mother asked, 'What happened?'

Matthew showed them the tag and the pack and explained what Mr Harper had said about only being allowed one companion. He looked from his mother to Steve and back again, knowing that one of them would have to stay behind. What had been described as a privilege, now felt more like a curse. How was anyone supposed to choose? What was he supposed to say? He said nothing.

'What will happen to the people who stay behind?' Steve asked.

'They've made plans.' Matthew said for the second time that day. They're coming back tomorrow after we've gone.' He tried to sound convincing

'Mum?' Steve put his hand on his mother's arm to get her attention, 'What are we going to do?'

‘That’s for Matthew to decide.’ She turned to her younger son, ‘Honey,’ *that word again*, ‘honey, you know I’ll always love you no matter what you decide to do. And it’s really not a difficult a decision to make. A young boy needs his mother and tomorrow they’re coming back, you said so yourself. We’ll *all* be okay’ She said it though he could tell she knew it wasn’t true. Matthew hated her for that. Only a few hours ago she’d babbled on about how important it was to leave in the first group. How could she trust so easily that someone would come back for Steve? If she really believed it and if she really loved her sons she’d stay herself. Steve started to shake. Matthew was aware of the power his mother had had over them since their father had left. He wanted to shout at her. He wanted to stand up to her for once in his life and scream *No way! You can’t make me choose you over Steve. It’s not fair!* But she always got what she wanted. The decision had already been made.

‘Please don’t leave me.’ Steve whispered. Their mother ignored this completely and started preparing dinner while smiling, at frequent intervals, in Matthew’s direction.

‘We need to keep our strength up,’ she said determinedly. ‘We’ve a busy day ahead of us tomorrow.’

And so it was decided without Matthew having to say a word. He would have to take his mother and leave Steve behind. Confusion clouded his mind. *What should I do? What could I do? How can they expect children to decide who to take, when we haven’t been given all the facts? If only I knew what would happen to Steve after we’ve gone, I’d feel better. Or would I? Maybe the authorities will come back, they said they would. But what if Mum had been right before? There were so many reds? How could they all be evacuated at once?*

That night Matthew barely slept, and not because of the heat. The usual sound of Steve’s snoring had been replaced by irregular whimpering and erratic breathing. Hard to imagine that tonight would be the last time he slept in his own bed, in his own room, in his own home and maybe even on this planet.

When Matthew got up, the smell of warm porridge and toast drifted up the stairs as usual. Only today, they would be eating as a family for the first time in ages, and, probably, for the last time ever. Matthew struggled to swallow anything. No one spoke.

At eleven o'clock, their mother strapped the second tag securely to her ankle and raided the kitchen for chocolate and crisps to take with them. Matthew packed a few things into his rucksack: his favourite hoody; a slingshot that his brother had given him on his twelfth birthday; a magazine that he hadn't finished; a bottle of water; three quarters of a packet of biscuits and an old photograph of his dad.

Steve locked himself in the bathroom and refused to come out. He'd always acted older than his fifteen years, especially in front of Matthew, but now he dropped the façade and wept. Matthew sat on the floor outside for nearly an hour. The brothers had never been close, but Matthew still felt more of a bond between himself and Steve than he did with his mother. He didn't want to leave without saying goodbye, but time was running out.

Noon came and went. Steve refused to come out. Mrs Jones paced the length of the downstairs hallway screeching at Matthew to hurry up or she'd leave without him. Her earlier attempt at speaking to Steve through the door had been met with an outburst of swearing followed by what sounded like the entire contents of the bathroom cabinet being hurled at the door. She appeared to be more worried about missing the one o'clock deadline than about what would happen to Steve. Reluctantly, Matthew allowed her to drag him away from the bathroom door and out of the house.

By quarter past, they were hurrying towards the town centre and its tallest building, Capital Tower. They had studied the green card and the map last night even though they already knew the way. The journey should take less than thirty minutes.

‘Come on Matthew!’ his mother urged. ‘We need to walk faster. We can’t afford to be late.’

As they got closer to the town, there were more and more people heading in their direction. There were also more people lining the streets, begging passers-by for help, desperate for a way out, obviously not trusting that all would be ok and ignoring the instructions to wait at home. Up ahead, Matthew thought he caught a glimpse of Mr Harper, going the wrong way. A minute later he saw him again, closer this time, and by his side stood the girl from the playground.

Mr Harper dashed madly from one person to another, pleading with them, and following them for a few steps before breaking away, changing direction and attaching himself to someone else. Matthew watched with interest as he’d never seen his teacher behave like this before. As they got closer he could hear him begging a teenage boy.

‘Please take her,’ he implored, ‘I’ll pay anything. Name your price. All you have to do is take my daughter with you and you’ll be rich.’

The boy took the hand of a young girl who already accompanied him and pulled her past Mr Harper.

‘Sorry.’ His eyes looked genuinely apologetic before he turned and disappeared, caught up in the ever growing crowds.

Matthew tried to avoid looking at Mr Harper and his daughter. Their desperation only fuelled the apprehension he felt inside.

A loud crash came from about fifteen metres ahead. A crowd of youths attacked a group of smaller children. Armed with rocks, some of the gang tried hammering at the tags on the children’s ankles. Cries of pain and fear rang out now in all directions. Matthew’s mother raced a little way ahead of him now so he quickened his pace. He followed her as she crossed the road and slipped down a side street.

Matthew caught up. ‘It’s half past twelve,’ he shouted above the noise of the crowd. ‘How much further do we have to go?’

'Not far.' His mother looked ashen. 'Keep on to the end of this road, turn right and we're there.'

They ran until they could see the large glass skyscraper, known as Capital Tower, in the distance. Growing chaos in every street forced them to slow as they drew nearer. Avoiding trouble makers took some skill, perfect timing and a lot of luck. On more than one occasion they managed to get past mobs of hooligans or protesters by pretending to be part of a larger group.

Capital Tower stood behind a large square which had been fenced off from the streets. Like bees around a honey pot, people flocked in, only to be corralled like cattle. At two of the three entrances, security staff had lost control. Only at the smallest entrance, on the west, were people still being asked to show their tags. A tidal wave was brewing. The square's capacity had been reached, and still they poured in.

'Stand clear!' shouted a uniformed guard, from behind the fence. 'I need to close the gates before someone gets crushed.'

The crowd surged forward, harder than ever, in an attempt to squeeze through before the gap in the fence disappeared.

'It's only temporary,' he tried to shout above the noise of the crowd, but one man alone did not have the strength to hold them back. The west gate had been breached. Matthew forced himself to look away as the man became trapped himself between the wire mesh of the gate and a small wooden hut inside the corral, his screams ignored by everyone in their determination to keep moving forward.

Once inside the fenced area, they were guided roughly towards the entrance of the tower by men wearing camouflage gear. They passed a soldier with a megaphone.

'Please be patient,' he announced, 'There's room for you all. Stop pushing. We can only let three thousand into the building at a time. If the doors close in front of you it's to allow those inside to be relocated. Do not panic. Please just wait for the doors to re-open.' His voice faded as the crowd swept Matthew onwards.

Looking ahead, Matthew watched his mother getting further away from him. Something caught his foot and he fell sideways. He grabbed the arm of a stranger and steadied himself. He realised to his horror as he glanced to the floor that he'd been tripped by the legs of an old man who lay with his hands up over his head. No one tried to help him up. Matthew pushed his back into the crowd to try to move them aside but the tidal wave pushed on. If he didn't go with it he'd be brought down himself.

He reached the main building from the North side. It looked different. A four metre high piece of metal stretched across the breadth of the building. Twenty sliding doors allowed access to the room beyond. Armed guards stood menacingly either side of every door. Matthew watched a group in front of him as they rolled up their trouser legs and, in turn, placed their tagged foot onto a small metal step. This action brought the tag in line with a sensor which made the large door release electronically. The guards would then step forward, brandishing their weapons to prevent anyone other than the tag wearer from entering the building. Matthew tugged at his trouser leg to reveal his tag and positioned it so as to activate the door sensor. He watched his mother disappear through the door on his right and hurried after her. Inside the large holding area he searched for her. Where did she go? Panic gripped his chest. He looked around the packed room and saw a sea of frightened faces, although none he recognised. Most were exhausted; some were injured. He turned on the spot, scared by the sight before him, but relieved to be among the lucky ones.

4

Delicate vines laden with exotic fruit decorated the enormous clock on the far wall of the grand entrance. As one o'clock arrived, two steel doors slid slowly across the front of the building, temporarily stopping the angry crowds outside from advancing further. Inside, the room darkened temporarily before several spot lights flickered on.

Matthew looked around for his mother and wondered what would happen next. He spotted her a short distance to his left, pushing her way towards the front of the room without looking back. Before Matthew had time to follow her, a large screen lit up, high on the front wall. Three thousand heads turned to look.

A woman's face filled the screen and when she spoke, she reminded Matthew of a TV presenter introducing a new and exciting game show.

'Welcome to the gateway. In a few moments you will be taken aboard Freedom 1, the ship that has been designed especially for us, not only to transfer us from our present home here on Earth but as a permanent home in itself, where we can live safely for the rest of our lives. Each of you, in your pairs, will be given your own apartment and key cards to access it. Your card will also permit you to enter the dining hall, recreation areas, and later, when you are settled, your school room or place of work. Children under sixteen years of age will go to school where skills for our future survival will be taught alongside more traditional subjects. Everyone else will be expected to work in exchange for their place here. Jobs will be allocated according to experience and you will accept whatever job you are given. You must, each of you, agree to this now before passing through the gateway. Does anyone have any questions?'

The room erupted questions. People shouted from all directions:

'Who are you?'

'Where are we going?'

'When will I see the rest of my family?'

'Where will the others, with the blue tokens, go?'

'What will happen to our friends that we left behind? Will they be joining us later? Are we coming back for them?'

'You can save everyone, can't you?'

The woman on the screen smiled and nodded. 'All very good questions. I promise, all will be explained in good time. We really need to get moving as there are still many thousands of people outside waiting to follow you through. Let me assure you, though, that we have been preparing for a very long time and our greatest efforts will be made to save as many people as we can. Now, if you look around, you will see four staircases, one in each corner of the room. Please take any one of the staircases which all lead up onto the ship. At the top of the stairs, there are guides who will show you to your quarters. Please remain inside your apartment until otherwise instructed. Oh, and try to make yourselves comfortable. It's going to be a long ride.' The screen flickered and went black.

Matthew scanned the room, looking for his mother but, before he could locate her, he found himself being moved along with the crowds towards the closest staircase. He saw Rowland up ahead, being pushed along by a short, plump, hairy man that Matthew assumed was his father. Both of them looked nervous. Matthew reached the foot of the staircase and gave up looking for his mother. He began the long climb upwards, already tired from lack of sleep over the past couple of nights. The climb seemed to last forever as the sheer number of people made progress very slow.

After an hour and a half, Matthew thought he could see the top, and as he got nearer, he noticed a small group of men, dressed in maroon uniforms, waiting on the other side of the door to guide people onto the ship.

On reaching the top, instead of being taken to his apartment like most of the others before him, Matthew was shown to a large room and told to wait. There were three others in the room. An elderly gentleman sat in the corner nearest the door, leaning heavily on his walking frame. In the opposite corner, a teenage girl listened to music through an oversized pair of headphones, and between the two, with his knees pulled tightly to his chest, sat Pete.

'Have you seen my brother?' Pete asked immediately as he entered the room.

'Sorry, I haven't.'

'Did you lose your brother too?'

Matthew's heart felt heavy with guilt at the thought of leaving Steve behind.

'No,' he paused, 'I came with my mum, but she wandered off. I don't know where she went. She must have used a different staircase.'

'Don't worry. Anyone who gets separated is brought here, the guide told me.'

'Where're your parents?' Matthew asked. 'Are they here too?'

Pete looked at his feet and shuffled uncomfortably in his chair. 'My dad's dead.'

'Sorry, I didn't know.'

'It's okay, he died before I was born. I never knew him.'

'And your mum? Is she here?'

'I wish she were. I wanted her to come with me, but she couldn't leave Arthur. She cried and kept saying sorry. She came with us all the way to the gates.' He sniffed. 'What else could we do? Not that I didn't want to bring Arthur, you understand. We're twins; we have a bond. It's just, sometimes he can be a pain in the *you know what*.' He hid his face behind his knees and whispered, 'I just wish I could have brought Mum too.' Then he lifted his head and looked Matthew in the eye. 'I don't have to tell you though. You were in the same position as me. How did you choose?'

The words wouldn't come. 'I don't want to talk about it,' he said quietly as he sat next to Pete.

'I get you.'

I doubt it.

They both sat in silence, watching the door. To Matthew's surprise it was his mother who entered the room next, arm in arm with one of the uniformed men and with a silly smile plastered across her face.

'Matthew, where have you been? I've been looking everywhere for you. If we don't hurry all the good rooms will be taken. You're not to go wandering off until we know our way around.' She turned to smile at the guard.

'I told you we'd find him,' he said, while gently rubbing her arm. 'Now, shall I show you your apartment?'

'Thank you Frank, you've been so kind. I don't know how I would've coped without you.'

'Don't be silly Mrs Jones, just doing my job. Now, let's get going. You're on 73, so we'll have to take the lift. Follow me!'

Frank led them to the lift and then through a maze of corridors, that all looked the same. Every floor, every wall, every ceiling was sparkling white. Matthew tried to remember where they turned and which way they were going but gave up quickly as each corridor was identical. They went past door after door, each one white with a silver number near the top. Eventually they stopped outside room number 23,777. Frank looked through a bundle of glittery cards and selected two from the middle of the pile.

'These are your room keys,' he said. 'Don't lose them. You have one each, and you must remember to keep it with you at all times.' He handed the cards to Matthew and his mother. The dining room is on floor 102. Dinner would usually be at six o'clock but today you have to stay in your room until given permission to leave. It's for your own safety just while we take off. There are seatbelts on the two chairs in your living area. Put them on whenever you hear the warning siren.'

Frank then produced a strange looking piece of equipment from his pocket and beckoned Matthew forward.

'If you could just roll up your trouser leg, I'll remove your tag before I go.'

The tag somehow loosened when placed in the machine so Matthew could easily slip it over his foot. Frank removed the other tag from Mrs Jones and then walked towards the door. He stopped for a moment, looked at Mrs Jones and said 'My office is at the end of the corridor, as is my apartment, number 23,800. Try to make yourselves at home and I'll see you soon.' And with that he was gone.

The large room was perfectly square and dazzlingly white, though minimalism didn't come close when describing the effect of the almost empty apartment. Matthew gazed at two sunshine yellow, high backed, padded chairs which sprouted seamlessly from the centre of the floor. Other than the chairs, the only additional item in the room was an enormous flat screen monitor on the right hand wall. Three doors led off the back wall. The central door opened on to a small bathroom and toilet. The doors either side each led to a single bedroom; both were decorated in neutral tones and contained only a bed, a small wardrobe and a chest of drawers. On the back of each bedroom door was what looked like a weekly timetable. School began at eight thirty and ended at four, Monday to Friday. Saturday mornings were set aside for exercise. The afternoons and Sundays were mainly free, except for meal times and anyone doing shift work. Breakfast and lunch had been given thirty minute slots and an hour had been allowed for dinner. Everyone had to be home by eleven in the evening, every day.

Matthew chose a bedroom and tipped the contents of his rucksack into his top drawer. As he carefully arranged his few possessions, he wondered what sort of exercise they'd be expected to do in space.

Once unpacked, all he could do was wait, so Matthew returned to the sitting area and studied one of the chairs. A gold coloured five point harness hung from the back of it. Matthew's gaze drifted across the room. A small sign on the back of their front door caught his eye. He hadn't noticed it before, so he moved closer for a better look. On it was a map of level 73. There were also directions on how to get to the dining hall and information on what times it would be open. In red writing, at the bottom was a list of instructions entitled: What to do in an emergency situation. The list was short. In fact there were only two instructions:

1. Sit in a chair and fasten your harness.
2. Wait for further instructions.

Matthew sat on a chair and adjusted the harness to fit. His mother was still in her bedroom. She'd shut the door, without saying a word, fifteen minutes ago. Matthew wondered what he could do to pass the time. Eventually he let the harness fall from his hand and trudged back to his bedroom. He pulled his magazine out of the drawer and lay on the bed to read it. Within ten minutes he was asleep.

5

Next door's Alsatian whined and scratched at the front window. He'd stopped barking now. Almost an hour after he heard the front door close, Steve slid back the lock on the bathroom door. A single fly sat on the kitchen table in the otherwise empty house. Steve stepped forwards to swipe it away and was surprised when his fingers actually caught the insect, which made no attempt to fly away.

Outside, the street was silent. Steve wondered how many others were shut up in their houses alone, waiting to be saved. Matthew had said they'd be back but Steve wasn't even sure who "they" were. And he knew Matthew had only said this to reassure him. What if no one came? Would he die in this house? Or would the heat soon be so unbearable that everyone would flock to the sea to keep cool. Steve imagined the beaches packed with people, fighting for space near the water. Now what should he do? He could stay here and wait. Someone might come. But what if they didn't? It would all be too late for him.

One o'clock. Matthew and Mum would be gone. He had to do something now.

Steve hurried out of the house and down the street towards the town. He soon realised that he was not the only one to have chosen this line of action. He could hear what sounded like a riot coming from the direction of the town centre. Vehicles raced past him in both directions and as he got closer there were people, dozens of them, lying injured by the side of the road or else fighting viciously, each one demanding something from the other, threatening, screaming or begging.

Steve's heart hammered loudly against his chest. As he stood watching, trying to decide what to do next, someone grabbed him from behind and pushed him to the floor. A tattooed teen in ripped jeans and with more piercings than Steve had ever seen before shoved him on to his back and sat astride him, breathing heavily.

'What do you want?' Steve whimpered, his elbow bloodied from the fall.

The thug growled in response, 'A token, green or blue, or a tag. Turn out your pockets.'

'But I don't have one.' Steve cried.

His attacker stood up. A second later, Steve breathed in sharply as the youth's steel toe-capped boot landed heavily on his ribs. Steve cried out in pain. Fearing the youth, and desperate to get away, he turned out his pockets onto the floor and pulled up his trouser legs to reveal his bare ankles. Once satisfied that Steve had nothing of value, the girl gave up and ran off into the crowds in search of another victim.

Steve sat up and tentatively nursed his painful ribs. As the realisation of what he would have to do to survive slowly dawned on him, Steve wondered if he was capable. Time was running out. Steve got up and moved as quickly as his bruised ribs would allow. He followed the main road towards the town centre until he reached a passageway that would lead him into a maze of smaller roads he knew well. He hid in the shadows of the back streets, trying to avoid large gangs of desperate thieves. A few minutes later, he passed through a narrow ally and almost tripped over the body of another teenager, this time a boy.

The boy lay on his front, unmoving. Steve bent down and rolled him onto his back. He wasn't breathing. Steve backed away slowly, panic rising within him. A sound from behind made him turn. Were this poor boy's assailants still there? He froze and listened, fearing another attack, then scanned the alleyway, looking for the source of the clatter. A small pink shoe was visible from behind a large recycling bin. He guessed that the shoe's owner could be no more than seven or eight.

'It's alright,' he said quietly. 'I won't hurt you. Are you okay?' Steve approached the bin slowly and the girl shrank back against the wall.

'Please leave me alone.'

'What happened here?' Steve asked. 'Do you know this boy?' He indicated the motionless body behind him but kept his eyes fixed on the girl.

'It's my brother. They killed him for a token but he didn't have one. They didn't believe him so they kept knocking him down until he just didn't get up any more,' she cried. 'He made me hide when he saw them coming. I didn't do anything to help him. I was too scared to move.'

Steve leaned against the wall next to her hiding place.

'It wasn't your fault. You did the right thing. If you'd come out to help they could have hurt you. They might have killed you too. There's chaos on the main road.' Steve reached out his hand towards the girl. 'You can't stay here. Why don't you stick with me for a while?'

The girl looked at Steve's open hand for a moment before grasping it and allowing him to lead her out.

'Stick with me,' Steve said in a voice that sounded more confident than he felt. 'I'll help you find someone. Where are your family?' he asked, trying to block the view of her brother's body with his own as he led her away.

'It was just us. Nobody else. He was all I had in the world.'

'Where do you live?'

'St Judith's.' Steve recognised the name of the local children's home. 'Since our parents died in an accident last year.'

'Do you want me to take you there? Is there still someone to look after you?'

'I'm not going back!'

Steve sighed, 'Well then we need to get to the other side,' He nodded towards the main road, which swarmed with people. 'Our best bet is to head away from the town. There's no point in going any further in if neither of us has a token. If you want you can come back to my house and we'll wait together. Someone will come for us eventually.'

The girl shook her head and looked Steve squarely in the eyes. 'We have to get to the tall building, you know, the one made of glass. That's where everyone is going. We have to try.'

'It's too risky, and even if we could get there, they wouldn't let us in without a token.'

'I know,' she replied, kicking off a small, pink shoe. She bent down, put her hand inside the shoe and when she withdrew it, she was clutching two, small, blue pieces of metal. 'I only said that Adam didn't have a token,' she added nervously. As she spoke, the girl looked across to where her brother lay, and then back to Steve. She slipped the tokens back inside her shoe, put it back on and fumbled with the laces.

Steve thought for a moment. 'My brother had a green token. He took it to the meeting at the church where they gave him two metal tags. Apparently you have to be wearing a tag to be evacuated. Did you go to your meeting point yet?'

'Adam went. He brought home a blue token from school and took it to the church yesterday evening. I've never seen him look frightened before, but yesterday, when he got back, he said people were going crazy. Everyone wanted a tag, and not just the people with tokens. There were soldiers, but they lost control. A group of men stole the box of tags, before any had been handed out, and ran off. In the end they said the whole batch of blue tags would be deactivated. They gave out more blue tokens instead, to anyone still standing and still with their original token. I think Adam had to fight to keep his. When he got home he had a black eye and a bloody nose. He gave the second token to me,' the girl sobbed. She pulled Steve's arm gently, 'Adam wanted me to get there so badly. I can't give up now. We have to be at the glass building by six this evening.'

Steve looked at his watch, 'It's quarter to two. We're four hours early. Maybe we should hide somewhere for a while.'

'What if it gets worse?

'Crossing town now could be dangerous.' Steve warned.

'And later? People are just going to give up and go home?'

'You're pretty smart for a . . . how old are you?

'I'll be eight in six sleeps. I think we should go, before anyone else finds us here.'

'Brave too, for an eight year old. Can you run?'

'Faster than you,' she said indignantly. 'Will you come with me?'

'Well, I'm not letting you go on your own.' He walked towards the other end of the alley. The noise had died down and he guessed the fighting was now going on a little further away.

'Let's go this way.' He looked around the corner to check the coast was clear.

The girl ran back to her hiding place, retrieved a small silver rucksack and then ran after him.

'I'm Grace,' she said as she caught Steve up and fell into step behind him.

'Steve.'

The next twenty minutes were uneventful. They managed to get within one hundred metres of the building without running into any of the gangs. The last stretch would be tricky. There were several entrances marked on the map, but to reach any of them they'd have to get back on the main road.

Steve paused at the final junction and thought for a moment.

'We should leave the rucksack here,' he said.

'But we were told to bring it with us.'

Steve looked worried. 'There're too many people. Someone will see that you have a rucksack and they'll know you must have a token. What's in it anyway?'

Grace listed the objects in her bag. There were a few personal items from home; a map showing the way to the large area in front of Capital Tower; a change of clothes and some toffees.

Steve listened carefully, considering their options. 'Well, we know where we're going,' he began. 'So we don't need the map. Can you put your photos and anything precious in your pockets?'

Grace nodded and stuffed the pictures into her jeans. She looked carefully at a selection of things she'd brought from home and selected a silver locket and a small diary which would easily fit into the pockets of her coat, which she wore tied around her waist.

'I think we'll have a better chance if we travel light. Leave the rest here with the bag.'

'What now?' Grace asked quietly, after dumping the bag under a hedge.

Steve could only think of one answer.

'We're going to have to run for it. If we're fast, we can make it. He pointed towards a fenced area just outside the tallest building. 'Once we get to that fence over there, there are guards and we should be safe.'

Grace suddenly sprinted towards the entrance to the fenced area. By the time Steve started to follow her, she was already about twenty metres ahead of him. For a few seconds, it seemed, no one noticed the pair of them running wildly down the road as though their lives depended on it, which of course they did.

They were halfway before a man and a boy spotted them and gave chase. Steve closed the gap and ran alongside Grace. He didn't dare look behind even when he heard heavy footsteps gaining on him with every stride. Steve grabbed Grace's hand and nearly pulled her off her feet.

The entrance was only five metres away when he felt her jerk backwards. The man grabbed her and searched her pockets. Steve turned around and launched himself at the man, shoving him as hard as he could and knocking both him and Grace to the floor. Grace stumbled as she got to her feet but was quicker to rise than the man and managed to make it through the gate. Steve was less lucky. The boy quickly caught up and wrestled him to the floor.

With the speed of a rabbit, Grace reached the safety of the enclosure and revealed her tokens to the startled guard, who let her pass.

'You know you don't have to be here 'till six,' he grunted. But Grace didn't answer. Instead, she shouted through the fence to where Steve rolled across the floor in an attempt to get away from his attacker.

Grace waved her arms wildly and screamed Steve's name.

'He's with me!' she shouted. 'He doesn't have the tokens. Look! They're here. I have them. Let him go!' Grace waved the tokens in the air and then jumped back, as everywhere arms snaked through the fence trying to claim her prize.

'Let him go!' she persisted. He doesn't have anything! Please!' Eventually the message got through and the boy sank back on his heels, panting for breath and with tears streaming down his face.

'I'm sorry,' he whispered, shaking his head.

Steve stooped to pick up Grace's photographs before taking his place beside her, behind the fence.

'You dropped them,' he said, handing over the pictures. He turned to watch the boy and wondered what would become of the weeping wreck they'd left behind.

6

There were no windows in the dimly lit room, making it impossible to tell the difference between night and day. So, when Matthew awoke he had no idea how long he'd been asleep. He got up and peered through the door into the living area where his mother leaned back in one of the chairs with her eyes shut. He crossed the room and touched her arm gently.

'Mum, are you awake?'

She opened her eyes, breathed deeply, and smiled. 'We've made it. We'll be okay now, you and me. It'll take a while to get used to, but it's better than being left behind.'

Matthew turned his head away and tried to hold back the tears that stung his eyes. He forced the images of his brother out of his mind. How he wished he'd been stronger and brave enough to bring Steve with him instead of this thoughtless, crazy woman he called his mother.

A large screen that looked like a television filled the top half of one wall in the living area. Matthew pushed a switch and it flickered on. In the bottom left hand corner a digital clock read 8:45. It had been hours since they'd eaten, though Matthew didn't feel hungry. In the centre of the screen, a countdown timer flashed on and off, displaying a little over an hour.

'Do you think it's counting down to take off?' Matthew asked.

'I guess so,' she replied. 'I'm sure they'll let us know when they're ready.'

Matthew removed the bottle of water from his pack, drank a quarter and then offered the rest to his mother.

She pushed it away. 'Maybe later,' she said.

Matthew sat in the other chair and watched the countdown timer ticking away the seconds. He closed his eyes and let his mind wander. He remembered things he'd done with his father. Fishing, cycling, even homework. Then he tried to imagine his brother safe somewhere and waiting to be saved. Next he thought about another of his mum's birthdays, several years ago, before his father had left, one of his few happy memories of the whole family together.

A deep rumble followed by a high pitched squeal came from a speaker next to the screen. Matthew opened his eyes and saw there were just twenty nine minutes left. After a short pause, a female voice filled the room:

'Good evening everyone. Welcome to Freedom 1. The time is nine thirty one and we plan to depart at 10pm. You must all strap yourselves into your chairs immediately. Please check your harness fits comfortably and adjust it as necessary so that you are tightly secured. If you experience any problems with your harness, please press the call button next to your screen and a member of our team will assist you. Please keep your harness fastened until further notice. We will launch when the timer reaches zero. Try to relax and enjoy the trip.'

Serene piped music replaced the voice, but it did little to calm Matthew's nerves.

'I'm scared.' Matthew whispered. 'What if something goes wrong?'

'Just relax and enjoy it. It's not every day you get launched into space. Tomorrow we'll be waking up among the stars!'

Tick, tick, tick ... the remaining time disappeared second by second until there were only thirty seconds remaining.

The voice from the speaker returned. 'Thirty seconds till take off. Ensure you are strapped down firmly. Try to relax. All systems are go. We are looking at perfect launch conditions!'

The countdown began: '10 ... 9 ... 8 ... 7 ... 6 ... 5 ... 4 ... 3 ... 2 ... 1 ... lift-off ...'

Nothing happened.

Matthew looked at his mother for reassurance but her eyes were firmly fixed on the wall. He held his breath…still nothing happened.

The screen turned green and a message appeared telling them that they could remove their seatbelts.

'What's wrong?' Mrs Jones' gaze switched between the screen and her son, searching for an explanation.

The speaker crackled. 'Thank you all for your compliance. The launch was successful. You may now remove your harnesses. We will continue moving towards our destination for approximately four weeks. You are now free to move about the ship as you wish. Remember to take your key cards with you as you can only access certain areas by swiping your card. You may only enter areas if your key card allows it. If you get lost, there are maps next to each lift and stairway.

'The dining hall, on floor 102, is not open yet but will be up and running by seven o'clock tomorrow morning, from which time breakfast will be served in shifts. Check your timetable to see when you will be allowed to eat.

'For this evening, I'm afraid you will have to make do with whatever you brought in your packs. Any problems you have in the meantime, feel free to go to your floor manager, who is situated in the room at the end of you corridor, nearest to the lifts. If no one is available, press the intercom button outside the manager's office. You will have two days to settle in before school and work schedules begin. You will be informed in due course when, and where to go. In the case of an emergency, a siren will sound and you will put your harness back on. Have a pleasant evening.'

Matthew couldn't believe that they'd really left their home on Earth for good. The take-off had been so smooth that they hadn't felt a thing. Matthew looked at his mother. 'I'm going to explore. Do you want to come?'

Slowly his mother opened her eyes and shook her head. 'I think I'll go to bed. It's getting late and it's been a long day.'

Matthew picked up one of the key cards, shoved it in his pocket and slipped outside the door. When he couldn't find Frank in his office, he continued towards a large map which covered most of the wall at the end of the corridor. It suddenly became clear how large the ship was, and Matthew wondered how the ship hadn't been visible from the outside of the Capital Tower. The map showed over fifty floors packed full of living areas, just like the one he shared with his mother. Below these were a further fifty floors made up of store rooms and areas for growing crops and keeping livestock which was a surprise as Matthew hadn't really considered what exactly it would take to provide for so many people long term. Above him, there were the kitchens, the dining hall, work rooms, factories, gardens, schools and nurseries, a library and even a recreational floor made up of a gym, swimming pool and sports hall.

There were small gold buttons scattered across the map. Matthew pressed the one next to a large arrow and the words: *You are here.*

A robotic voice announced: 'Floor 73. Living accommodation for civilians, Floor Manager, Mr Frank Gibbon.'

Matthew tried several other buttons and found some that gave similar simple descriptions, and others simply said: 'No access for civilians.'

He stepped into the lift, and looked at the key pad and a digital display where a scrolling message instructed passengers to enter the number of the floor they required. A red light flashed next to the number 73, indicating the floor on which he currently stood. Matthew keyed in the number 102 and pressed enter. The lift moved up, slowly at first, and then accelerated smoothly. Matthew watched the numbers on the display rise. A few seconds later the lift slowed to a gentle stop at floor 102. The doors slid open and Matthew took a moment to absorb the colourful sight that greeted him. A rich, red carpet spread out into a gigantic room. The cream walls were hung with numerous enlarged photographs, which included the Seven Wonders of the World, the London Eye and members of the royal family. A shiny silver and glass serving area took up most of the right hand side of the room and a sign on the counter read: *Open for breakfast from 7am.*

Matthew strolled around the edge of the large room, looking at the artwork and wondering what would be happening in some of those places right now. The thought depressed him so he decided to try another floor. Matthew got into the lift and went up to floor 120, where the map showed gardens. Matthew gasped as the door opened and he saw the enormous space before him. He actually felt a breeze in his hair and could smell the grass beneath his feet. He heard the faint humming of insects as they flew from plant to plant. Hundreds of varieties of flowers in all colours, many of which Matthew had never seen before, filled the area around the lift. He strained his eyes to try to see the other end of what must have been the biggest room that Matthew had ever seen, but all he could see was a perfect blue sky.

Matthew walked briskly through the garden, stopping from time to time to wonder how certain parts of it could have been created. After walking for almost a mile, Matthew thought he could make out the distant end of the gardens, and as he moved closer to that end, he realised that it wasn't the sky that he'd been gazing at this last half hour. All the walls and ceilings were painted sky blue, and there were thousands of tiny lights shining through in all directions. Matthew ran his hand along the wall, momentarily lost in thought, but brought back to reality by a familiar voice.

'Hey! Matthew, wait up!' Pete yelled as he ran to catch up. He looked towards where Matthew had been touching the wall. 'It's amazing, isn't it?'

Matthew nodded. 'It all looks so real.' He turned to face Pete. 'Did you find your brother?'

'Yeah,' Pete replied, 'he'd gone back down the stairs to look for me. I had to wait for ages. We've got a room together on floor 62. Have you seen the size of the pool on 135?'

'Not yet.' Matthew replied. 'I only looked at the dining room before I came here. That's huge too, though nothing like as impressive as this. Everything about this place is massive.'

'Come this way!' Pete jogged towards a cluster of trees and Matthew ran to catch up.

Pete pointed to the bottom of a grassy slope. 'Look!' he grinned.

It was unbelievable.

At the bottom of the slope stood a wood which was certainly large enough to get lost in. The wind rushed through the boys' hair as they sprinted down the hill. The mowed grass was replaced by long wild, flowering grasses as they grew nearer the trees. Matthew recognised Oak, Sycamore, Beech and Horse Chestnut trees, growing between varieties he knew didn't exist on Earth. A strange tree with lilac bark stretched out from between two smaller cherry trees.

Pete jumped to grab the nearest branch and snapped off an orange, star shaped fruit. 'I wonder if it's edible!' he thought aloud.

'I wouldn't risk it.' Matthew said. Maybe you could take it to school in a couple of days and ask.'

Pete shoved the strange fruit into his pocket and they continued to explore. A little further into the wood, he stopped at the base of an apple tree, lifted an arm and let his hand trail over the bark while circling the tree. 'We were going to get some apple trees,' he mused, 'before it got too hot to grow stuff. Mum always wanted an orchard. She would have loved it here.'

By 11pm the lights in the garden dimmed, so the boys strolled back to the lift.

'Can we meet up tomorrow?' Pete asked. We could look around the rest of the ship.'

Matthew nodded and yawned. 'Sounds good; I'll meet you at breakfast.'

The lift stopped on the 73rd floor and Matthew waved goodbye as he stepped out. Once inside room 23,777, he turned off the main light and crept to his bedroom. The door slid closed behind him and he crawled into bed, pulling the thick, white duvet over his head. The soft hum of the ship's engines soon sent him into a deep sleep.

***

The following morning, Matthew arrived in the dining room before Pete, and joined the queue. While he waited, he read a notice which informed customers that their key cards would only allow them to pass through if they presented it within their allotted time on the timetable. He reached the turnstile and swiped his card. A light turned from red to green and the bar moved down under his hand. As he stepped through, two things happened: the square section of floor beneath his feet sank slightly under his weight, and a thin ray of green light zigzagged down his body. The process took no more than three seconds. Matthew tried to move forwards, but a robotic arm snaked out of a hole in the wall to his left and handed him a rectangular piece of plastic. The hand withdrew smoothly and a monotone voice came from a small speaker next to the hole. It said:

'Height – One metre forty.
Weight – Forty six kilograms
Age – Twelve years
Body Mass Index – Within normal range
Diet code – Maintenance
Meal size – Child's, regular
Enjoy your meal. Please proceed.'

Matthew turned the piece of plastic over in his hand. It had the word "child" printed on one side and "regular" on the other. He reached the counter and the girl behind it held out her hand.

‘Meal ticket please.’ She said cheerfully.

Matthew handed it over and watched her serve a portion of porridge that he considered too small to be regular. He took the bowl and sat down to wait for Pete.

***

Over the next couple of days, the boys spent much of their time together in the woods. They also explored other levels of the ship together, some of which they were free to roam, like the gardens; others could only be accessed with a key card. They searched these levels with limited success. They did find one level where the door slid open upon inserting their cards. The level marked on the map only as “School”. Needless to say, they didn’t spend too much time exploring there.

On the second evening, after eating a simple meal in the dining hall, Matthew lay on his bed. A knock on the door roused him. He knew at once that it wasn’t Pete; it was too late and anyway, Pete had an unusual and rather annoying way of knocking to the tune of his favourite TV show. This knock was louder and slower.

Matthew heaved himself up, opened his bedroom door, and found to his surprise his mother already answering the door. It slid open to reveal Frank, in his freshly pressed maroon uniform, holding a clipboard and smiling in a way that gave Matthew the creeps. His mother stepped aside to allow Frank to enter. He made himself comfortable in one of the yellow chairs and gestured to Mrs Jones to sit in the other.

‘Mrs Jones,’ he began, ‘I’ve come to issue your work permit.’ Matthew leaned against the wall as Frank went on to explain that everyone over the age of sixteen would be expected to begin work the next day. He then gave Mrs Jones a questionnaire to assess her skills. After filling it in, he looked through a booklet, and asked for her key card, which he scanned with a small machine that appeared from the depths of his pocket. After that, he explained to Mrs Jones that she must report to level 39 at six o’clock every morning. Frank then turned to Matthew and gave him the details of his new school, Hawking Middle School. He, and everyone else from Newdale, would be required to attend between eight and four, Monday to Friday, starting the next day.

***

A month passed with little excitement. Matthew, Pete, and the rest of the evacuees settled into their new routines.

School was hard. Their teacher, Miss Rose, was strict, but fair. Matthew, Pete and his brother Arthur were in the same class as Rowland who quickly became popular with the other boys. They laughed at his smart remarks and positively encouraged his silly behaviour. Matthew and Pete avoided him as much as possible, so it wasn't long before they became the subject of many of his jokes.

One Tuesday morning, for example, Miss Rose asked the class to suggest words they thought were frequently misspelled.

Rowland's hand shot up so fast, it almost launched him into the air.

'Yes Rowland?' Miss Rose asked nervously.

'Diarrhoea!' he said proudly.

The room erupted into peals of laughter. Rowland waved his arms trying to silence his friends, long enough to explain further. 'Matthew's always had trouble with diarrhoea!'

Rowland took a minute to look around at his admiring fans as they clapped and cheered, before returning to his seat.

Matthew sunk lower in his chair and felt his face grow warmer.

Pete stared at him in disbelief, before leaping out of his seat and launching himself at Rowland, who ducked, but not quickly enough to avoid contact with Pete's fist.

Later Pete admitted that he'd missed his target, Rowland's nose, but was satisfied with the end result.

Rowland, who arrived the next day with a black eye, was far from satisfied. He used his gang members to deliver increasingly ridiculous threats to Pete throughout the day.

Pete spent most of the next week dodging Rowland and hiding in the toilets, until one unfortunate afternoon, when they came face to face, alone, in the changing rooms.

Pete was struggling to get his PE shirt over his head, so didn't see Rowland until it was too late. The fight was over before it began. Pete tried to fight back, but Rowland finished the battle by sitting on Pete's chest and delivering two black eyes and a bloody nose.

Pete learned two things that day: Never fight someone three times your weight, and it's better to ignore Rowland than to react.

***

Saturday mornings turned out to be fun. The 'exercise' on Matthew's timetable was surprisingly varied. Three weeks out of four you could choose from a long list of activities. Some days he swam, others he played football and once a month there were team games and competitions. The rest of the weekends could be spent however they wanted. Many, including Matthew and Pete, escaped to the gardens, the one place that felt like home, and where they could run free for a while.

Weekdays became dull. School was just like it had been on Earth and Matthew's mother no longer spoke to him. Their days were timetabled and boring. The food was bland and the novelty of being in space soon wore off.

One day rolled into the next, until one ordinary Friday evening, when something happened that certainly was not dull, and would cause everything to change again — because this particular Friday was the day that the boys met Ludo.

7

Dinner consisted of watered-down vegetable soup, stale bread and an over-ripe banana, which, the girl behind the counter kindly informed them, had come from their first harvest since leaving Earth. After a difficult day at school, the boys hungrily cleared their plates in record time, then dumped them through the "to be washed" hole in the wall near the exit. Matthew hastily leapt through the lift's sliding doors as they opened, only to come face to face with Rowland and three of his sidekicks.

'Look where you're going moron!' Rowland put up his arms in a defensive manner, and then shoved Matthew as hard as he could back through the door into Pete.

'Keep your hands off me Neilson!'

'Or what, Matilda? What you gonna do? Tell your Daddy? Oh no, you haven't seen him in years. Maybe you'll get your big stinking brother to rescue you, except he got left behind, didn't he? You know he's probably dead by now, don't you? So, what *are* you gonna do?'

'Don't talk about my family like that,' Matthew warned. 'You don't know anything about them. Just leave us alone!' Matthew stepped back, leaving the gang room to go past.

'And you're very quiet Petal,' Rowland rounded on Pete as he entered the room.

'Shut up, Rowland!' Pete snarled as he grabbed a sodden mop from a plastic bucket by the wall, and thrust it towards Rowland and his cronies, spraying them with smelly brown water. Rowland froze for a moment, shocked, as water ran down his face and dripped from his chin.

Matthew grabbed Pete's sleeve and dragged him past Rowland and into the lift before the saturated boys had time to react. He hammered the button for floor 120 and ducked as a bright yellow *caution wet floor* sign sailed straight towards his head and crashed into the already closing doors. As the lift rose, Pete chuckled, and by the time the lift reached the garden, both boys were laughing hysterically. They tumbled out onto the newly mown grass and took turns at impersonating Rowland as they strolled down the now familiar path to their favourite spot in the garden.

'We shouldn't be laughing,' Matthew said. 'He'll be even worse at school on Monday.'

'Serves him right after what he's been like lately.'

School had been particularly troublesome for Pete recently. In befriending Matthew, Pete had automatically become a new target for Rowland's gang. Only the day before, one boy had somehow managed to get Pete's trousers wet and then convince the entire class that poor Pete had wet himself.

But all thoughts of school were left behind as they entered the small, grassy clearing in the woods. The boys had found it by chance while exploring. They almost missed it completely because, from even just a short distance away, the long grass and several rambling blackberry bushes obscured it completely. To get to this part of the garden, the furthest point away from the enormous sliding doors, took about thirty minutes at a brisk walk.

Matthew stretched out and kicked off his shoes. Pete sat beside him, deep in thought. They often passed an hour or two here after school in this way, chatting, thinking, relaxing and generally unwinding after a hard day's work. Sometimes Pete would vent his anger by ranting for a few minutes. His favourite topics included how to get his own back on Rowland, what Matthew should do about his mother, and do we really still need to learn history at school? Other times Pete quietly grieved for his mum.

About twenty minutes passed in companionable silence, when a twig snapped only a short distance away. The rustling noise that followed grew suddenly louder, as though someone or something moved towards them rapidly, but neither boy saw anything. Matthew sat up and looked at Pete, who put his index finger to his lips. Holding their breath, both boys prayed that their secret retreat would not be discovered.

As suddenly as it began, the noise stopped.

Matthew stood up slowly and moved towards the bushes that hid them from view. He squinted through the brambles and, for a brief moment, saw movement, about ten metres to his right. A branch from a willow tree swung back into place, like it had recently been disturbed. But, whoever lurked behind the tree had now changed direction, and was slowly moving away from them. Matthew relaxed a little, shoved his feet back into his trainers and retied the laces, curious about what this other person had been up to.

'That was strange,' he remarked, more to himself than to Pete. 'No one but us ever comes this far.'

'Maybe they were lost,' Pete said. 'It was probably just a little kid.' Then he added unconvincingly, 'We should probably check it out though.'

Looking braver than he felt, Matthew marched in the direction of the willow tree, with Pete scurrying along like an excitable puppy at his heels. From the other side of the tree, the boys had an uninterrupted view to the top of the grassy slope, about two hundred metres away. There was no one there. Whoever they'd followed must have doubled back into the woods. For a moment, Matthew wondered if it might have been Rowland and his gang, extending their fun into the evening by tracking them to their sanctuary to torment them further.

'Ridiculous!' Matthew reprimanded himself.

That surely couldn't be the case, he thought. If Rowland *had* followed them, he wouldn't have just left . . . *But has he gone? Is he hiding somewhere nearby?* Another branch swung to their left, this one closer than before. Both boys turned on the spot and stared. Nothing moved for a minute, then a shrub rustled, this time to their right, and so close that Matthew felt the leaves brush his arm, then a scraping noise from behind. Why couldn't they see anyone?

'Maybe it's some sort of animal,' Matthew whispered, 'you know, a fox or a rabbit. It has to be something small that can move quickly and is difficult to spot.'

'I still don't see how it could have got from there,' Pete indicated the tree on their left, 'to there,' he pointed to where the most recent rustlings had come from, 'without either of us seeing anything.'

The bush, which was about four feet tall and densely covered in dark green foliage and strange yellow flowers, began to shake. Pete indicated for Matthew to circle around the back of the bush while he slowly moved towards the front. The bush stopped moving. The boys reached the bush at the same time from opposite directions.

Pete pointed to the bush and silently mouthed, 'One . . . two . . . three . . . now!'

Matthew dropped to his knees, trying to get a look under the bush. At the same time, Pete separated the branches rapidly, eager to discover whatever was hidden beneath.

'I see it!' he yelled. 'It's heading towards you! Grab it!'

Matthew lay in wait, arms stretched out towards the centre of the bush, unable to see anything other than Pete jumping around like a hyperactive monkey. Then he felt it, just for a second . . . something brushed against his hand. He made a move to grab it, but then cried out in pain as something sprayed his face.

It was a strange liquid that burned his skin and made his eyes sting. He withdrew from the branches, arms flailing wildly, and crawled blindly away, tears streaming down his face.

'Pete,' he shouted, 'Pete, where are you?' His breathing increased rapidly and his throat felt raw. He thought he might be sick.

Once the feeling eased off a little, he sat back on the grass. His eyes were still streaming and everything looked blurry.

'Pete!'

Again no answer.

'Pete,' he whimpered, 'help me, I can't see!'

Several minutes passed before Matthew's vision returned. Relief swept through him. He blinked away the tears and, to his surprise, he saw Pete striding towards him grinning. In his hands, he carried something unlike anything Matthew had ever seen before. It was the same size as a chimp, brown and completely hairless, its hind legs were short, though it had large feet with long toes which resembled human fingers. It had large tear-shaped ears which stuck out either side of its wrinkled face. Its arms were skinny compared to its body, which looked like that of a Buddha. It was obviously not going to come quietly. It wriggled and it shook. It hissed and spat like a cobra, spraying what looked like water from its mouth. It aimed for Pete's face but he held the wild creature at arm's length and seemed to be unaffected.

'Be careful, it's dangerous,' Matthew rasped. 'What do you think it is?'

'I dunno but it's kind of cute, don't you think?'

'Cute! You've got to be kidding! It blinded me with that stuff.'

'What do you think we should do with it? I can't just let it go; it could hurt someone.'

'It did hurt someone,' Matthew snapped. 'Me!'

'Maybe we could keep it, you know, like a pet. We could train it to do tricks and stuff.'

Matthew shook his head in disbelief. 'Train it? It's not a dog. It doesn't look like something you could train. I think we should ask Frank. He might know what it is and what to do with it.'

'No, I don't think we should tell anyone. They might take it away, or worse still they might kill it.'

'Good,' Matthew retorted. 'Let them have it!'

The creature's aggression faded with each passing second. Clearly exhausted, its chest heaved as it glared first at one boy, then the other, before tensing its body and growling quietly for just a second. Slowly it lifted its head and smiled, just long enough to convince Pete it had given up fighting. Pete adjusted his hold on the thing, pulling it in close to his chest, while careful to keep its mouth pointing away from him. Suddenly, the creature wriggled around in Pete's arms and released one last poisonous spray in his direction. Pete stumbled backwards, but fortunately his grip on the thing's monkey-like arm stayed tight and the escape attempt failed. Just to be on the safe side, Pete restrained it further by wrapping it tightly in his jacket and tucking it backwards under his arm. Finally, the creature stopped struggling, and, apart from its heavy panting, remained still.

'There, there,' said Pete soothingly. 'I'll look after you. Don't worry, you'll be ok. We'll both look after you.'

'Actually, I'm quite capable of looking after myself,' came a muffled voice from under Pete's jacket. 'Now, if you would be so kind as to let me go, we can pretend that none of this ever happened.'

Pete almost dropped the thing in shock. Matthew's mouth fell open and he stared at the creature's furrowed rear end, which poked out from under Pete's arm.

'You can talk!'

The thing sighed. 'Well, you're a bright one aren't you? Talk about stating the blooming obvious. Make a great pair you two, don't you? One with the brains and the other with the brawn. Now are you going to turn me around so I can see my captors, or are you going to continue this conversation talking to my posterior?'

Carefully, Pete turned the creature round, being sure to keep its face at a safe distance from his own.

The thing turned its head towards Pete, sniffed deeply, and then as if revolted, leaned away.

'Look,' he continued. 'The thing is, you were not supposed to see me. We are supposed to stay completely hidden at all times and I am going to be in *so* much trouble if they find out, so please, as a favour from one intellectual to another, let me go and don't mention this to anyone.'

'We?' Matthew said, taken aback. 'You said "we". Are there more of you?'

'Well you didn't think I could fly this little ship all by myself, did you?'

Matthew laughed. 'You? Fly the ship? That's the funniest thing I've heard since we've been here.'

At this, the creature looked genuinely hurt.

'We may be small but our technology is infinitely superior to anything human made.'

Pete, who was obviously enjoying himself a little bit too much, grinned from ear to ear. 'What exactly are you anyway? And where are you from? Oh, and do you have a name, and did you and your friends help to build the ship or do you just fly it? Do you work for the government? Where do you live? Are you going to stay on the ship forever or do you have to go home?

Matthew glared at Pete. 'You don't really believe it do you?'

'*I* am not an *it*,' said the creature, indignantly. 'And if you put me down, I'll be more than happy to answer your questions.'

'Don't put it down!' Matthew shouted. 'It's a trick! It'll run away as soon as it gets the chance, or spray us with that stuff.'

Ignoring Matthew, Pete turned and gently rested the creature on a small smooth rock, before sitting down in the long grass next to it.

The creature took a few moments to get comfortable, stretched its skinny arms and then leaned back against a tree with its hands behind its head.

'I'm Ludo, an inventor and a scientist. I come from the twelfth planet from the largest of the sister stars, Zelda, in the third quadrant of the Zama Galaxy. We are collectively known as hissing changelings although we don't actually hiss, we spit, and only when attacked. We consider ourselves a peaceful race, so, over time, have dropped the hissing part and now prefer to be called just *changelings* and to be left to ourselves.'

'Then why are you here?' Matthew asked, 'and why were you hiding in the bushes?'

Ludo rolled his eyes and sighed impatiently.

'You asked if we worked for your government. Well, to be precise, we are repaying a debt. We owed your planet a favour. Many centuries ago, before we first discovered the extent of our abilities, which is another story, we were suffering. Our planet could not sustain us and your planet had an excess of what we needed to survive: Insects, to pollinate our crops, since all our bugs had died off and you had swarms of them. They were pests to your crops, but they brought life to ours. With your world's permission, we gathered millions of insects and brought them back home. Our planet has thrived for many years because of yours and so now, with your world dying, we felt we had no choice but to help in any way we could. Your government requested ships and we built three hundred and ninety two of them to their specifications. Some of us agreed to remain with you for the first few months to make sure everything went smoothly. Eventually, when your people get the hang of things here, we'll go back home.'

'Okay,' Matthew had to admit Ludo's story sounded plausible. 'But that still doesn't explain what you were doing in the gardens.'

'Oh that's simple,' the changing smiled. 'I was blackberrying. We don't have anything like them on Zelda Twelve; they're delicious.'

Matthew laughed. Strange as the whole story sounded, he was starting to believe it, and what's more, he was starting to quite like the small brown creature.

'So what now? Will we see you again? We come here most days after school and often at the weekend too.'

‘Maybe. I haven’t had much free time lately, but if I do get down here and I see you, then I’ll say hello, as long as you promise not to attack me next time.’

Once Pete had promised and they’d both agreed to keep their meeting a secret, Ludo said goodbye. He scurried to the nearest bush, but stopped just before he disappeared from view. He turned back and looked at Matthew.

‘I probably should warn you, you’ll not be feeling terribly well — quite soon I expect. Side effects of the venom. But don’t worry. You’ll be fine by tomorrow.’

And with that, he was gone.

8

Nineteen hours had passed since Freedom 1 had vacated the planet, taking one hundred thousand lucky passengers with it. Steve and Grace waited outside the steel doors at the front of the building with hearts full equally of hope for the future, and sadness for what they were leaving behind. They waited, expecting to be given a way out, a chance to escape the fate of the planet. They waited, until long after their water ran out and their bellies rumbled. They, along with many others in the crowded square, came up with numerous reasons to explain why they had had to wait so long.

‘They had to deal with the first load of people before they can let us in,’ said some.

‘It’s bound to take a long time to organise so many people,’ said others.

‘They need to load our food and all sorts of other equipment first,’ Steve overheard a man telling an elderly woman, who he presumed was the man’s mother.

Steve tried to reassure Grace, but as time went by she grew more and more restless. At six o’clock, twenty four hours after the blue token holders had been instructed to gather, Steve was relieved to see a group of soldiers arrive. They handed out rations of food and water. They refused to answer any questions, their only words being: ‘Wait one more day.’

After four days of being told to wait just one more day, a plump, blond woman emerged from behind a closed curtain onto a balcony, high above the crowds. A microphone squealed as she adjusted its position. The woman told them how governments and great leaders from across the world had come together to deal with the crisis at hand, and of their plans to evacuate as many people as possible from all over the world. She told them how hundreds of great ships had been built and prepared to take vast numbers of people to safety. Two ships had been prepared for every country across the world for those lucky enough to gain a place in the lottery. She spoke of the future of mankind in a way that, under normal circumstances, would have had an audience chanting and cheering, but today the captive crowd listened on with suspicion and uncertainty, whispering among themselves, some daring to hope, others already given up. The woman tried her hardest to inspire the crowd, then zapped away their last drops of hope by informing them that for some reason only one ship had landed here, and that ship had left five days ago.

They had waited, but already their time had run out. Steve's heart sank. He listened to Grace sobbing and knew he must stay strong for her.

The woman continued, though the crowd grew louder and broke away into smaller groups.

'Unfortunately, there isn't enough space for everyone, but please, do not despair. We have made alternate arrangements for everyone who managed to secure a blue token. We are still hopeful that our second ship has merely been delayed. Time on the surface of the Earth is running out for us and, although we cannot hope to escape the effects of the rising temperature forever, we have come up with a plan to buy us some more time.

'Deep below the Earth's surface, where the temperature has remained constant for billions of years, we have excavated a space large enough to house a significant number of people. This is where many of those who received a red token should have ended up. Instead, we offer it to you. We believe we can survive the extreme temperatures on the Earth's surface by staying deep below layers of cool rock, a natural barrier to the heat. This solution, however, is not permanent. We will have, at best, two or three more years before the temperature will reach levels that will be dangerous for us even deep below the surface. We hope to be rescued long before that time, or to have come up with a more permanent solution. We will be taking an impressive team with us below the surface. The team includes some of our most talented scientists and mathematicians, as well as many creative and imaginative people from a wide cross section of society, who we hope will solve any problems we may encounter.'

The woman retreated through a small door at the back of the balcony. Shortly afterwards, Steve, Grace and the others were led to the outskirts of the town, flanked by a patrol of uniformed men. Across the town, windows were broken, shops had been looted and stood empty, and an unnatural quiet had descended on the wreckage. An empty crisp packet skittered across the deserted road and joined a small collection of rubbish that swirled near an upturned wheelie bin.

And so, the mass evacuation of the town began.

Thousands of people moved as one.

Those at the front followed the soldiers that had previously brought their rations. Those at the back followed those at the front.

From time to time, a desperate man, woman or child would try to join the procession, only to be beaten back unsympathetically by soldiers.

Live and let die.

When the soldiers reached the underground station to the west of the town, they slowed, causing people to suddenly bunch closer together.

They were funnelled through the narrow entrance and poured down the stairs to the platform. Again, Steve and Grace waited. Whispers spread and eventually Steve overheard a man talking about a train with more than fifty carriages.

By half past midnight, after six hours on their feet, they reached the platform. Few of the lights worked properly so Steve found it difficult to keep track of Grace. He wanted nothing more than to curl up on a bench and sleep, but didn't want to risk losing Grace or his place in the queue. He yawned and jumped up and down on the spot to keep himself awake.

By their turn, at least eight different trains had been seen, each with fifty carriages. The trains had already made four trips and Steve estimated they would probably have to do the same again.

The journey lasted a little over an hour and Grace slept. Steve stared out of the window, trying not to think.

They whizzed by numerous stations without slowing until they had gone way beyond the outskirts of the town. The train had come above ground about halfway through the journey, not that it made much difference to the view at this time of night, but eventually, it pulled into a dimly lit station that looked vaguely familiar.

'I've sure I've been here before,' Steve said to himself.

Grace stirred as the soothing motion of the train ended.

'Where are we?' she yawned.

'Lark Valley station. Come on, we're getting off. The last time I came here was on a family day out. Have you been here before?'

Grace shook her head. 'Whatever they have planned for us,' she told him, 'It's no family outing.'

They walked with the crowds, out onto the street. By three o'clock in the morning Steve was exhausted. He couldn't believe how strong Grace had been. He had only known the girl a few hours, but already felt strangely attached to her. She needed him now more than she had ever needed anyone in her life, and he didn't want to let her down. He was nothing like his mother.

It was cooler here than it had been in town. A light breeze ruffled Steve's hair. They were walking downhill towards what looked like a building site. Dried mud marked the road and through the darkness, various pieces of machinery could be seen, scattered around a large stone building. Above the building, a battered sign had come loose at one end and now hung precariously over the entrance. Lit by a single bulb, it read: Black Spring Caves.

The weary travellers pressed on like a flock of sheep being herded into a cramped pen. A small skirmish ahead caught Steve's eye. As they moved nearer he could hear a man begging to be let in.

'Not without a token!' A guard jabbed a truncheon into the man's chest, knocking him to the floor. The man started to rise, then, collapsed to his knees, shoulders quivering as he buried his face in his hands and sobbed.

After showing their tokens Steve and Grace were allowed through a heavily armoured fence, before being led through two sets of titanium doors and then down numerous flights of stairs. The walls were dark and water ran down the rough stone surfaces. Candles burned at irregular intervals in some places. In others, they could hear the hum of a generator and single bulbs were dotted about.

There were none of the luxuries of Freedom 1 down here, only vast open caves joined by endless tunnels. Eventually, roughly cut stone stairways gave way to metal ladders, and wooden handrails were replaced by ropes in only the most awkward of passageways. Eventually, after what must have been at least six hours, they reached a flatter path. As they rounded another bend, the flickering candle light faded into blackness. Steve gripped the rope tightly as he inched his way forwards. With every step came a new challenge. Sharp rocks, at unexpected angles, slowed their progress, and occasionally the low ceilings bumped and scraped Steve's face and head. He could hear Grace's laboured breathing close behind, but had no words left to ease her suffering.

A faint glow suggested the tunnel turned sharply to the left, a little way ahead. Steve took Grace's hand when the rope ended, just before the corner. In the distance, enough light shone from beyond the next corner to allow him to see the floor a metre or two in front, only his view remained blocked by a tangle of sweaty bodies. Even so, the journey now became slightly easier. Once round the bend, they were allowed a brief rest, before continuing down the path. With the next dip, appeared another rope to guide them onwards.

The light increased as they neared the bottom, where the narrow tunnel opened into an enormous cave.

Steve strained his eyes, trying to gauge the size of the place through the gloom. The dense train of people slowly diffused, filling the void. Steve guided Grace along the left hand wall until they reached an opening. Three passages led off in different directions. Each one, they later discovered, led to hundreds of smaller caves, some of which were strewn with blankets, others had picnic benches in rows. Steve and Grace would have to sleep in one of these caves with dozens of other people and with nothing more than a blanket for comfort. This would be their new home.

Time passed slowly below ground. The first day frightened Steve. The second day was worse. After three weeks, Steve's eyes had become accustomed to the lack of sunlight, but his head had not. He felt claustrophobic, and the thought of being down here indefinitely filled his heart with dread. There were some who had cracked after just a couple of days and had begged to be released from the stone prison. Then, monitors had been brought down to some of the larger caves to show pictures and film from the surface. There were no signs of life. No insects. No animals. No people. No hope. The complete lack of vegetation surprised him most. A few trees stood bare, but most had been burned to the ground. Without grass and plants the Earth looked like a planet from an episode of Dr Who. As Steve stared at the screen, he realised everyone had fallen silent. All eyes were facing the same way. People were in shock. They had known for a long time that the end was close, but seeing it made it real.

Inescapable.

Nobody else would try to leave now. They were stuck here; either until someone found an answer to the most impossible of problems, or until they all died. It didn't look hopeful. Steve wondered if it would have been better to have stayed outside. The end would have been horrifying, but at least it would be over.

Now, with nothing to do to pass the time but eat and sleep, not that anyone had much to eat, Steve sat against the cold damp wall. Food had to be rationed, water too. The seas had dried up almost completely, so they only had the water stored in great tanks beneath them to rely on. Steve had heard a rumour that the guards collected their urine daily, and a small team were currently working on a way to recycle the water. He hoped they would be rescued before they became desperate enough to want to drink anything other than the water held in the storage tanks.

Grace had spent much of the last three weeks mourning the loss of her brother. Steve had tried to talk to her many times, not only to try to help her through, but also for his own sanity. Despite this, Grace had become increasingly withdrawn and hardly moved from her bed. She probably wouldn't have eaten either if it hadn't been for Steve bringing her food twice a day.

Life became almost unbearable. Steve thought of different ways to end it all, in case things got any worse. He thought about drowning himself in the water tanks, but they were heavily guarded and besides, he didn't want to contaminate the water supply for the others. He considered climbing up high enough to have a terminal fall, but he worried it would be upsetting for the children in the group to have to witness and anyway, he really didn't think he could go through with it. Instead, he did nothing. Just like hundreds of others in the caves alongside him.

9

In mid-February, the passengers on board Freedom 1 reached their destination. According to an exciting video announcement, the engines had been turned off and they would be forever in orbit around the star called Zelda. Had there been windows on the ship, passengers would have marvelled at the sight before them, for Zelda, though smaller than her sister, Zina, shone like a giant glitter ball emitting a swirling pink radiance that enveloped the ship. Dozens of identical ships surrounded them, more joining all the time; each one loaded with grateful passengers from Earth.

At school the children studied Maths, English, Science and History, just as before. They no longer needed lessons in Geography, Music, Drama or Religious Education. Instead, they learned how to make small electrical components that were used in the construction and repair of the ship. They learned how to create electricity, how to make their own clothes and also spent many hours on the lower levels of the ship, where they worked with the animals and were taught how to tend the crops. Sometimes, Matthew would see his mother working with the cows, connecting their udders to the giant milking machines, feeding them or mucking out their pens. He liked watching her work; she looked just like any of the other workers down here. Normal. He tried to imagine talking to her at the end of the day about work, school, and everyday things. In reality, though, his evenings were usually spent alone. In silence.

Matthew enjoyed the lessons on the farm more than being in the classroom, but Rowland and his cronies, who had no intention of doing anything physical, hated them. Rowland looked for any opportunity to get out of them completely. This had not gone unnoticed by Miss Rose, who today insisted that they would not return to the school room until every child had mucked out at least two of the pig sties and one cow's pen. Matthew and Pete had both finished in a little over an hour and sat in the artificial sunshine with a beaker of lemonade and a biscuit. Rowland refused to even start. Miss Rose had had enough. She ordered everyone back to the school room and calmly informed those students who hadn't managed to complete the task that they would be returning to the farm at 4pm and would remain there for as long as it took. Rowland scowled.

Matthew wiped the crumbs from his mouth and put his empty beaker into the basket, which Miss Rose used to carry down their snacks. 'Come on Pete!' he called as he got up and brushed some loose strands of straw from his trousers. 'Looks like the fun's over.'

Pete grabbed the basket, and then both boys followed Miss Rose towards the main gate.

Miss Rose stopped and turned. Then, seeing Pete with her basket, she smiled and said, 'Thank you, boys.'

At that precise moment, Matthew noticed movement just behind his teacher. A broom slid slowly out from Rowland's pen directly into the path of Miss Rose. As she started towards the gate, Rowland's end of the broom shot up suddenly. Miss Rose lost her balance immediately as both of her legs came into contact with the broom together. She fell, heavily, onto the concrete yard. Her hand shot out to break the fall, but she cried out in pain as she landed on her wrist. The colour drained from her face as she sat up and caught her breath. Then, she nursed her arm, gently touched her fingers one by one. She grimaced as she tried to move her wrist, while struggling not to cry in front of her class.

Pete dropped the basket, and rushed to help his teacher.

Matthew picked up the broom and propped it against the wall. He peered into the pen, which was now empty except for the six large brown and white cows. A small wooden door in the back corner slammed shut. Rowland had gone.

***

The following morning, at eight thirty, Matthew settled himself behind his desk and pulled his electronic work book out of his bag. He turned it on and clicked on Maths, followed by today's date, 26th February 2128. At the back, Rowland said something quietly, and his gang fell about in hysterics.

The classroom door slammed shut, the room went quiet and everyone turned to face the front, as Mr Harper strode towards the smart board. He stopped abruptly, and turned to address the class just as Rowland reached his seat in front of Matthew.

'There will be no foolish behaviour or practical jokes while I am in charge. I do not want to hear your whining voices unless I have spoken to you directly. I do not expect to see you out of your seats unless you are following my instructions,' He paused and looked at them balefully. 'Do I make myself clear?'

'Yes Sir,' chorused the class, with little enthusiasm.

'I said: Do I make myself clear?'

'Yes Sir,' they repeated, louder this time.

Mr Harper paced the room slowly with his hands clasped behind his back. A sharp tapping noise came from his tan, tasselled cowboy boots, the most colourful item of clothing he owned, which echoed around the room. As he paced, he focused on intimidating individual students using only the depth of his glare.

'Miss Rose will be incapacitated for at least the next two weeks as she has fractured her wrist. I will be covering until she returns. Some of you already know me but for those of you who don't, I am Mr Harper and I expect certain standards. I do not expect you to like me; I know I'm not going to like all of you.'

Matthew groaned and looked at Pete, who shook his head in disbelief.

Rowland turned around and sneered at Matthew. 'Who's going to be teacher's pet now then? Not you, that's for sure. I think we could have a little fun over the next couple of weeks. It'll be just like old times.' He laughed and turned his attention back to Mr Harper, who explained that in today's lesson they would cover calculating the area and perimeter of circles.

Matthew slowly drifted off into his own thoughts. Seeing Harper reminded him of Jess and he wondered what had become of her. Hard to believe by looking at him now, that the last time he'd seen Mr Harper he'd been a desperate wreck. Matthew remembered feeling sorry for him and his family.'

'Jones?'

Mathew snapped out of it. 'Yes Sir?' he asked cautiously.

'Before we start, perhaps you'd be so kind as to recap last week's lesson. Miss Rose informs me that you should all be familiar with working out the area of a parallelogram. Remind the class please of the formula.'

'Sorry Sir, I can't remember.' Matthew looked at his feet.

'What a waste of valuable space. Why they did the lottery at all is beyond me. It should have been a test of intelligence. Then, we'd have brought the brightest students on board instead of idiots like you. That would have given us a little more hope for the future, don't you agree Jones?'

Matthew remained silent.

'Never mind. Tonight Jones, I expect you to complete an extra homework on the area of quadrilaterals, which I'll download especially for you, along with the class homework on circles.'

For the first time since they left, it was just like being at home.

***

After a long hard week, the boys were desperate to spend a day in the gardens. They hadn't spoken of Ludo at all because Mr Harper made them stay late at school every day. Saturdays were Matthew's favourite time of the week — just him and Pete, in their remote hideaway, where no one could spoil their fun, not even Mr Harper.

Saturday morning after breakfast, Matthew raced to complete his compulsory 64 lengths in the pool before knocking for Pete.

Arthur answered the door. 'He's in the shower,' he said standing aside to let Matthew through. Since his brother had befriended Matthew, Arthur didn't go out of his way to instigate trouble at school, though he often got dragged into it by his so called friends. Arthur was something of a sheep. Quick to follow, keen to keep his reputation and his place in Rowland's gang, desperate to be popular, but he got little pleasure from tormenting anyone. To an outside observer, he appeared the stronger, braver twin. But, to Matthew he'd always be a coward. Of course he'd never say so to Pete.

Pete appeared half dressed, 'Sorry, I overslept. Just got back from the gym. I'm ready now though,' he said as he pulled his shirt over his head. 'Let's go!' Then, as he reached the doorway he turned to his brother. 'I'm off! See you later.' He waved in Arthur's direction with one hand and dragged Matthew into the corridor with the other.

They hurried to the grassy clearing, chatting excitedly, although they were careful not to mention Ludo when passing others in the garden. When they were sure they were alone, they whispered his name, expecting him to appear as if by magic. They called and searched for twenty minutes, then gave up and lay in the long grass.

'Maybe he has to work,' Pete suggested.

'Maybe he wasn't real. Do you think we imagined him?'

'What? Both of us? Don't be daft.'

The morning passed quickly. It was nearly lunch. Reluctantly Matthew got up. They'd have to hurry if they wanted to make it to the dining hall. As they walked towards the bushes surrounding their clearing, a small voice stopped them in their tracks.

'You're not leaving already are you?'

Pete turned towards the voice and grinned. 'Ludo!' he exclaimed. 'We called for you ages ago. Where have you been?'

'Where have I been? I thought you said you came down here most evenings. I've been looking for you all week.'

Between them, the boys explained what had happened to Miss Rose and how her replacement enjoyed making their lives difficult. In their excitement, they forgot they were supposed to be going to lunch and sat down again. Matthew wondered why Ludo had been so keen to find them.

'Was there a reason you were looking for us every day?' he asked.

Ludo looked serious. 'Why yes of course,' he said, licking his puffy brown lips. 'It's the blackberries. In case you haven't noticed, I am only 18 inches high and have already consumed every blackberry within my reach. You boys, being tall and kind and helpful and handsome and brave and willing to please and—'

'Alright, enough already!' Pete laughed. 'Lead us to the blackberries. Do you have a basket or something to put them in?'

Ludo picked up a small woven bag that had been hidden in the grass, and passed it to Pete. He led the two boys down a narrow path to where several blackberry bushes stood. Fifteen minutes of hard picking later and the little bag was full. It took Ludo only two minutes to gobble the whole lot down and pass the bag back up hopefully. Matthew sighed and reached for more of the berries.

'You'll be sick.' he said as Ludo finished licking his lips.

The second batch lasted much longer and Ludo decided to save the third bagful for later. He relaxed back into the grass and sighed contentedly.

'Now,' he said. 'What can we do to resolve your little problem?'

Matthew and Pete looked at each other and then at Ludo expectantly.

'What problem?' Matthew asked.

'Why, Miss Rose breaking her arm of course. We don't want you staying behind every day next week as well do we? Obviously, I want to do something to help you after all you've done for me and I'm just getting used to your funny ways. I'd miss your charming company.'

‘As well as the use of our arms and legs,’ Pete retorted with a chuckle.

‘I would never say no to a few extra blackberries and if you don’t come till next weekend, half of those blackberries will be lost to the birds and insects. However, now I feel we are friends, and friends help each other, am I right?’

Matthew nodded but Pete looked doubtful.

‘What exactly could a changeling do to help improve our lives?’ asked Pete.

‘What would you like me to do?’

Matthew thought for a moment. ‘Get rid of Harper for a start. Could you do something to him that would keep him away from school too? Perhaps you could break his arm.’

‘Or his leg,’ Pete added, helpfully.

‘It’s possible, but not really necessary. The simplest solution would be to get Miss Rose back.’

‘And you could do that?’ Pete asked.

‘If that’s what you really want.’

The boys both nodded eagerly.

‘Then let’s do it!’

‘How?’ Pete asked,

Ludo looked at them sternly. ‘I’d need you both to help, obviously, but it shouldn’t be too difficult. Fairly simple, I’d say. We just need Miss Rose back and for that her arm needs to be usable.’

‘Oh, I get it!’ Matthew exclaimed. ‘You said you had abilities. Can you heal Miss Rose’s hand?’

‘Yeeeeeees,’ Ludo replied, ‘Only, not in the way you think.

10

Ludo sat perfectly still; his small wrinkled body moved up and down slightly as he breathed. A gentle breeze bent the grass and Matthew wondered if the changelings had anything to do with the weather conditions in the garden. He knew that sometimes it must rain overnight because often the grass would be wet in the morning.

Ludo leaned forward, as if he were about to begin a bedtime story for a small child.

'Did you not wonder why exactly we are called changelings?' he asked.

The boys glanced at each other before looking back to Ludo. Matthew shook his head.

'I never thought about it,'

'Me neither,' added Pete.

The changeling continued, 'Well . . . we have a rather unusual ability. No one knows exactly how we can do it. It's not magic. It's more like time travel, only I can't actually travel through time myself. I like to think of it as a gift, passed down from generation to generation. For many years changeling scientists have studied it and written lengthy research papers and books, though no one has proof of how it works.

'So what exactly can you do?' Pete wanted to know.

'I can take others back . . . to change things. If you want, I can take you back to the day your teacher broke her arm, but that's all I can do.' He paused. 'What happens on that day would then be up to you. Somehow you would have to change something, either be in the right place to catch her, or stop her from falling. You'll have to work that out between yourselves. Think about it if you need to and then let me know what you decide.'

'What happens after?' Matthew asked. 'If we manage to change something, what happens next? How do we come back?'

Ludo took a deep breath. ‘Once you arrive in the past,’ he told them, ‘you can stay as long as you want, depending on how far back in time you have gone. A day, a week; a year if you’ve gone back far enough. I can only take you to the past, not the future, and you must be sure to return before the point in time from which we started. When you are ready to return, one of you needs to say: “Ludo, I’m ready!” and I’ll bring you both back. You can only revisit a time once, so if you don’t get it right first time, that’s it.’

Matthew glanced at Pete who grinned from ear to ear.

‘Will we have to avoid bumping into ourselves in the past?’ Pete asked.

‘No, no, you will go back to exactly where you were and repeat that time. There will only be one of each of you. One thing to remember though, try to travel back from somewhere you can’t be seen. It would lead to lots of awkward questions if you suddenly disappeared in front of a crowd. Once you are back here, the you from the past will take over, but there is usually a second or two before that happens, so to anyone watching it will look like you disappear and then reappear a couple of seconds later.’

‘Okay, let’s try it.’ Matthew grinned, ‘What do we have to do?’

Ludo looked at Pete. ‘What about you? Are you willing to go back too?’

‘Are you kidding?’ Pete replied, almost bouncing with delight. This is the most exciting thing that has ever happened in my life. I’m not sure if I believe it yet, but if there’s a chance we could get rid of Mr Harper, let’s go for it. I don’t know exactly how we’ll do it, but I’m sure we’ll work something out when we get there.

The changeling nodded. ‘Good, good. Now come and stand either side of me and hold my hands.’

Matthew bent down to reach Ludo’s hand. It was warm, leathery and incredibly sweaty to touch. Pete crouched on the other side and took Ludo’s left hand. He pulled it away sharply and made a fuss about wiping his hand on his shorts. The strange creature seemed oblivious to Pete's reaction and reached out, catching hold of Pete's flailing arm. Pete reluctantly gave in, wrinkling his whole face as Ludo's grip tightened on his hand.

Ludo spoke softly, his voice seemed to have an instant calming effect on the boys. 'Now think back to the day in question. Try to imagine whatever you were doing just before Miss Rose tripped.'

Then, Ludo began to hum.

An invisible force tugged Matthew backwards. The light disappeared and his feet left the floor. He was aware of his body hanging in the darkness. Slowly, the light came back and he could make out the farmyard and the animals, only everything appeared in black and white. He looked to his left and saw Pete, gazing into the distance. It reminded him of one of the really old photographs that his Nan used to show him. Then, slowly, the colours returned, one by one. Yellows then reds, greens then blues. Like a paint-by-numbers picture, being filled in bit by bit until you could see the whole farm as it should be. Matthew realised he had been holding his breath, so exhaled, just as the ground rose to meet his feet. The weight of the fork that appeared in his hand caused him to stumble, wildly to his left, where he bounced off of a disgruntled cow before regaining control of his body. He scanned the yard and found Miss Rose some distance away, trying to persuade a group of boys to work a little faster.

Matthew put down the fork and looked around. To his left, he saw a large barn which housed eight cows. Somewhere amongst them, broom in hand, hid Rowland.

Matthew waited.

Miss Rose's voice grew louder as she got cross with the boys. Matthew ducked out of his pen and slipped into the barn where he knew Rowland was crouching behind the cows, skiving.

***

Pete lost his footing and landed heavily on his bottom. Embarrassed, he checked to see if anyone noticed him and recognised the cow shed at once. He looked around, trying to work out when exactly he'd appeared, then slipped out of his almost clean cow pen and made a bee line for Miss Rose. He marched up behind his teacher and coughed to get her attention.

'Peter, have you finished already? There's lemonade some and biscuits in the shed. Run along and help yourself. I'm sure some of the others will join you as soon as they are finished. Her voice rose in volume towards the end of the sentence as she turned back to face the boys she'd been in the middle of scolding. Pete just stood there, not sure of what to do or say.

Miss Rose smiled. 'Is there something wrong Peter?'

'I . . . I . . . I . . . just wanted to say . . . It's just that . . . Thank you for being a really good teacher.' Pete retreated. He could have kicked himself. *Thank you for being a really good teacher?* What an idiot, he thought.

Miss Rose's attention returned to the boys who still refused to work. Pete listened as she really lost her temper.

'Alright!' she shouted. 'Enough is enough. Everyone back to the school room *now*!'

The boys downed tools and trailed back.

'Oh, and one more thing,' she added. 'Those of you who haven't managed to complete your task will be returning with me at four o'clock and will remain here as long as it takes you to get finished.' She turned and walked towards the pen where Rowland crouched, hidden, broom in hand.

***

Matthew silently closed the door to the barn, picked up an orange plastic shovel and carefully advanced on the tubby boy's position, still not exactly sure how to stop him. The front of the barn consisted of a long, five bar metal fence so Matthew had a clear view of the yard.

Fortunately for Matthew, Rowland's focus never wavered from the yard, so he didn't notice Matthew creeping up on him from behind. Unfortunately, Matthew could see Miss Rose getting closer and closer to Rowland's position. He had to act now. Not caring if he made a noise, Matthew shovelled up a pile of cow manure, and without hesitating, threw it at Rowland's head. Rowland, who'd heard the shovel scrape the concrete floor, turned to face Matthew at exactly the wrong moment and ended up with a face full of manure. He dropped the broom and wiped his face on his sleeve. Then coughed several times trying to clear the bits of straw from his mouth. Furious, Rowland jumped on Matthew and knocked him to the floor before pounding the smaller boy's chest and face with his fists.

'Rowland! Get out here right now!' Miss Rose was livid. 'What on Earth do you think you are doing?'

'I think you must have forgotten Miss.' Rowland spat. 'We're not on Earth anymore.'

More punches rained down on Matthew's already bruised body until the lights faded and Matthew passed out. When he opened his eyes, Matthew saw two men hauling Rowland out of the barn and Miss Rose sitting in the straw beside him. Pete rushed into the barn, startling the cows. He looked worried and then relieved as Matthew cautiously sat up.

Miss Rose helped Matthew to his feet.

'Are you alright?' she asked, looking Matthew up and down.

'I'll be fine. Nothing's broken just a few bruises.'

Miss Rose turned to Pete.

'Will you take Matthew to the medical room on floor 134? I need to deal with Rowland.' She smiled at Matthew. 'I'll be up to check on you in a little while. Do you think you can manage the walk to the lift?'

Matthew nodded, and then the two boys slowly walked away from the farmyard. As soon as they were out of view, the boys giggled.

'We did it!' Matthew exclaimed.

‘What did you do to Rowland?’

‘I’ll tell you all about it once we’re out of here. Are you ready?’

‘Yes. As much as I’d love to stick around to see what happens to Rowland, I think we should go before anyone comes to check on us. This could be the only chance we get for ages.’

Matthew agreed and together the boys said, ‘Ludo, I’m ready.’

For the second time, Matthew felt himself being pulled backwards into darkness. Wind rushed past his body, though he couldn’t tell if he was sinking or rising and for a few seconds he forgot to breathe. Suddenly, solid ground crashed into his feet and everything spun like a merry-go-round. He recovered quickly as the colours poured back into the familiar picture of the garden. Matthew laughed out loud as he saw Pete struggling to stay upright, and then giving up and toppling to the floor. Matthew felt giddy and collapsed in a heap beside his friend. They swapped stories and both boys were laughing uncontrollably by the time Ludo appeared behind them. Matthew couldn’t wait to tell Ludo about their adventure and launched himself into a vastly elaborated version of events which ended up as a full scale story of good overcoming evil.

Pete butted in from time to time adding extra details and confirming how well Matthew had managed to time his attack on Rowland and completely change the outcome of that day. They both especially enjoyed describing Rowland’s dung covered face.

‘The more he tried to wipe it off,’ Pete laughed, ‘the worse he made it look. It was spread . . . all over . . . his face.’ He managed between giggles.

‘Did you see him spitting?’ Matthew asked, holding his side as he now had a stitch. ‘He must have got some in his mouth.’

Matthew roared with laughter as Pete tried to do an impression of Rowland. The image of this alone would be enough to keep the boys smiling for days afterwards.

'Rowland's going to be impossible now,' Pete chuckled, when he finally calmed down enough to speak. 'It'll probably be best if we avoid him for a while.'

'Don't forget,' Ludo reminded them, 'That what you changed happened last week. You never know, Rowland may have got his own back already and you've missed it.'

'Even better for us,' Pete laughed.

Matthew agreed. They both thanked Ludo and said their goodbyes after making him promise to meet them the next weekend.

'I suppose we're too late to get anything to eat.' Pete said gloomily.

They took the lift down to the 73rd floor. Matthew retrieved his key card from his pocket, but before he had time to use it the door slid open and his mother stepped towards them.

'Hello, Mrs Jones.' Pete stretched his hand towards Matthew's mother. 'I'm Pete Kettle.'

Mrs Jones nodded a greeting but said nothing, nor did she take Pete's hand. She brushed past him and wandered off down the corridor. Pete glanced at Matthew, who looked away, embarrassed by his mother's behaviour.

'Sorry about her,' he said quietly. 'She's not been herself lately.'

Pete shrugged and followed Matthew into the room.

'Bloody hell,' he said as he looked around the room. 'It's exactly like our room looked when we first moved in.'

'What do you mean?' Matthew asked.

'It's empty and white. Why haven't you collected your stuff or changed the walls?'

'Changed the walls? I don't understand.'

Pete led Matthew to the wall nearest the front door. He touched a flat, square white button that Matthew had never noticed before. A small section of plastic rose away from the wall and slid upwards, revealing dozens and dozens of multi-coloured buttons, each one clearly labelled. Among them, Matthew saw a silver button marked living room wall colour. Pete pressed it once and the walls changed from white to pale yellow. A second press and they turned bright pink. Pete grinned at Matthew as he pressed the button again and again, changing the wall from corn flower blue to fire engine red. He laughed loudly as he pressed the button faster and faster.

Matthew laughed too as the room flashed between colours, but after only a couple of minutes, he felt sick and shouted for Pete to stop. Matthew took over and slowly worked the button. He settled on a shade of green that reminded him of his living room at home. Next, he chose a sky blue for his bedroom and yellow for the toilet but decided to leave his Mum's room white. Then Pete took Matthew down in the lift to collect his soft furnishings. On the way, he told his friend that Robbie, the floor manager on 62, had knocked on his door one day whilst the boys had been in the garden and had shown Arthur how to make the place more like home.

'I assumed all the floor managers did the same. Maybe yours missed you by mistake?'

'He probably tried to show my mum. You've seen what she's like at the moment.'

As they entered a vast storage room, a short plump woman asked for their key cards.

'It's just for him.' Pete pointed at Matthew, who dug his card out of his jeans pocket and handed it over.

'Take two of each,' the woman indicated rows of shelves, mostly empty, that had previously held enough linen to supply the whole ship. 'Sorry there's not much choice. Most people came within the first couple of days,' the woman apologised. 'You're lucky to have found me here at all. This room's being stripped tomorrow and will be used for storing food from Monday.'

Matthew selected a bright orange pillow case and duvet for himself and a brown set for his mother. He took some sage green cushions and a set of bright purple towels and flannels. Matthew handed blue blankets and a pair of multi-coloured light shades to

Pete. Finally he picked up a small basket containing cleaning equipment and a couple of wash bags, each complete with toothbrush, toothpaste, soap and shower gel.

One hour later and the rooms had been transformed. Matthew had even attempted to clean up a little bit. By now, both boys were hungry. Matthew looked at the clock. 6.40.

'We'd better hurry. I don't want to miss two meals in one day.'

Matthew put the cleaning things into a small cupboard and sighed. He hoped there would be more days like today. Not being bullied by the boys at school, obviously, but the time travel and the revenge on Rowland, he could get used to.

The front door slid open and his mother walked in. If she noticed the changes then she didn't mention them. She walked directly through the bedroom door and closed it firmly behind her. Matthew sighed and caught the front door before it slid shut. The boys rode the lift to the dining hall in silence.

11

The bedroom clock said 6:20 am and although there were no windows on the ship, light crept into the room. Hidden all over the walls were small LEDs that came on and off on a time switch to mimic the hours of daylight on Earth. Matthew noticed, as the weeks went by, and they moved towards what would have been summer, the lights were coming on earlier and staying on till later every day. He wondered if their orbit around the new star, Zelda, would be longer or shorter than that of an Earth year and if the light patterns on Freedom 1 would eventually reflect this, or carry on as though they were still at home.

From the other side of his bedroom door, Matthew could hear his mother getting ready for work. She always left at 6:45am and returned about ten hours later, when her shift had finished. Matthew had tried to show an interest in his mothers work, but she rarely spoke more than a few words. All he knew was that she helped to feed, muck out and milk the cows, nothing more. Same routine day in, day out, but she preferred it to having nothing to do.

Matthew would definitely prefer to have nothing to do today. The end of the school term grew nearer, and even in deep space, exams took over his life. With all his weekends of late being spent in the garden, Matthew had spent little time revising. Instead, he planned to fit in half an hour's cramming before school. He waited until he heard his mother close the front door before going to get washed and dressed. His new school uniform, which had been delivered the night before school opened, was much more comfortable than his previous one, though not pretty to look at. Grey shorts, grey shirt, grey jumper, grey socks. Did no one have any imagination these days?

Matthew sat for twenty minutes with his electronic text book in his hand before deciding that he probably already knew as much as he ever would about algebraic equations. He snapped the book shut, and after a quick stop at the dining hall for breakfast, where a young girl served him the usual small portion of porridge with no sugar, he sprinted to the school room and arrived just in time for registration.

The day dragged. The class spent the whole time in silence, either revising or working on the test. Miss Rose, who hadn't tripped or injured herself in any way in her recent past, sat at her desk busily writing reports. Matthew frowned as he looked back over his answer paper and saw how many questions he'd left out. After a few feeble attempts to fill in the blanks, Matthew put down his pen and let out a deep sigh.

After school, and a meagre dinner, Matthew and Pete escaped to the garden in the hope of seeing Ludo. They called for a while, but heard no response, so soon gave up and sprawled out on the grass. The afternoon sunshine was somehow projected across the garden leaving long shadows under the trees.

***

Mrs Jones pushed her key card into the slot next to the front door. It had been a busy day at the dairy, as several of the other farmhands were off work with a sickness bug. She yawned and headed straight to the shower. Ten minutes later, cleaner and smelling less like the farmyard, Mrs Jones intended to go directly to bed. As she crossed the living area, the screen on the wall came to life. Mrs Jones paused to look at the screen and then changed direction and moved towards it. She sat down and stared at the display with curious anticipation.

Without warning, a computerised voice explained that there had been news from Earth about a second group of survivors — those who had selected, or been given, a blue token. The voice, which sounded neither male nor female, went on to give a brief description of where the others were. Mrs Jones heard 'Somewhere safe . . .' And '*in a beautifully designed underground hotel . . .*' As the voice continued, a long list of names began to scroll across the screen. Her gaze dropped to the floor and she rose from the chair to look for an off switch. Finding none, she shuffled back to the bathroom. As she closed the door, the voice faded to a murmur. To drown out the sound further, Mrs Jones turned the shower back on. Soon steam, and the hiss of the water, filled the room. Mrs Jones got undressed and stepped into the shower again. She swayed backwards and forwards under the warm, comforting spray.

***

At 6:30pm, on her way to get dinner, Mrs Jones ran into Frank.

'Oh Mrs Jones,' he greeted her. 'You must be so relieved.'

Mrs Jones stared blankly at Frank.

'It was your Steven, wasn't it? Oh my God, it wasn't, so thoughtless of me. I'm so sorry. I saw the name Steven Jones with the others from Newdale village I just assumed it was your son.'

Mrs Jones blinked. 'Where did you say you saw Steve's name?'

'On the list, of course, the blue list of survivors . . . the second group.'

'I didn't see it . . . I mean . . . I did, but I didn't think to check. Are you sure? He didn't have a blue token. He didn't have anything. How could he be on the list? It has to be him though. Newdale's a small town. I'd know if there was another Steven Jones. Are you sure that's what it said? I don't see when he could have found a token. He didn't have one when we left. Where would he have got it from at the last moment? We left so late that Matthew and I only just made it ourselves. And Steven . . . Steven . . . he was still at home. Are you sure it said Stephen Jones?'

'Quite sure. But if you want to check for yourself, it'll be broadcast again at eight.'

'He's my son. I need to know now!' Mrs Jones raised her voice.

'Okay, I'll take you to see Gordon. He's a close friend of mine; we shared a room at Uni and he's in charge of broadcasting the information. I'm sure he'll let you look at the list. I'll have to come with you, though, as your key card won't let you into the control room.'

Mrs Jones' hand trembled slightly as she tucked a stray strand of hair behind her ear. She stood, like a child waiting for permission, her head down, but her dark eyes pleading, until Frank took her by the arm and led her towards the lift. Once inside, Frank pushed the top button on the control panel. The label read 198, the highest floor on Freedom 1.

Mrs Jones thought it curious to have such a large ship with 198 floors. *If you're building something this big, why not round it up to a perfect 200?* But before she could voice her thoughts, the lift door opened and Frank stepped out.

'This . . . is where it all happens.' Frank said proudly, swiping his card and waiting for the glittering green door to reveal the restricted area. 'The control room.'

Mrs Jones followed, eyes wide with wonder as she saw the vast number of screens, controls and flashing lights in all colours of the rainbow. As they reached the front of the room, she noticed a large screen playing black and white images. A small green light blinked in the corner and written next to it were the words, "Live feed".

A red haired, athletic looking man stepped in front of Mrs Jones, blocking her view. He scowled at Frank.

'What do you think you're doing, bringing a civilian up here without clearance?'

'It's okay, Gordon. Mrs Jones is a friend of mine. I'm hoping you can help us out. You see, she missed the broadcast of the names and we think her son might be on the list.'

'It'll be broadcast again at eight. She'll have to wait. The Captain's furious already, so now is not a good time to go around breaking the rules.'

'Gordon, have a heart; how would you feel if you had no idea whether your kid was alive or not?'

'That's exactly why I broadcast the list, to put people's minds at rest if I could. But when the Captain found out, he exploded. I've never seen him so mad.'

While Frank and Gordon continued their exchange, Mrs Jones managed to manoeuvre herself into a position where she could see the screen more clearly. It reminded her of one of those films you see on nature programmes where they show footage of the animals at night. A strange glow, like a torch about to run out of batteries, came from the picture, making it look eerie. She could make out people moving in the background and every so often a face would come into view.

'Is that them?' She asked Gordon. 'Are they the ones who got the other tokens?'

'I'm sorry, lady, you do not have clearance to be here. You should leave now before I have to send for security.'

Ignoring his warnings, Mrs Jones moved closer to the screen. 'What have you done to them? Why are you keeping them in the dark?' She stared at the image before her. 'That's not what you've told people. It's nothing like a hotel. Where are they?'

And that's when she saw him, just a glimpse, but she knew Steve was alive.

'Quick, turn it back! I think that's him!'

'We can't, we don't control the images. We get whatever they send.'

'But I need to be sure. I still want to see the list; it should be available for everyone to check. And why haven't you shown this footage to anyone? People would want to see this. You have to show everyone.'

'Mrs . . .' Gordon began.

'Jones, and that was my son, Steven Jones.'

'Mrs Jones, you have to understand. We can't just—' Gordon continued.

An imposing figure, dressed in all black, appeared from nowhere and cut him off.

'No we certainly can't. Come with me please ma'am.' The man had a deep authoritative voice. He indicated a small room behind them. Once inside, he introduced himself.

'I'm Captain Blackstone.'

'Oh, I'm sorry to have caused so much trouble, but I need to know if my son is on that list and I missed the broadcast.'

'I believe it will be repeated this evening,' he said through gritted teeth.

'Yes, I heard. Do you have children? I'm sure if you did, you'd understand. I can't wait. I need to his name in writing and I have to see it now!'

'Look, I understand your need to know, but *you* have to understand that you've put me in a very difficult situation. If people found out about the conditions their loved ones were living in, it could lead to mass hysteria.'

'No, I'm sure they'd just be relieved.'

'Trust me, I know what I'm doing and I *am* the captain. I can't possibly allow the footage to be seen by the public. I'm sure they would be relieved initially, but eventually someone will ask about their long term prospects and I don't know how to answer that yet. Do I have your word that you'll keep this quiet? I mean, I'll check the list of names for your son if you swear that you won't tell a living soul about what you've seen here today. And I need your assurance that you will never enter an unauthorised part of the ship again.'

'I won't tell a soul.'

'You must understand how important this is. One day, when I have a more solid plan for saving them, I'll show people the footage without making them panic. Until that time,' he continued, 'I need your word that you will tell no one.'

‘You have my word, I already said, they won’t hear anything from me. One more question though, if I may — What happened to the people who weren’t saved? Is it over yet?’

‘We don’t know for sure. Our outdoor cameras stopped working several days ago. It’s unlikely that there’s anyone left.’

‘Please, show me the list and you won’t hear from me again.’

‘Wait here.’ Blackstone left the room. As he walked away, Mrs Jones noticed his hair, which she’d assumed he’d combed off his face, was actually pulled back into a long grey ponytail. Blackstone returned a minute later with a laptop, which he placed on a desk in the middle of the room. ‘What’s your son’s full name and date of birth?’

‘Steven Jones, no middle name. 13th of January 2112

Blackstone scrolled down the screen until he reached the Js and then slowed down.

‘Jones, Steven, 13th of the 1st, 2112 from Newdale. He’s definitely on the list.’ Blackstone turned to Gordon, ‘I’ve got work to do, so make sure I’m not interrupted any more today.’ He started to move towards the door, but stopped and turned back. ‘Oh, and if anything like this ever happens again, *you’ll* be mucking out cows for the next fifty years! See that she leaves.’

Mrs Jones left the control room. A strange nagging sensation chipped away at her. Something familiar…from a long time ago. Something like love, but not love, with a hint of guilt, but not too much. She felt relieved that her eldest son was alive, even though it hadn’t bothered her at all to leave him behind. Hearing he was alive had changed her somehow. Seeing him in the cave, sensing the despair, momentarily made her feel more human than she had in a long time. In a brief moment where confusion clouded her mind, Mrs Jones decided to do perhaps the first decent thing that she had done for a long time. She would break her vow of silence to the Captain and she would tell Matthew that his brother was alive.

***

Under the shadow of a small oak tree, Matthew shivered. He looked at his watch; the dining hall would be closing in half an hour. Pete pulled his shoes and socks back on. His feet had dried out after paddling in the stream earlier. As they neared the familiar path which led through the trees and back to reality, they heard movement from behind.

Gasping for breath, Ludo collapsed at their feet.

'Wait up,' he panted. 'I thought I'd missed you.'

'You need to get more exercise mate,' Pete grinned. 'What's the hurry anyway? We'll be back in the morning.'

'I'm working a double shift tomorrow. Some of the other changelings are sick. Nothing serious, but they'll be out of action for a while, which means that I won't get here much over the next few days. Just wanted to let you know in case you were worried.'

Matthew reached for a couple of blackberries and tossed them to Ludo, who ate them greedily.

'Thanks,' he said, wiping his mouth on his forearm.

A rustling of leaves caught Matthew's attention. He glanced over his shoulder at the same moment as his mother appeared in a gap between a willow tree and a row of blackberry bushes.

12

The only sounds were the trickling of the stream; the buzzing of the occasional insect; the leaves rustling in the alien-made wind, and the heavy breathing of one small, brown, unfit changeling, who had tried to run for cover after the appearance of Matthew's mother. Her panicked screams proved that it was too late to hide. Ludo had been seen . . . again.

'It's okay,' Matthew said, grabbing his mother's arm to try to calm her. 'He's with us, a friend of ours. He's harmless.'

Mrs Jones backed away.

'Get away from it!' she ordered, hysterically. 'It could be dangerous!'

Ludo stepped forward. 'I'm only dangerous if provoked or attacked. In self-defence, I could spray a toxic liquid which will blind you long enough for me to escape.'

'Ludo!' Pete interrupted. 'I don't think she needs to know the specifics.'

Mrs Jones was already marching back towards the entrance to the gardens, half walking, half running, with a panicked expression on her face.

'Mum!' Matthew ran after her, leaving Ludo to watch the situation unfolding from the safety of the trees. 'He's okay. He won't hurt you.'

'Matthew, it just said it was poisonous. We need to get away and let security know,' she began to hyperventilate. 'Someone needs to capture it and take it away.'

'No Mum, you don't understand. You can't tell anyone. He'll get into trouble.'

Pete caught up with the pair of them.

'Mrs Jones, please listen.' He added. 'You really don't know anything about Ludo. He works on the ship. We promised that we wouldn't tell anyone that we'd seen him. His kind are supposed to stay hidden from us to avoid people getting scared, just like you are.'

'*He* works on the ship? A strange-looking, talking creature tells you he works on the ship and you just believe him without question? That thing's obviously brainwashed the pair of you. For all you know it could be an alien.'

'He is an alien. At least, he's not from Earth, but this far from home technically we're all aliens. And he's not an *it*. He's a changeling and he's called Ludo and we've been seeing him for weeks. He's our friend and he's completely harmless,' Matthew insisted. 'In fact, we wouldn't even have this ship if it weren't for the changelings, let alone be able to fly it.'

'And how would you know, you're just a child. It could be plotting against us all, telling you lies just to get close to you.' She continued marching towards the doors.

'He's not like that. We really know him. He—'

'Not another word Matthew.' She turned and held up her hand to silence Pete. 'And not from you either. You're just children, easily fooled. You haven't got the life experience to make the right decision. Trust me, I know what's best for all of us and that is my final word on the matter.'

Mrs Jones refused to say another word, no matter how much the boys pleaded with her. By the time they reached the corridor on the 73rd floor, they were physically trying to stop her advancing. Pete kept standing in front of her, only to be crossly pushed aside, and Matthew tried desperately to hold her back by hanging on to his mother's arm and dragging her backwards. Their efforts were, however, in vain. Mrs Jones knocked briskly on Frank's door and within minutes the whole story came pouring out.

Frank ushered them all inside and questioned the boys for twenty minutes on their dealings with Ludo. They answered his questions as briefly as possible but left out their whole time travelling adventure. Despite the boys' pleas, Frank decided that the best thing to do would be to report the whole incident to the captain. He eventually managed to quieten Mrs Jones down by reassuring her that a team of experienced humans were at the helm, all under the expert control of Captain Blackstone, who has years of experience in space travel, being the youngest ever astronaut to walk on Mars some forty years previously. 'We're lucky to have him. He's piloted, and captained, numerous ships over the last four decades.'

Matthew couldn't work out if Frank genuinely believed all this or if he was just trying to prevent his mother from running round frightening the rest of the passengers on the ship.

Frank insisted that he had never heard of a "changeling" and that the idea of aliens flying Freedom 1 was ludicrous. He told Mrs Jones and the boys to wait there while he spoke to his supervisors.

They waited.

Matthew looked at the clock and sighed when he realised that they had missed yet another meal.

'I bet the captain's eaten.' Pete moaned.

Matthew pictured the Captain negotiating his way through a large three course meal.

Two hours later, the door slid open, and an imposing figure filled the door frame.

'How did you get in?' Matthew asked.

The man stepped forward with a grunt, 'What you meant to say is — How did you get in, *Captain Blackstone?'*

Blackstone towered above the boys. His long grey hair and several days' growth of stubble framed his tired face. He spoke abruptly, reminding Matthew of Mr Harper. 'Tell me exactly what you told your manager.'

Matthew took a deep breath. 'We've met one of the changelings. I don't know what you're worried about. I think that…'

'Did I ask what you thought?' Blackstone asked menacingly, his top lip curling slightly.

Captain Blackstone's visit lasted no more than five minutes. Matthew noticed a brief moment of recognition between the Captain and his mother and made a mental note to ask her about it later.

He refused to let the boys speak other than to answer his direct questions.

When he left, Matthew breathed a sigh of relief and then he and Pete raced back towards the gardens, hoping desperately to see their friend. Ludo sat quietly in the centre of the clearing looking depressed.

'Well?' he said hopefully, as Pete sat beside him.

Pete shrugged. 'I don't know what they're going to do, but I get the feeling it won't be good news for you.'

Ludo's gaze dropped towards the floor. 'We were all told, when we first came on board, and we're reminded every day that the number one rule is not to be seen. Not only have I broken that rule, but I have spoken with you on many occasions. They'll have no choice but to punish me.'

'That's ridiculous!' Matthew protested. 'You haven't done anything wrong. None of us have.'

'Promise me one thing?' Ludo begged, holding Matthew's gaze with his eyes. 'If you don't see me anymore, will you send a message to my sister, Yahtzee. I promised my mother I'd look after her. Tell her I'm sorry. Tell her what happened, she'll be worried and please, *please* don't let her actually see you. I don't want her to get into trouble too.'

Before Matthew could promise anything, a man in a sky blue uniform with silver buttons stepped into the clearing, his protective trousers rustling as he moved. Ludo got up and walked towards him.

'Stay still!' the man bellowed, waving some sort of weapon towards the changeling while simultaneously pulling out what looked like a large silver sack from one of his enormous pockets. He snatched up the small creature in one swift move and threw him into the sack.

'Stay still and I won't have to restrain you further.'

'Restrain him further?' Pete looked at the man with disgust. 'He's only a tenth of your size and completely harmless. Is the sack thing really necessary?'

'Young man, you really don't know what we are dealing with here and I suggest you don't tell anyone anything about your little friend here unless you want to be spending the next six months in solitary confinement and have all your friends thinking you've got a highly contagious disease.' The man turned to Matthew. 'If we hear one word about this from anyone on the ship, your feet won't touch the ground. Do I make myself clear?'

The boys nodded reluctantly, and without another word the man turned and disappeared down the path. Pete shook his head.

'What now?' he asked.

'Well, it's too late for dinner.' Matthew gave a lopsided grin. 'I suggest we go and look for Yahtzee.'

'Didn't you just hear what he said? I mean the bit about six months in a cell somewhere and all our friends thinking we're really ill.'

'What friends?' Matthew scowled briefly and then sighed.

'Alright,' Pete agreed. 'So we have no friends. That's not the best reason I can think of to go looking for trouble. And what's the point anyway?'

'We promised Ludo.'

'Actually we didn't promise anything.'

'But we would have if we'd had more time.'

'Speak for yourself.'

'Okay I will. If you don't want to come, I'll go by myself.'

'But *where* exactly will we go? Ludo has never said where he works or where they all live. How are we supposed to find Yahtzee? They're not supposed to be seen, remember?'

'So you are coming then?'

Pete gave up the argument. 'I suppose someone will have to keep you out of trouble. What's the plan then?'

By the time the boys left their spot in the garden, they had agreed on a vague plan of action. Matthew trod carefully as the darkness descended and the path merged with its surroundings. The boys said their goodnights before going home to get some sleep. On his way down the corridor, Matthew realised this was the first time that he'd thought of his room on the ship as home.

***

There were two problems: One — the tightly secured straps on the sack, and two — the guard who refused to put said sack down. Apart from that, Ludo's plan was fool-proof... Except for not knowing where they were; who else was in the room; if the door was locked and whether the guard knew about his spitting ability. Okay, so there were more than two problems. Ludo always found it best to deal with one problem a time. So far his plan, though a little vague, involved lots of spitting and running. Spit in their eyes and run away. Not that that had worked out for him last time. *Yahtzee is going to be so cross with me when I get back.*

Before he had a chance to put phase one, chew through sack, into progress, his world, or rather the sack, turned upside down, depositing him unceremoniously in a heap on the ground. Startled, he blinked, jumped to his feet and spun round, taking in the details of his unfortunate situation.

The smell of apple and blackberry pie filled the air in the most extravagantly decorated room on the ship — the captain's cabin. Blackstone lounged behind the glass dinner table and dabbed at his mouth with a silver napkin. Subtle pink tinged chandeliers reflected off the silver and purple flock wallpaper, lighting only one end of the room. In the gloom of the other end, Ludo made out a four-poster bed, complete with purple and silver patchwork quilt and covered in dozens of mix and match patterned cushions.

‘As much as I appreciate the lift, Captain, all you had to do was ask. I’d have happily walked here to join you for dinner.’

A rough hand shoved him to the ground. ‘Don’t speak unless you’re spoken to,’ the guard whispered gruffly in his ear.

Obviously the guard had never dealt with a changeling before. Ludo only had to turn his head to come face to face with the guy. He took his time, while the guard revelled in trying to intimidate him, to draw from all sixteen of his salivary glands.

And he spat.

At point blank range.

The guard screamed like a baby in need of its dummy, and fell to his knees, rubbing at his already streaming eyes.

Blackstone sat up straight and reached for his phone. ‘Now,’ he said calmly.

Suddenly, the lights brightened and the door slid open. Four more guards entered, all dressed in white bio-hazard suits, complete with masks and respirators.

Ludo didn’t stand a chance.

Within seconds, and despite his wildest efforts, Ludo was restrained in something resembling a straitjacket and fixed securely to a small metal chair.

Blackstone stared at Ludo.

Ludo stared at Blackstone.

‘So,’ Blackstone finally broke the silence. ‘This is the one?’

‘This is it,’ a woman’s voice wheezed through the respirator.’

‘I’ll have you know, *I* am *not* an—’

‘Silence it!’ Blackstone snapped.

A thick blanket covered in pin prick lights appeared in the corner of Ludo’s vision.

‘Okay,’ he relented, a thread of panic creeping into his voice. This was not a game. He’d seen blankets like this before. ‘I get it. I won’t talk.’

Too little, too late. The guard behind his right shoulder launched the blanket in one sweeping arc and brought it down over Ludo's head.

There would be no talking his way out now. This was a one way blanket. He would be able to see and hear everything that went on in the room, but no matter how loud he shouted, nobody would hear him. He sighed.

'This is it,' the woman continued. 'The one that's been seen.'

Blackstone turned to face the quivering blanket. 'You are here to be sentenced. You are accused of not only allowing yourself to be seen, but of initiating a relationship with two children, which goes directly against your original orders. You have also released your poison on a member of my staff, proving you cannot be trusted in an environment such as ours, here on Freedom 1.

'There is no defence for your actions. You may not speak.'

Ludo shifted uncomfortably under the blanket. Blackstone's stare sent shivers down his spine. This was bad.

'Your sentence has already been decided, and will be carried out immediately.

***

The next morning, after a breakfast of porridge, toast and fruit juice, the boys set off towards the lift. Since they had found the garden, they hadn't really spent much time anywhere else and didn't know their way around the majority of the upper levels at all.

Fortunately, school had finished for Easter — though they only had one week off instead of two — which gave them some much needed time. Their plan involved starting at the top of the ship and working their way down. Matthew had bought a pen and notebook to make a map of the ship and to record what they found on each level. The lift had quite a few labels for different floors, which Matthew copied down into his note book. During a general sweep of the ship, they would mark off all of the restricted access areas on their map. The boys figured that if the changelings were supposed to stay hidden, they wouldn't be living or working somewhere that just anyone could get to.

***

Searching the ship took a lot longer than they thought. By dinner time, they had only managed to get as far as level 180, and of those top eighteen floors, they had only managed to map out a few. Levels 190–198 were completely inaccessible to civilians. They had discovered, by asking around, that these floors housed the control room, a command room and the staff quarters. Floors 180–189 had many areas they could get to and some they could not. Their own school took up the centre of floor 182 and several other schools surrounded it. As far as they could tell, these floors were all similar in layout. On the next floor a signpost over the main door read: Nursery and Pre-school, and above that were several floors taken up by places set up for further education. These floors were not accessible without going through a door that used palm print recognition instead of a key card.

By the end of the week, the boys had a pretty good map of the ship. There were lots of areas still left blank, but they had managed to rule out many of these by hanging around and watching people come and go. Some of the unmarked areas on the map simply weren't big enough and others, Matthew felt, were much too far away from the control room. This meant that the area still to search had been narrowed considerably. It seemed most likely to Matthew, and Pete agreed, that the changelings would be somewhere near the top of the ship. Somewhere close enough to get onto the control room without being seen by the general public. A whole week passed with no sign of Ludo or any of his friends and family. Tomorrow, they decided, they would try to find a way to explore the hidden rooms.

13

Five months earlier: The day of the lottery.

Jess had only been at Newdale High school for half a term. It wasn't ideal to switch high schools part way through the year, but it had been the only option left. Besides, she was used to change. A year before she had been forced to change schools when her father had been offered a job as head of maths at Newdale. It meant moving across three counties which, to Jess, may as well have been the other side of the world. It had been decided that she would go to the Grange, an all-girl school about half a mile outside of Newdale. It was easier for everyone if she wasn't attending the same school in which her father taught. The problem was, she hadn't settled at The Grange. In fact, she hated it. The girls were mostly stuck up, spoilt brats with swimming pools and ponies in their gardens. Jess felt out of place and so kept to herself. Unfortunately, her quietness had been mistaken for rudeness and she soon was excluded from all of the previously established friendship groups.

As time went by, she became more and more isolated and at home she was miserable and withdrawn. Her parents decided to move her one more time. This would be her last chance to try and fit in and this time it would be harder, having her father there. Had she known how unpopular her father was with the students, she may have thought twice before agreeing to move schools, but today, for the first time, she was actually glad to be at the same school as her father.

He had warned her about the lottery, told her what it meant and promised she would be safe. He and his wife, her mother, already had their places on the escape ship.

Jess's mother's place was guaranteed as her own father worked at the United Kingdom Space Agency. The UKSA had been contacted by the government eighteen months ago to assist with evacuations. Jess didn't know exactly what her grandfather did, he had never had much time for her or even for his own daughter, but she knew he was an influential man who had an important role in the Space Agency, and it was because of him that her parents would be leaving in the first group.

Mr Harper had reassured his daughter that no matter what colour token she received, he would be taking her with him and her mother and they would all leave this place together. Jess believed him.

***

As the whole school lined up, Jess looked from one classmate to the next, wondering which, if any, of them would be among the lucky few. She didn't have any preferences; she didn't have any friends.

Jess neared the front of the queue. As she looked up, she noticed the boy from the playground earlier. He looked nervous as he, in turn, stepped up and reached into the box on the large wooden table. A few seconds later, his hand emerged, holding a green token and Jess smiled to herself. She had a feeling about this boy. She didn't know his name but she had seen him around school and she believed him to be a lot like her, another outsider.

Three quarters of the students had passed the box before Jess took her turn. She closed her eyes and plunged her hand deep into the darkness. There were only nine rows of children left now. Each student silently held in place by their form tutor. There would only be a few green tokens left by now. Jess had tried to keep track of how many had been withdrawn, but couldn't always see clearly from her position near the back of her row. Knowing what all the different colours meant, Jess hoped to select a green and take her place fairly, without her father's help. Her hand seized the first token it touched and closed around it. Jess pulled her hand out and found herself too scared to open it, wanting to keep her hopes alive by not knowing. Too scared to think about what her father would have to do if she hadn't managed to secure a place for herself. She held her breath and opened her hand.

Red.

Jess's eyes searched the school yard frantically for her father. He stood near the oak tree, watching her from a distance. Her eyes caught his and in that split second she sensed his fear. Her heart sank. For the first time that day she felt scared and she wondered what her father would have to do. She hoped he had a plan that wouldn't involve hurting anyone else, but she knew what sort of a man he could be and it frightened her. With nothing left to do, she went home to wait.

The first of the street lights flickered on outside the house. Jess sat on her bed. She turned the TV off as every channel played either re-runs of lotteries from all over the country, or showed over animated presenters discussing with various "experts" what it could all mean. They were clearly guessing. Jess wondered how many people actually knew the awful secret — that the reds would probably never make it. The greens would be saved, followed by the blues. The government spokespeople still insisted the lottery only gave people a slot. Her parents had discussed it in hushed voices many times over the last few weeks. The reds were doomed, destined to go down with the sinking ship that was planet Earth.

Jess shuddered. The only people that knew the secret were those that had already booked their place in the future and wouldn't risk losing it by letting anything slip to the press. She wondered what stories would be on the news after all the Greens and Blues had left.

Jess heard the soft click as the front door closed and rushed downstairs. Her parents looked exhausted. Her mother's smudged make-up ran down her puffy cheeks. Jess looked to her father.

'What's wrong?' she asked, though in her heart she already knew. Her father shook his head and in that moment Jess realised the terrible truth. He couldn't keep his promise. Jess would be going nowhere.

She ran to her mother and they cried together.

Her father broke the silence first. 'We have to leave early in the morning. There's still a chance. We mustn't give up hope. I've got money, and people don't yet know what is happening. I'll buy another green token, whatever the cost.'

When Jess awoke after a restless night, she still felt tired. She had heard her father leave long before the sun rose and wondered what news he would bring with his return. She knew they had to be at the Capital Tower by one o'clock. It would usually take twenty minutes on foot, but her mother had planned for them to leave at eleven thirty, just to be on the safe side. Her bag had been packed since last week, so with nothing to do, she sat and she waited.

Twelve o'clock came and went. At five minutes past, Mr Harper finally arrived home to be met at the door by two desperate faces. He had dark rings under his eyes which avoided Jess's gaze. He looked at his wife and shook his head. 'Everyone's panicking. It's dangerous outside and it's getting late. We need to start moving towards the town. I've taken out all of our life savings in cash. We'll try to buy a token on the streets. We'll have better luck in town as all the people with green tokens will be in one place at the same time. They still believe that the coloured tokens are just to allocate a departure time, but everyone wants to go first. I think when we're all out there people will be more sympathetic. We'll have to really play on the "keeping a family together" thing.'

At twelve thirty Jess and her parents abandoned the car and started to walk. She saw no sign of sympathy on the streets. Money meant nothing anymore. Jess couldn't bear to see her parents behaving like desperate beggars. She didn't notice Matthew watching them from further down the road. Shocked by the level of violence on the streets, she closed her mind to the sights and sounds of a town in despair. Desperate times called for desperate measures.

She would never forget this day for as long as she lived. She reminded herself that might not be very long.

They made their way towards the tallest building in the town, Capital Tower, the headquarters of the UKSA. Her father had brought her here once before. They had been on their way to the shopping centre to buy Jess's school uniform for Newdale High and had stopped off to collect some paperwork for her grandfather. It looked different now, with crowds gathering from all directions. People were shouting and shoving, fighting and begging. Once again, tears welled up in her eyes.

Ten to one. They needed more time. Her parents would be leaving and she would be alone. She had never seen her father cry before and she knew she couldn't blame him for anything. When he promised her she'd be safe, he'd meant it. He truly believed that his money could buy him anything. He hadn't lied; he believed he had the power to change things. She mustn't blame him.

She hugged her father and studied his face for the last time, burning his features into her memory. She allowed his unsteady hand to cup her face before she broke away and turned to her mother. Tears streamed down her cheeks. 'You have to go before they lock you out,' she cried softly, looking at her mother's anguished face and then burying herself deep in her arms.

Mrs Harper pulled her daughter close. Without letting go, she turned to her husband and smiled. Somehow she found the words. 'I won't leave her here alone. Take Jess; I'll stay.'

'We can't...' Mr Harper stammered. 'I mean...you can't...the tag won't come off until you're on board!'

Mrs Harper threw herself to the floor and clawed desperately at the tag until her daughter sat beside her, covered her mother's frantic hands with her own and eased them away from her now bleeding ankle.

Jess shook her head, smiled, stood and offered her hand to her mum. 'I'll be ok,' she said calmly to the defeated woman at her feet, though the words were lost over the hubbub.

Mrs Harper let out a wobbly sigh, then stood decisively and faced her husband. 'Don't worry about us,' her voice wavered. 'We'll be okay. I'll take care of Jess. You have to go now; you'll be needed.'

Understanding crept up on him and he shook his head. 'I'm not going without you, Sarah.' He croaked. 'I could never . . .'

'And I'm not going without Jess!'

After a moment's awkward stillness, he pulled them both into a ferocious bear-hug.

'Go John.' She whispered into his ear. 'I want you to go.' Then she pushed him gently away. 'If you don't…it's all for nothing. So senseless. Do this for me . . . for us.' Their eyes locked. 'I'll be happy if I know you're there helping others.'

Sarah kissed him tenderly and then gently pushed him towards the open gates. 'It's time John.' She put her arm around Jess's shoulders and led the girl away. It took a concentrated effort to move her legs, one at a time, away from the gate. She swallowed her sobs and hid her face from her daughter, knowing that looking into her eyes would send her over the edge. Mother and daughter slowly weaved their way through the crowds, against the flow of people, still trying to enter the enclosure. Knowing she would never again look upon her husband's face, she still refused to look back.

14

On Saturday morning, the boys met in the garden before breakfast. Matthew wanted to go to the clearing in the little wood. They hadn't been since the day Ludo had been taken away. Memories of their few short weeks of fun with the changeling came flooding back.

'I can't believe he's not here.'

'It's so quiet without him,' Pete agreed.

'Did you have any ideas overnight?'

Pete looked serious. 'Well, we know there's no way onto the restricted floors without a key card.' He sat down looking troubled. 'I can only think of one way,' he continued. 'We need a key card so we'll have to get one. Who do we know that might have access?'

'Only Frank, and there's no way he'd let us borrow his, especially now.'

'Who said anything about borrowing it?' Pete said with a wicked smile.

'You mean we should just take it, without asking?'

'Don't you think that would be best? I'd much prefer it if nobody knew what we were up to. That way we stand a better chance. Now, where does he keep it and when does he use it?'

'Maybe we should follow him for a while and see where he goes.' Matthew said. 'There's no point stealing his card until we know it'll work.'

'The problem is *how* we follow him without making it obvious. We can't very well go up to the control room with him in the lift, can we?'

'I've had a better idea.'

'What?' Pete asked.

'We'll just ask him about the ship. He might tell us if he thinks it's just an innocent question.'

After some thought, Pete agreed. 'Okay, but let me do the talking.'

It took a while to track down Frank. They tried his office first and then his room, with no luck. The boys waited for him in corridor 73 for nearly an hour before giving up and going to get some breakfast. When they reached the front of the queue, they noticed Frank tucking into his breakfast, a much larger portion of porridge than either of the boys had ever received.

'Quick!' Matthew urged. 'Let's go and sit with him before he finishes. We can pretend we're interested in becoming a manager like him when we're older. Ask him what the job involves.'

'Hi Frank, do you mind if we join you?' Matthew asked. 'I know you must be busy, a man in your position, but do you have a few minutes to talk? We want to ask you a few questions.'

'Questions eh, what sort of questions?' Frank asked while scraping porridge from the sides of the bowl.

'We've been thinking,' Pete started slowly, 'that what you do must be quite interesting, and I wondered, well I thought that when I'm older it might be something I could do.'

'Me to,' Matthew continued, 'only we're not sure exactly what the job involves, so we were wondering if—'

'You were wondering if I could fill you in, is that it?'

'Yes, if you don't mind.'

'Well, I suppose it's quite varied. I spend a lot of time dealing with people's problems and concerns. I have the whole of floor 73 to deal with, that's nearly two thousand passengers you know. You'd have to have good communication skills.'

'Do you ever get to work anywhere other than floor 73?'

'Sometimes, but only if someone needs my help, or if another manager is off sick.' Frank leaned back in his chair and stretched out his legs.

'Have you seen the whole ship? I bet you're important enough to go anywhere you want. Have you ever been in the control room?'

Frank laughed. 'Yes, a few times I've been called there to run errands for the crew. It's an amazing place. I remember the first time I saw it; all new staff received a guided tour of the ship before we took off. It's full of computers and gadgets and flashing lights.'

'Do many people work there?'

'I've never counted, but I guess around fifty. I don't think you're likely to get a job there though, they're all geniuses.'

Frank finished his porridge and put his spoon down. 'Been pleasant talking with you,' he nodded at the boys. 'But I've a full day ahead of me and I need to get going. I'm always here early if you want to chat.' He gave Pete a wink, put on his jacket and walked cheerfully towards one of the canteen staff, a pretty young girl with long brown hair, tied back in a ponytail that reached halfway down her back.

Pete grabbed Matthew's arm. 'We don't have much time.' He jumped to his feet and dragged a confused looking Matthew towards the lift. As they went past Frank, they heard him thank the girl, who had a badge with the name "Alice" printed in gold letters. Then he asked her if she would still be on duty at lunchtime. Matthew never heard the response; Pete pulled him into the lift and punched the number 198 into the keypad.

'What are you doing?' Matthew asked, panting slightly.

Pete's hand disappeared up his opposite sleeve and retrieved a plastic key card from its hiding place.

'Fancy checking out the control room?' he grinned.

'What? When? How did you get it?' Matthew gasped.

'Frank left his blazer hanging on the back of his chair. I searched his pockets when he started waffling on about the control room. We have to do it now before he notices it's gone. Hopefully he'll think he lost it and won't suspect us for a while. Eventually he's sure to work it out, so we've only got one chance at this. Are you ready?'

Matthew nodded though he didn't feel ready at all. They'd already been in trouble once and he didn't fancy spending time in solitary confinement. True, Ludo had been a good friend to them, but wasn't this asking a bit too much? The lift slowed down and the door slid open to reveal a short, green corridor with an emerald encrusted door at the end. Two smaller corridors led off to the right, but the door in front oozed character and importance. *This is it*. The corridor stood empty. A small slot to the left of the door looked the right size for the key card. The boys pressed themselves as flat as they could into the walls either side of the door before Pete plunged the card into the slot. The door instantly sprung open.

Cautiously, Matthew peered around the solid metal doorframe. His jaw dropped as he took in the sight from back of the room. Dozens of people bustling around in organised chaos. The crew moved purposefully, like ants searching for food, each one knowing their role. Numerous long worktables jutted out at 45 degree angles from either side of the room, allowing everyone — including the boys — a view of the central control panel on the front wall. Each person watched, and responded to, the various messages and data that scrolled, like breaking news bulletins, across the bank of screens which lined each table. No one lost focus long enough to notice the boy's heads in the open doorway behind them. Mesmerized by the activity before them, Matthew struggled to concentrate. He tried to pay attention on the layout of the room. Three doors led off to their right. Two of which were firmly closed, the third, and closest, stood slightly ajar. He ducked down low, sped towards the door, slid through the gap and then sat on the floor of what appeared to be the men's toilets. Pete joined him a second later and pulled the door almost closed.

'Now what?' Matthew asked. 'There's no sign of Ludo or any of the changelings. I don't think they come in here at all or Frank would know about them.'

'Ludo said the changelings controlled the ship, and this is the Control Room, but it's full of people. There must be somewhere else. We need to see what's behind the other doors, but I don't know whether they're locked. If they are, I doubt that Frank would be allowed in, so his card's probably useless. Who in here looks important enough to have access to the whole ship?'

Matthew looked around the control room. 'I think we can eliminate all those that are wearing the same maroon uniform as Frank. If his key card doesn't work, then theirs probably won't either.'

'Good thinking,' Pete whispered. 'So who's left?'

Matthew pointed at a man with a long grey ponytail, who sat with his back to them in a black, leather swivel chair. The man studied a large monitor and then moved several switches.

'His uniform looks quite impressive and over there . . .' he indicated a small group of men and women wearing dark green. 'They're our only other option. What do you think?'

'I vote for the man in the chair, he's got to be in charge. If anyone's got access, it's got to be him.'

'Okay, we're agreed that he's got access, but what can we do about it? How can we get his key card? We were lucky with Frank, but something tells me that the man in that chair won't be so easy to fool.'

Without warning, the emergency alarm sounded from a speaker over Matthew's head making him jump so violently that he struggled to keep his balance. It was a siren rather than a bell and much louder than the alarm they'd heard on their last day at school. It sounded on for about five seconds, and then went quiet for the same amount of time. It repeated continuously, but in some of the silences, there were messages such as, 'Security breach.' or 'All members of staff to your places.' and 'sending message out now for all civilians go to their rooms and fasten their harnesses.'

Another message followed, 'Please do not panic. This is just a drill.' But from the way the staff were scurrying around and shouting strange numbers or codes at one another, Matthew remained unconvinced.

‘Now what?’ Pete asked. ‘We’ll never get out without being seen.’

The man in the chair stood up. Matthew recognised his black uniform, ‘It’s Captain Blackstone! He looks different with his hair tied back.’

‘Yeah, scarier!’ Pete agreed.

They watched the Captain as he walked towards one of the doorways the boys had noticed before. He slipped his key card into the slot by the door. Then he placed his hand on to a small screen and waited for his palm print to be recognised. Slowly the door slid open and the man disappeared into the darkness within.

Without thinking, Matthew dashed for the door. He could sense Pete close behind. A chorus of cries from the staff only spurred him on quicker. I slender young woman and a short, plump, bespectacled man, both in Maroon uniforms tried to block them, but Matthew dodged first one way, and then the other, reaching one hand forward just in time to block the door from sliding shut. As a sensor detected his hand, the door slowed and then sprang open again, allowing the boys to pass through. Pete prised the woman’s hand off his sleeve and shoved her roughly into the man, sending them both off balance long enough for the door to close unhindered.

As his eyes adjusted to the darkness, Matthew searched for somewhere to hide. The small room offered no protection and no way out except for a metal, spiral staircase leading upwards from the centre of the small room in which they stood. Blackstone’s long, black shiny boots clattered up the steps well above them by now so he didn’t notice the boys.

Matthew stared at the door. ‘If someone other than the captain can open that, we’re dead!’

‘We’re already dead,’ Pete whimpered. ‘They all saw us!’

‘But none of them know who we are. If we can get out without Blackstone seeing us we might stand a chance.’

A series of loud thuds and muffled shouting from the doorway started them moving.

'And the only way to go is up there?' Pete asked nervously.

'This was your idea!'

'We have to find a place to hide.'

'Agreed.'

Quickly, they crept up the stairs, which led them into a long dark room. The room reminded Matthew of an overcrowded charity shop with random pieces of furniture dotted about. Three quarters of the left wall housed a muddle of sideboards, dressers and bookcases, each one overflowing with a mixture of antique and modern looking junk. There were rows of leather bound books, whose spines were covered in strange symbols instead of words.

Floral plates were hung on the opposite wall, and the floor was covered in a maze of brightly coloured rugs. An unusual collection of chandeliers hung from the ceiling, which was noticeably lower than ceilings everywhere else on the ship.

Glass display cabinets towards the back of the room housed what looked like game counters and chess pieces of all shapes and sizes, and a large framed jigsaw, of Earth from space, took up most of the back wall.

Jumbled pieces of furniture were dotted about making the room a great place for a game of hide and seek.

Matthew crept along the shadowy back wall and hid behind a large grandfather clock. Pete ducked down behind a battered, old piano. A large green Persian rug stretched across the floor towards where the Captain had stopped.

Slowly, a group of small brown creatures surrounded him. They all watched him carefully as he spoke to them. Matthew couldn't hear him, but he guessed they were being given orders, because suddenly they all leapt into action around him. The man turned towards the corner where Matthew was hiding and marched across the room, straight towards the clock. Matthew's heart beat so loudly that he thought it would be heard. The man briefly stopped next to the clock, causing Matthew to hold his breath for what seemed like an eternity, before heading back down the stairs. He passed so closely that Matthew could hear him breathing.

When the sound of the captain's footsteps faded, the boys crept out from their hiding places and approached the changelings. Matthew thought back to his first encounter with Ludo. He covered his eyes, before coughing quietly, to get the attention of the group.

15

The siren continued to sound on and off. A monotonous grinding sound that hurt her ears. All over the ship, people immediately stopped what they were doing and made their way to their rooms.

'Where are you?' Mrs Jones muttered as she strapped herself into her chair. 'I'm not coming to look for you!'

The monitor came on and the sirens faded. The ringing in Mrs Jones's ears continued for a few minutes after the noise had stopped.

The familiar cyber face appeared on the screen. 'This is only a drill; there is no need to panic. We urge you to stay in your seat until given permission to move by your floor manager, who will be coming round shortly to conduct a head count. As soon as everyone on board is accounted for, you will all be released.'

'Ridiculous! A head count! As if anyone could go anywhere. I don't know where Matthew is.' Mrs Jones said to the screen. 'You can't keep me locked up in here if I don't know where he is.'

'Please stay calm.' The voice continued. 'This is just a practice to make sure you all know what to do in an emergency.'

The screen blackened, and again Mrs Jones thought of her son and remembered that she still hadn't told him about Steve. She decided that once Frank had officially released her, she would go and look for him . . . or perhaps she'd have lunch first.

***

The changelings all become aware of the presence of the boys at the same time. They slowly turned to face them, their eyes inquisitive. The only noise came from the grandfather clock, which ticked rather irregularly, as though it needed winding up. They didn't appear to be surprised by the sudden appearance of two strangers among them.

Matthew spoke first. ‘My name’s Matthew and this is Pete. We don’t have much time; we’ve been seen, and as soon as Blackstone goes back to the control room someone will be after us.’

One of the taller changelings spoke first, ‘What do you want?’

‘We came because Ludo sent us. He wanted us to give you a message. We didn’t know how to find you. We really don’t want to cause any trouble for you and we know you’re not supposed to talk to us.’

One changeling stepped forward. She looked smaller than the others and wore a thin patchwork dress over her hairless brown body. She looked at Matthew.

‘What’s your message?’ she asked

‘Ludo asked us to give the message to the one named Yahtzee. Is that you?’

She nodded. ‘I’m Yahtzee, Ludo’s sister.’

‘We promised Ludo that we wouldn’t actually let you see us so that you wouldn’t get into trouble, but we didn’t know how to contact you as we never had time to ask him.’

Pete stepped forward to stand beside Matthew. ‘He wanted us to tell you he’s sorry. He wanted to look after you, but they took him away.’

‘When . . .? What happened to him? Where did they take him?’

‘We don’t know.’ Matthew shook his head sympathetically. ‘But, they took him because he’d been speaking to us. It’s our fault. We’re so sorry.’

Yahtzee smiled at them. ‘It’s not your fault,’ she said reassuringly. ‘I’m sure Ludo knew the risks. He liked you and so he took a chance. I don’t blame him or you. He told me about you, you know, and he said that you are good, kind boys. Thank you for delivering his message. Now you really need to hurry home. Apparently, someone stole a key card, but as yet they don’t know who.’ Yahtzee raised her wrinkled eyebrows. ‘I don’t suppose you know anything about it? They’re carrying out a search right now to see who's missing. If you're not in your room when they check it, you'll be in trouble. Why don't you give me the key card and I'll return it.'

Sheepishly, Matthew pulled the shiny card out of his pocket and handed it to her.

A deafening roar from the staircase and the heavy clatter of boots on metal could only mean one thing. A furious Blackstone would be upon them any moment.

'Hurry,' Yahtzee urged. 'Follow me!'

She led the boys to a small lift and pushed them inside.

'One more thing,' she added, her hand hovering over the lift buttons, 'If you should ever want to contact me again, go to the stream at the bottom of the garden. Under the footbridge are some large pebbles. Pile them high to signal that you need me and I'll meet you at 4:30 the following evening. Now please, hurry!'

She waved goodbye as the doors slid shut.

***

Matthew emerged on floor 73, leaving Pete in the lift to continue down. It took him a while to get his bearings as this lift had not been marked on the map and they hadn't noticed it before. The paint on the outside matched the colour of the walls and at only half the size of the regular lifts, to a casual passer-by it looked like a strange kind of air vent. Matthew checked the door number closest to him 21,698. He figured he was two corridors and nearly one hundred rooms away from his own.

Matthew leant against the wall to think. Franks men would probably start from the other end of his own corridor because both the lifts and his office were in that direction. Matthew imagined them working their way from one room to the next. Getting closer. Time was running out, so he pushed himself off the wall and dashed to the end of the corridor. He rounded the next bend, but pulled back when he saw them. Four men, in maroon uniforms. They were each clutching shiny silver clipboards and working their way systematically closer.

Matthew peered round the corner cautiously. The men entered each room in turn, disappearing for only a minute or two before moving on to the next. This would all be down to timing and luck.

Matthew dug his key card out of his pocket and gripped it as he prepared to make his move.

Frank and two others entered rooms at the same time. The fourth guard emerged a few seconds later and walked briskly to the next door.

Matthew got ready to run.

The door slid open and the man disappeared from view.

Matthew made his move.

Forty doors away from home — He heard a door slide open. It was too late to turn back, so he ran faster.

Twenty doors away — He saw the back of a guard's maroon blazer and heard him thank the room's occupier for their time. He ran on.

Ten doors away — The guard started to turn. Matthew would never make it and he had nowhere to hide.

Five doors away — The guard's radio bleeped. He unclipped it from his belt as Matthew reached his own door and scanned his card. The door slid and Matthew practically fell through the gap before it fully opened.

Matthew glared at his mother as he strapped himself in with only seconds to spare. He tried to steady his breathing as Frank entered the room.

The floor manager read from a list of questions without making eye contact. At least Matthew's mother backed up his story and told them he had been with her for the last hour. They left after only a few minutes and Matthew allowed himself to relax a little. His mother sat with her eyes closed.

‘Where were you?’ she asked. ‘I thought something had happened to you.’

‘You didn’t look very worried.’

‘We need to talk.’

‘Why? We never talk.’

His mother turned her head sharply towards him and their eyes locked. ‘It’s about—’

The screen flashed on, this time showing pictures from home, on Earth. First they saw it as it had been when they left. Then new images came, of how the Earth had changed and what it had become. There were no signs of life anywhere. A few patches of shrivelled brown grass remained here and there between vast dusty spaces. A dried up river bed snaked between sun scorched trees, and the rotten corpses of sheep, or cows (it was impossible to tell which) littered a field. As the camera panned to the right, it revealed a blackened figure, almost certainly the remains of a man or woman, hunched over the steering wheel of a Land Rover with peeling paintwork.

Matthew fought back tears forming in the corners of his eyes and wiped his sleeve across his face.

‘Steve,’ he sobbed. ‘Where’s Steve? What must have happened to him? They said everyone would be okay, but that man in the car . . .’

‘No!’ his mother shouted, leaning forward into her harness. ‘You don’t understand. I’ve seen Steve. He’s okay.’

‘What? How can you have seen him? Where?’

‘In the control room.’

‘Steve’s here, on the ship?’

‘No, I went to the control room. I saw Steve on the monitor.’

‘What were you doing in the control room? You don’t have access.’

‘I went with Frank. I don‘t know how he did it, but Steve must have got a blue token. He‘s with the other group now. For now they're safe under the ground and they're already working on plans for a rescue. He's going to be fine.'

'But you knew Steve was okay, and you didn't think to tell me until now.'

'I came to tell you last week, but that thing got in the way.'

'Last week! You've known for a whole week and didn't think to mention it.'

The expression on his mother's face remained passive.

'And as for that thing,' Matthew continued. 'That thing . . . is my friend, and thanks to you, he's been sent away! Matthew unfastened his harness and stormed towards his room.

'You can't go yet; we have to keep our harness on until Frank says it's safe.'

Unbelievable.

'It is safe!' Matthew yelled, tears now blurring his vision. 'Don't you see, you…you…? This is all your fault! They were trying to catch *me* out of the room. They're scared we're on to their secret. There *is* no emergency,' he sighed. 'If you'd just kept quiet we wouldn't be in this mess. And I, for one, am not sitting around here all evening waiting for Frank. I'll be in my room.' The door slid shut behind him.

Matthew threw himself on to his bed. He didn't love his mother; he didn't even like her that much. The thought of being without her didn't bother him at all. He felt as though he had been without her all his life anyway. Maybe he'd been too harsh. She hadn't cared for them on Earth, so why should he expect anything more here? He realised he hadn't asked her about Steve. The thought of facing his mother made him feel sick, but Steve's face filled his head and his heart hammered loudly in his chest. He needed to find out what she knew. Matthew got up, wiped his eyes with the heel of his hand, and went back to the living room. His mother still sat in the same place, as though nothing had happened.

Matthew stood behind his chair. 'What did you see?' he asked quietly.

His mother answered his questions in short sentences, giving no more detail than necessary. Matthew thanked her coldly and went back to his bedroom. He thought of Steve huddled in a dark, damp cave and hoped he'd be okay. How long could a person survive in the conditions his mum had described without going insane? But the important thing to remember was that against all the odds, Steve had survived and that meant he had a chance. For the first time, Matthew felt a flicker of hope. He dared to think of a future that Steve would be a part of. Steve was safe for a while longer. Eventually he would be rescued.

***

As he slept, moments from Matthew's last days on Earth, filled his dreams. He relived his last hours at school and his last night at home with his brother. But then, more troubling scenes flashed before him, of the fighting in the town, of absolute chaos, and then of Mr Harper and his daughter, desperately searching for a way to keep their family together.

Matthew awoke and sat up. Darkness surrounded him, and it took him a while to remember where he was. He lay down and tried to get back to sleep, but his dreams troubled his mind. He just couldn't switch off, and so found himself wondering what happened to Jess, and whether she had made it into the underground centre like Steve or if she was already dead. Matthew actually felt sorry for his old teacher. He knew how it felt to leave someone behind. True, he and Steve weren't exactly close, but they were family and he didn't deserve to be left behind, alone, to have to fend for himself.

Pete's mother had sacrificed herself for her children. Matthew hadn't known Pete's mum at all, but he believed she was more like what a parent should be than his own selfish mother. Pete's mum had laid down her life so that her children might stand a chance. That's what parents did. His mother didn't consider anyone other than herself. Then it occurred to Matthew that Mr Harper hadn't given up his place on the ship for his daughter. He carried on as though nothing happened, knowing Jess never made it. He stopped feeling sympathetic and covered his head with a pillow.

After another two hours of drifting in and out of sleep, Matthew got up. A quick shower revived him. He dressed quickly and went to knock for Pete. They talked about Ludo over breakfast and then went to the garden. They stopped where the bridge crossed the stream and looked beneath the shady archway. There were half a dozen flat stones under the bridge, which Matthew stacked into a small pile.

'What are you doing?' Pete asked. 'I mean, what do we have to say to Yahtzee if she comes?'

'I've been thinking all night,' Matthew replied. 'And I think I have an idea. Anyway, we have until tomorrow to work out what to say.'

16

Mondays were always the same: maths and history before lunch then electronics in the afternoon. Matthew had always struggled with maths at Newdale, but Miss Rose explained things in a different way, which seemed to make more sense. It would never be his favourite subject, but at least he didn't enter the classroom with that feeling of dread hanging over him.

During history, instead of concentrating on Oliver Cromwell and the Civil War, Matthew daydreamed about history lessons of the future, when the story of their lives now, would be told to future generations. A story of bravery, sadness and hardships. He wondered how interested children would be in lessons about "Changelings and their Powers", or maybe "How Changelings Shaped the Future". He doubted they would be given that much credit considering how much help they had already given and how badly Ludo had been treated in exchange.

'And for homework . . .' Miss Rose's voice echoed in the high-ceilinged classroom, bringing Matthew sharply back to the present, 'Use your notes from today to write an essay entitled "Oliver Cromwell, Hero or Villain" and please give arguments for both side of the story before giving your own opinion, which of course, must be backed up by evidence. You have until Friday.'

Matthew sighed; he'd have to borrow Pete's notes, or else admit he'd not been listening.

***

After lunch, they moved to a different classroom for electronics with Mr Brown. Matthew had finished his automatic lights project, so tried to help Pete fix the mess he had made of his work last week. Matthew enjoyed electronics, partly because he seemed to have a natural flair for the subject, and partly because Rowland was in a different group for technology. The hour went by quickly, and with

Matthew's help, Pete managed to finish soldering his variable resistor and LEDs to his circuit board *and* write up his work.

At four o'clock, the bell finally signalled the end of the day, and the boys left level 182. They rushed down to the little bridge over the stream, hoping to see Yahtzee as they approached. Nothing. They searched under and around the little bridge, but saw no sign of her.

'I don't think she's here.' Matthew said looking a little disappointed.

'We're a few minutes early.' Pete looked at his watch, 'it's only twenty past.'

Matthew sat on the side of the bridge and let his feet dangle over the edge. Pete followed him but, before he could sit down, a rustling noise caused him to turn and Yahtzee appeared from behind a tree. She walked confidently towards the boys, extending a long, slender hand as she drew near. Cautiously, Matthew took her hand and shook it gently.

'Pleased to meet you, properly I mean. I'm Matthew Jones.'

'Pete Kettle. Pleased to meet you too. Ludo is a good friend, and any relative of Ludo is a friend of ours too. That is, if you want to be friends.'

Yahtzee smiled. 'Ludo liked you and that's good enough for me. I'm very pleased to make your acquaintance.' Yahtzee bowed as she spoke. 'Now, is there anything in particular you want from me, or is it just the pleasure of my company?'

'We should be more careful this time,' Matthew suggested, 'Before I say anymore, we should go somewhere more private. I think we should go deeper into the woods, and we have to keep watch along the path at all times. We mustn't let anyone see us together. I promised Ludo that I wouldn't let you see us, but I can't keep that promise, not if we have a chance of helping him. We'll just have to be careful.'

Matthew led the way down to the woods, but instead of stopping at their usual place, he headed deeper into the trees. He brushed branches aside, pressed back leaves and trampled a new path through the previously undisturbed undergrowth. He only stopped when it became impossible to go any further, not due to the dense woodland, but because they had reached the wall at the end of the garden room. It looked as though no one had ever been there before, at least not since the room had been built. The overgrown grass brushed against his legs and the untended plants grew thick, blocking the light. Matthew shivered.

'Now, is somebody going to tell me what this is all about, preferably before we all get caught and I end up going the same way as Ludo?'

Matthew explained his plan, which was more of an idea than an actual plan. He hadn't really worked out all the details yet.

Pete looked impressed. 'I don't know why we didn't think of it sooner.'

The shadows masked Yahtzee's face, making it difficult to tell what she was thinking. They all sat in silence for a while, the boys waiting to see if Yahtzee would agree to help them. If she refused, they would have to forget the whole thing and Ludo could be lost forever. Without Yahtzee's help, they may as well forget the whole thing.

The changeling stood up. 'Let me get this straight,' she began, 'You want me to take you both back in time to the day you were caught with my brother. Then, you will make sure he's hidden before you get caught, so that when I bring you back, he will have never been taken away and we all carry on just as before. Nobody else on this ship will find out about him or us and we'll all live happily ever after. I don't know what my brother told you about our ability, but changing things is always risky. One small change to the past can have a knock on effect on everything else. What if you don't like the way your new version of events turns out? Did Ludo tell you that you can only go back to a given moment once? If you mess it up you could be permanently stuck with an even worse future than having no Ludo on the ship. Ludo has been sent away and I miss him. I love him, but the Captain has assured us that he's safe at home. In a couple of years we'll see each other again.'

'A couple of years! Ludo said he'd only be here a few months.'

'A couple of years is only a few months when you live as long as we do.

'Did Ludo tell you that we've already been back? Pete asked, steering the conversation back on track.

'What?' Yahtzee's attention snapped towards Pete.

'It's okay.' Matthew jumped in, trying to reassure her. 'We made a change and everything turned out well. Things are much better now than before.'

'He should *never* have let you!' Her eyes blazed with anger. 'It's not a game! Changing little things can affect so much of what is important.' Yahtzee softened her voice, 'I'm sorry. As much as I want to help, and I want to bring Ludo back, I'm afraid the answer is no.'

Pete started to object but Yahtzee cut him off.

'I'd really like it if we could still be friends. If you want to see me again, you know how to contact me.'

Matthew couldn't think of anything else to say that might make her change her mind.

'Of course we want to be friends,' he answered, accepting defeat for now.

Feeling deflated, the boys trudged down to the dining hall. Frank stood at the front of the queue, flirting with a waitress who looked less than half his age. Matthew took a tray and joined the queue and Pete followed behind him. They both received meagre portions of some kind of pie with lumpy mashed potatoes before sitting down in the far corner of the room. A sickly sweet smell filled the air making Matthew wonder what delights to expect for their pudding. They ate in silence. Once his pie had disappeared, Pete asked thoughtfully, 'So, what are we going to do now?'

'Carry on as normal. What else can we do?'

Frank winked at the blonde waitress, then sauntered over and sat at the end of the boys' table.

'You look like you're up to something,' he said accusingly. 'You should try to keep your noses clean for a few weeks. You don't want to get a reputation for being trouble makers.'

'We're not up to anything more than eating this . . . what do you think this is?' Matthew replied, digging at the remains of his dinner with a fork.

'Just take this as a friendly warning,' Frank continued. 'Trouble makers will not be tolerated on this ship.'

'Yeah we noticed. Poor Ludo, sent home just for talking to us. That was a little bit over the top don't you think?'

'Keep your voice down!' Frank glanced around nervously, then whispered, 'What makes you think they sent him home?'

'Are you saying he's still here,' said Pete getting excited, 'Because Yaht—' Matthew kicked Pete hard under the table. ' . . . because he's been missing for days? You sent someone to get him. They carried him away in a sack like a piece of rubbish.'

'We have no police force on this ship,' Frank hissed, 'no judge and jury. Just one Captain who makes all the decisions. Those who do not stick to the rules forfeit their right to be on this ship. Space here is limited. We will not keep anyone who breaks the rules.'

A strange feeling crept into Matthew's mind and his heart began to beat a little bit faster. 'What do you mean by "keep"?'

'Anyone who breaks the rules or causes trouble will be ejected. Like I said earlier, I give you fair warning. If you cause too much trouble, or upset the civilians with stories of E.T and changelings you'll be going the same way as your buddy Ludo.' Frank smiled wickedly and raised his eyebrows. 'And for him, I'm afraid, there's no way back.'

'Why didn't you just send him home? I'm sure it must be possible.'

'Possible, yes it would have been possible, but really not worth the effort. It's much easier on everyone to have him ejected.'

'But what about his family?' Matthew shook his head in disbelief. 'What will they say when they find out?'

'They're not expecting to see him for another two years. By the time they realise, it will be too late. We won't need his kind any more. We won't need to have anything to do with them ever again.' Frank's chair scraped back across the shiny lino floor as he stood up. 'Oh and one more thing, we never had this conversation.' And with that, he marched briskly out of the dining room.

Matthew sat open mouthed, staring at Pete. 'What just happened? I'm not sure I understood that properly.'

Pete rested his head in his hands. 'Ludo's been ejected and he can't get back!'

'I can't believe they forced him off the ship. Maybe they're just trying to frighten us.'

'Pete looked up. 'I don't think Frank was lying. He's not smart enough to pull it off. I wonder how they . . . Do you think they sent him out in some kind of pod?' Pete asked, 'to float around lost in space until he fades away, or did they shove him out with nothing, with no way to breath. Is he dead already? Do changelings even breathe oxygen?' Pete clutched his chest as if he were struggling to breathe. 'I don't know what's worse, dying instantly or floating around in space, knowing that no one's coming to help you.'

'I refuse to think about it when I know we can change it,' Matthew banged his fist on the table. 'We have to try to get him back. We have to tell Yahtzee!'

Pete nodded and made small whimpering noises. 'Okay, what's the plan?'

Ten minutes later, and more than a little out of breath, they reached the bridge and began piling up the stones. They worked in silence, each boy lost in his own thoughts, before solemnly walking home.

The next day dragged. To make matters worse, Miss Rose kept them both back for forgetting to do their homework. Somehow fractions hadn't seemed so important the previous evening. Matthew sat watching the second hand on the clock, wondering how long Yahtzee would wait for them.

By the time they returned to their hiding place, Yahtzee had been there for over an hour.

'You're late! I've got to be at work in twenty minutes.' She said crossly. 'Ludo may have had time to chat every day, but I have other things to do, you know!'

Pete apologised and briefly explained why they were late. Then he looked at Matthew, willing him to take over the story, not wanting to tell Yahtzee of her brother's fate.

'Yahtzee,' Matthew began, 'please stay. We really need to talk to you again. It's important.'

'Well if it's got anything to do with time travel I'm not interested.'

'It's Ludo,' Matthew continued, 'he hasn't been sent home.'

For a moment Yahtzee looked excited.

'He's still here?' She asked.

Matthew shook his head. 'There's no easy way to say this,' he looked at Pete, who stared blankly at him. Clearly he would have to tell her himself. 'Look, I'm really sorry Yahtzee, but Ludo's been ejected from the ship.

17

Yahtzee looked unwell.

Matthew didn't know if changelings had circulatory systems that were in any way similar to humans, but her brown wrinkled face suddenly looked pale, as if all the blood had drained away.

Yahtzee turned from the boys. 'No!' she shouted, shoving the pile of stones and sending them tumbling into the stream.

The ripples faded.

Yahtzee grabbed the hem of her long cotton dress and used it to wipe her nose. Slowly, she turned towards the boys, meeting their gaze with her coal black eyes. Her mouth opened, as if to speak, then closed. Yahtzee swayed a little before allowing herself to sit with a bump. 'When Ludo took you back . . .' she began slowly. 'When Ludo took you back, you managed to change something small.' She looked thoughtful. 'And when you came back, did everything seem okay? Did you have problems adjusting to the new timeline?'

'Everything was fine,' Matthew reassured her. 'There were no problems at all. Please Yahtzee, let us help Ludo. Let us at least try. I don't understand why you're so worried. Things couldn't be any worse, whatever happens.'

'Oh believe me, things can always get worse. That's something I know for certain.' Her long skinny fingers fiddled with the fabric of her dress. 'When we were young, our mother told us stories of how great disasters were caused by small, innocent changes.'

'But not all changes lead to bad things. You must know that. How many times have you changed something and had trouble afterwards?'

'You don't understand. As a child, my mother's stories frightened me so much I decided never to change anything — *ever*.'

'You've never taken anyone back?' Matthew whispered.

'No, and I didn't realise that Ludo had either until I met you. He always agreed with me, said he would never take the risk.' She looked at them sternly.

'Perhaps he didn't want to upset you,' said Pete.

'Maybe,' she agreed. 'One thing I do know, if the situation were reversed, Ludo would go back for me without hesitation.'

'So we're agreed?' Matthew asked.

'I didn't say that!' she snapped. 'You don't seem to realise how complicated this process can be. I don't know if I should. I'm not sure if I can.'

'You said yourself that Ludo would do it for you. He's your brother! How can you not do this for him *and* for your family? Think about how they will feel if he's lost forever.'

Yahtzee closed her eyes for a few seconds, then nodded in agreement. 'If you think you can do it, I'm willing to try.' She tried to sound confident. 'Do you remember what you have to do?'

Pete nodded and Matthew said that he did.

'Then let's do this before I change my mind.' Yahtzee took each of their hands in hers and asked if they were ready. Matthew saw Pete close his eyes and did the same. He thought back to the day his mother saw Ludo, and tried to block out everything else. He didn't even notice when Yahtzee began to hum.

Matthew felt himself being tugged backwards, off his feet, and a wave of excitement passed through him. As he waited, hanging in mid-air, he opened his eyes and a black and white picture developed in front of him. Within a few seconds, it had been filled in, one colour at a time, with all the shades that brought the scene to life. Pete stood shakily beside him. The place looked right, but he couldn't see Ludo.

Matthew looked all around. They had arrived in their usual hiding place.

'I wonder when we are.'

'I hope we're not too late,' said Pete.

‘Let’s just wait for a while. We could be a little early.’ Matthew peered through a gap in the trees and saw no one.

‘Do you think Yahtzee knows what she’s doing?’ Pete asked. ‘I mean, she’s never done this before. I wonder if they have lessons in time travel at school. What if she messed it up? Maybe we should get her to bring us back,’ he said anxiously. ‘And what if we’re lost? What if she doesn’t know where we are and she can’t bring us back?’ He paced the clearing franticly.

‘No!’ Matthew shouted. ‘Remember we can only come here once, so we mustn’t waste it. Let’s think about it before we do anything hasty.’

They sat down in the long grass. The temperature rose steadily in the garden throughout the morning. Matthew hoped they’d come to the right day. They decided to paddle in the stream to cool down and were just taking off their shoes when they heard footsteps behind them. Matthew jumped up and looked through the gap in the trees, frightened that his mother might already be on her way. He relaxed instantly when he saw Ludo. He laughed out loud and rushed to great his friend. He hadn’t realised until then how much he’d missed the changeling.

Pete ran forward too, sweeping Ludo off his skinny feet and into a clumsy hug. Ludo looked stunned.

‘What’s all this?’ he laughed. ‘Anyone would think you hadn’t seen me for months.’

‘Well, it’s been a while,’ Pete chuckled.

‘It’s been less than twenty-four hours!’

‘For you maybe; it’s been a lot longer for us.’ Matthew enjoyed watching the confused expression on Ludo’s face as he began to explain what had happened.

At first, Ludo didn’t believe them, especially when they told him of Yahtzee’s involvement. ‘But she said she never would,’ he insisted.

‘You have to realise that when you were gone forever, she had no other choice. What happens after my mother sees you is terrible. We’ve been through days of worry.’

‘You were really that worried about me?’ Ludo asked curiously. ‘I’ve never had friends like you two before, and for as long as I live, I’m sure I’ll never meet another human being as kind and wonderful and caring and thoughtful and—’

‘Ludo, we have to hurry.’ Matthew urged. ‘We don’t know how much time we have, and we need to stop the chain of events that spirals out of control from the moment you’re seen. You have to go home now!’

‘What if I never see you again? I couldn’t bear it.’

‘If you don’t hurry, that’s exactly what will happen,’ Matthew said, realising they had spent too long talking. He went to the gap in the trees to check if they were still alone. He could see his mother walking towards them only fifty metres away.

Matthew felt sick; panic rose up inside him as he turned towards Ludo and shoved him away from the approaching disaster that was his mother.

‘Run,’ he whispered, looking over his shoulder. ‘Run! Run!’

Ludo dived for the cover of a blackberry bush and the boys watched as the dancing of leaves grew further and further away from them.

‘Pete sighed. ‘Do you think we’ve done enough?’

‘There’s only one way to find out; let’s go!’

‘We’re ready Yahtzee,’ they both whispered together. Nothing happened. Pete opened one eye and quickly realised they were still in the garden.

‘Let’s try again,’ he whispered, ‘Maybe we need to say it louder.’ But before they had time to speak the words, Mrs Jones burst through the undergrowth and stood, brushing pieces of plant matter off her cardigan. The boys stood silently, waiting for Mrs Jones to speak. She glared at Matthew.

‘I can’t imagine for one minute why you two would want to hang around here — it’s so dark. The rose garden is much prettier and it’s a lot warmer in the sun.’

‘How did you know where to find us?’ Matthew asked.

‘I didn’t. Frank told me he’d seen you walking through the garden earlier. I followed the path until I heard someone laughing. Anyway, I came because I thought you would want to know that I’ve seen Steve.’

Matthew thought for a minute, of course he already knew about Steve but he couldn’t admit that without his mother getting curious about how he knew. He didn’t want to confuse things just as they were starting to make progress, so he decided it would be best to play along.

‘Seen him where?’ he asked, shielding a quick wink to Pete from his mother’s view. He’d already filled Pete in with the news of his brother.

The boys let Mrs Jones tell them her story of how Frank had taken her to the control room and about the live feed she had seen on the monitor. It was actually quite interesting, as this time she gave much more detail. As she went on, she became more animated, and talked of how good his chances of survival were. She said that they had been given an extension on life which should give them enough time for a new escape plan to be thought up and executed.

‘So, there’s nothing more for us to worry about, is there?’ she finished, smiling brightly. ‘We’re all okay.’

‘Steve could be stuck in a cave for two years, and even then they might not rescue him.’

‘You always were a pessimist, Matthew Jones. Have a little faith. Try to enjoy yourselves a little. Oh, and I might not be home till late. Don’t wait up.’

Mrs Jones turned on her heel and marched away.

‘Let’s get out of here before we see anyone else.’ Pete suggested.

Matthew agreed. ‘I’m ready when you are.’

They closed their eyes, and together they shouted, 'We're ready Yahtzee!

18

He was hungry, but he didn't want to eat. He was cold, but he didn't want to move. He was tired but he couldn't sleep. He was depressed. Nothing could lift his spirits.

It was impossible to tell the difference between night and day in the caves, so the days rolled together forming a never ending hell.

Not far from where Steve laid his head, water dripped, ever so slowly, from a crack in the top of the cave to a shallow pool on the floor. The noise echoed around the cave and through Steve's head, reminding him of a book he'd read once about Chinese water torture. Although he couldn't feel the drips, they tormented him just the same, preventing him from having any peace, even as the others slept.

Grace thought they had been here about two and a half months. It seemed a lot longer. Steve wondered whether death would have been a better option than this. He rarely thought about Matthew or his mother. He needed to keep his head clear if he was going to survive this without going mad, but then, he thought, maybe he was mad already.

A bell clanged on the other side of the cave wall. Not the sort of bell you heard at school, or the kind you heard in a fire drill, but a single tone from a simple hand bell and it signalled that food would be served soon. This happened only once a day, in the morning. You then had to decide whether to eat it all in one go, or to try to make it last the whole day until they received their next tiny portion. Water would come a few hours later. Steve guessed they staggered the giving out of provisions just to break up the monotony of the day, to give them something to look forward to, and they really did look forward to receiving their tiny bowl of cooked rice and beans. People were losing weight. It didn't show the first few weeks, but now people's clothes were starting to hang off them and Steve could feel his ribs were a little more prominent than they used to be. He had become used to the smell of so many bodies in such a confined space, but would have been grateful for a little more water to wash away the layers of grime that covered him from head to toe, just to make himself feel a little more human. He looked across the cave, at the filthy men, women and children who were sprawled across the floor like animals around him. Then, forced himself to get up and collect his food.

19

Once again the colours faded; once again they all crept back. Matthew took a couple of seconds to catch his breath and balance himself before looking around, relieved to be back. Pete crouched beside him, legs wide and arms flapping wildly, trying not to fall. For a while, Matthew felt content. They were back and they were okay, only something about the scene before him didn't seem quite right. Matthew couldn't work out what had changed. They were in the right place, but were they in the right time? Then he realised what, or rather who, was missing from the picture.

'Where's Yahtzee?' he asked.

Pete, who had regained his balance by now, searched the horizon for movement. 'Yahtzee?' he shouted. 'If you're hiding, you can come out now. There's no one else here.'

'She's gone!' Matthew said, shaking his head.

Eventually, the boys gave up looking and went back to Matthew's place. The clock in the living room said 6pm.

'If it's still Tuesday, then we only left school an hour and a half ago. We can't have missed her.' Matthew said.

'Maybe she had to go home suddenly. Maybe she went to look for Ludo,' Pete suggested.

Matthew looked doubtful.

'She wouldn't have just vanished without saying goodbye. Besides, she didn't even know what we were going to change or where to find Ludo if he's back. I half expected to see him standing there with her when we arrived.'

'I don't think it works like that.' Pete looked thoughtful. 'It's not magic. Remember what Yahtzee said about how changing things can have knock on effects.'

'Something's wrong.' Matthew's heart fell into his stomach. 'How far back did we go? Six days? Think how much could have changed in all that time. Most of the stuff we remember from the last week wouldn't have happened if Ludo hadn't been taken away.'

Pete considered this for a while. 'So what do we do?'

'Whatever's happened, I don't think we're going to find out tonight. We should go for dinner before it's too late and just see what happens tomorrow. We'll go to the garden after school and maybe one of them will be there.'

Pete agreed. After a reasonable-sized portion of shepherd's pie, the boys said their goodnights and went home. As Matthew passed Frank's door it occurred to him that if all had gone well, then he would no longer be in Frank's bad books. He doubled back and knocked on the door. To his surprise, a middle aged woman with mousey brown hair answered the door and greeted him with a smile.

'You're the young man from 23,777, ain't ya? I've seen you around. How are you doing?' She offered a pale hand and shook Matthew's with a firm grip.

'Fine thanks. Sorry, I don't know your name.'

'Mrs Beecham, pleased to meet you.'

'I'm Matthew Jones. I'm looking for Frank. Is he here?'

'After what he's been up to, I'm surprised you'd want anything to do with him. He's lucky they haven't ejected him, though there is talk that they still might. Is there something that I can help you with?'

Matthew didn't answer. He raced back towards the lifts, but one was going up, and the other had stopped on floor 143. Not wanting to wait, he took the stairs instead, three at a time, until he reached floor 62 where Pete lived. He sprinted to Pete's door and hammered on it. After what seemed like forever, but was actually only two or three minutes, Pete appeared wearing a pale blue fluffy towel, his hair dripping and a series of wet footprints trailing across the floor. He stepped back, allowing Matthew to enter the room.

‘What’s the emergency?’

‘Something’s not right.’ Matthew panted. ‘Other things have changed. Have you noticed anything unusual?’

‘No, but I haven’t seen anyone since I left you. What’s happened?’

‘Frank’s gone. He might get ejected. I don’t know why but maybe it’s our fault.’ Matthew pushed past Pete and collapsed into the yellow chair on the left of the room. ‘Something’s happened to him because of what we changed.’

‘What?’ Pete stared, open mouthed in disbelief. How do you know? Who told you?’ Pete wobbled on one leg as he pulled on his shorts.

‘There’s a woman in his office, doing his job. He’s not coming back.’

‘What should we do?’ Pete asked as he towelled his hair.

‘Nothing,’ Matthew decided. ‘At least not for now. Try not to panic. We’ll find Ludo tomorrow and if anything bad has happened we’ll just change it again.’

‘You’re right. Let’s wait and see what happens tomorrow. There’s nothing we can do now anyway.’

As Matthew lay in bed, later that night, he went through the endless possibilities. Life is a complicated series of actions and reactions. If a gradual change in temperature could finish off the Earth, who knew what chaos could be caused by a couple of time travelling children.

***

The next day proved to be more troublesome than they had hoped. Getting information from others without looking like total idiots was almost impossible. They separated, hoping they would find out more if they split up — Matthew took the park, while Pete headed to the canteen. They met mid-morning, by the lift on floor 73.

Pete couldn't wait to spill his news. 'That girl in the canteen, you know, the one Frank's always chatting up?'

Matthew nodded.

'Once she started, I couldn't shut her up. She's none too happy, I can tell you. I can't repeat some of the names she called Frank. The last time she saw him, he dumped her, which was Tuesday, by the way. The next day he was arrested and taken away, and she says no one's seen him since.

'So he's been gone five days!' Matthew said. 'What did he do?'

'They accused him of breaking several of the ship's strict rules, the most serious among them being inappropriate use of privileges, stealing and skiving off his duties.

'Then that's not our fault.' Matthew said, relieved. 'He messed things up for himself.'

'Here's a thought,' Pete slapped the table with his palm, 'think back to the day your mum found Ludo and we all went to see Frank.'

Matthew nodded and Pete continued. 'What if Frank was just about to skive off work or do something that broke one of the rules when we all turned up with a story that makes him change his plans. But now, things are different. We didn't make him change his plans and whatever he did that day, he got caught. We changed it, that's true, but I don't think that makes it our fault.'

Matthew had to agree. 'He probably would have been caught sooner or later anyway.'

***

That afternoon, lessons passed without incident, probably due to the fact that Rowland was absent. According to Shane West, who sat opposite Pete, he'd been off all week. When the bell rang, Matthew piled his books into his bag and followed Pete towards the door.

Miss Rose stopped Matthew before he could get outside. 'Have you got a minute? I won't keep you long.'

‘I’ll catch you up outside.’ Matthew called after Pete before turning to face his teacher. His shoulders slumped as he dragged his feet towards the large wooden desk at the front of the classroom.

Miss Rose smiled. ‘How are you holding up?’ she asked.

Puzzled by the question, Matthew simply shrugged.

‘I know things must be hard for you,’ she continued, ‘but I wanted to let you know that I’m here if you ever need to talk to someone.’

‘Thanks, but I’m okay.’

‘Of course you are. You’re a fighter. You’ll do well in life. My granny used to say that you prune a plant to make it stronger, and it’s the same with people. You can knock them down from time to time, but they come back tougher and wiser.’

***

Matthew pondered over that last statement as he hurried after Pete. Together they strolled down to the stream and stopped when they reached the little bridge. Pete scrambled down the bank and piled Yahtzee’s stones carefully.

‘I don’t think that’s going to work,’ Matthew said sadly.

‘It’s worth a try.’

‘Yes, but if Ludo hasn’t been seen, then we have never have met Yahtzee to discuss the stones. I think that may be why we didn’t see her yesterday when we came back.’

‘I still think it’s worth a try,’ Pete insisted. ‘We’ve got nothing to lose.’

Matthew waited until Pete was happy with his arrangement of shiny pebbles before continuing down the path to the trees. They reached their usual spot and didn’t have to wait at all. Ludo sat in the centre of the clearing and a second changeling stood beside him. For a minute, Matthew assumed Yahtzee had come to see them, but he soon realised that the second changeling was not only taller than Yahtzee, but quite definitely male. The second changeling wore a shiny, purple, three cornered hat, which glistened in the sunshine. He turned to face away from the boys as Ludo rushed forward.

'Ludo,' Matthew called, 'You're back. What happened to Yahtzee? We haven't seen her since she brought us back.'

'Slight problem, but nothing we couldn't fix. Don't worry about Yahtzee, she's fine.'

'Where is she? We want to thank her for helping us.'

'That's the problem. She doesn't remember you or any of what happened. You changed her when you saved me — thanks for that by the way. Being ejected must be a horrible way to go. I'm quite glad I don't remember it. Anyway, from the moment you hid me, Yahtzee stopped knowing you. She didn't even remember to bring you back.'

'We wondered what happened to her,' said Pete. 'If she didn't remember us, how did we get back?'

Matthew had completely forgotten about Ludo's companion until he walked forward, with a regal gait, and interrupted the reunion.

'I am Mah-jong,' he bowed low. 'I am the eldest of the changelings on this ship.' He spoke slowly, enunciating every syllable perfectly, though his voice quivered slightly, confirming his elderly status.

'Are you their King?'

'No,' he chuckled, 'we have a queen, back home on Zelda 12, but it is customary among our kind for the eldest of any group to take charge.'

'Mah-jong?' Pete asked, 'Are all changelings named after games?'

'It's an ancient tradition going back many centuries. Those of us blessed with the gift, are given a new name, picked by the Queen, and the Queen loves games from all over the multiverse, although Earth games were a particular favourite for quite a few years.

'I digress, the reason I'm here today is we need your help. We've heard all about you from Ludo and we believe *you* could be exactly what we need. You've had experience at past travel — two successful missions, I believe — and with a little training we could work together to make significant changes to the past that could benefit everyone in the future.'

'Why us?' Matthew asked. 'Why not the Captain or—'

'I get the feeling he's more used to giving out the orders than following them. And you already know of our existence. If you were to work with us you would have to agree to only change things in the precise way instructed by us. You did well to rescue Ludo, and for that we thank you, but mistakes were made. You are lucky that we managed to bring you back at all. With Ludo rescued, Yahtzee never became involved, so how could you expect her to bring you back? You'd never even met. That's what caused the delay in your return. Ludo and I have been working together to bring you back. It took a little time as we had to wait till Yahtzee fell asleep. We worked from her room because we needed her presence. That's why no one met you in the garden when you came back. We had to stay with Yahtzee. I hope you've managed over the last twenty four hours and grown accustomed to any secondary changes. Remember, a week has passed in which your memories will be different to everyone else's. You won't remember any conversations with friends, or day to day stuff. I suggest you don't say too much to your friends for a few days. Wait until you get used to things as they are.'

'What kind of things would you want to change?' Matthew asked impatiently. 'And what would we have to do?'

'Oh, so many things could have been done better. We owe your people so much and have really tried our best to save you all, but your leaders are greedy and selfish. We have inadvertently played a part in their wicked games and would like to change that. Somebody has been working against us. We need to find out who and stop them. You didn't think it through last time and there have been consequences. Next time, if you agree, things will be planned out for you. We will give you a few days to make up your minds. Ludo will be here on Saturday morning, when you must give us your answer.'

'Will it be dangerous for us?' Pete asked.

'We will look after you well. If you follow our instructions you should be safe, but there are no guarantees.'

'Basically, we'd be helping to put things right.' Pete said. 'It's got to be worth a try, and if Rowland dares to give us any more grief, we get the chance to sort him out again. It's a win-win situation.'

Matthew looked at Pete, who grinned as though he'd just won the lottery.

'We don't need a few days.' Pete said excitedly.

Matthew agreed. 'When do we start?'

20

Matthew woke early on Saturday. On his way to the bathroom a strange feeling came over him. Something else had changed, but he couldn't quite put his finger on what? He knocked on his mother's bedroom door, hoping that if he spoke to someone it might put his mind at rest. He hadn't seen her at all since his little adventure, as she always left for work early, returned briefly to shower and change, then went back out until well after Matthew had gone to bed. She didn't answer. He wondered what she had been up to for the last few days.

Even when they were still on Earth, days would often pass where they had little or no contact. Half of him wondered if she had been secretly planning something to mark his passage into teendom. Today, after all, happened to be his thirteenth birthday. He pushed the thought from his mind. His father had moved abroad more than three years ago and since then she had rarely even remembered his birthday, let alone celebrated it. He hoped to see her today though, so that he could ask her what had happened to Frank.

Matthew looked into the bathroom, and then he realised. Everything was *exactly* as he had left it yesterday. His mother usually made some sort of mess in the morning for him to clean up. Every day he picked up clothes from the floor, cleaned the sink, or replaced the toilet roll, but he hadn't done any of these for a couple of days because he'd been so tied up in his own life. The bathroom was tidy, and his mother hadn't cleaned it once since they'd been here.

He wondered how long she'd been gone.

***

After spending an hour in the gym, imagining all sorts of possibilities, Matthew decided to ask someone — but who? His considered talking to Miss Rose as she'd always been nice to him, but he didn't know where to find her at the weekend and he couldn't wait until Monday, he needed to know now. Then he remembered Mrs Beecham. She didn't know him at all. If he played it right, he thought, he might be able to get her to talk.

A 'closed' sign hung in the office window, but it also gave Mrs Beecham's room number. Matthew hurried down the corridor and rapped on the front door. It took several minutes before the new floor manager opened the door. She appeared wrapped in a fluffy white dressing gown and with a sleep mask pushed up on top of her head. Without makeup, she looked about twenty years older.

'Unless this is an emergency, I am off duty until ten,' she snapped.

Matthew looked at his watch. It was a quarter to ten, and he thought it unlikely that fifteen minutes would be enough for the woman to make herself look presentable.

'I'm sorry to bother you,' Matthew mumbled, 'I'll come back later.'

Mrs Beecham fumbled in her pocket and pulled out a pair of dainty spectacles. She balanced them on the end of her nose and a smile slowly spread across her face.

'Matthew,' she said in a much softer tone than before, 'Sorry if I was a bit harsh. I didn't get much sleep last night. How are you coping? Missing your mum, I'll bet. Still, you've come to the right place if you need help with something. What can I do for you?'

'It's about my mum. This may seem like a silly question, but I can't sleep for thinking about it,' he lied. 'Would you mind telling me exactly what happened so I can get it all straight in my head. No one's really told me the full story and everything is in such a muddle.'

'Why don't you come in and sit down. I've got some chocolate somewhere if you'd like it.'

Mrs Beecham reminded him of his next door neighbour back home. He wondered what had happened to her as the old lady ushered him into a soft floral chair. She offered him a small bar of chocolate which he took, and sat opposite him, leaning forward to see him better. She started at the beginning and told the whole story, shooting him sympathetic glances at regular intervals. He heard how Frank had taken his mother to the dining hall late after closing time. They had hidden and waited for the last of the staff to go home, and then gorged themselves on whatever they could find in the fridge: pork pies, cakes, fruit and ice cream.

'They even managed to polish off an entire board of cheese and a large bottle of red wine that was reserved for the Captain,' Mrs Beecham said. 'The cook discovered the missing food the next day and reported it to her supervisor. When they checked the records to see whose key cards had been used to access the dining hall since the previous evening, Frank was the last one to enter, and he quickly confessed when questioned. He couldn't explain why he was there so late. Unfortunately for your mum, he named her as his accomplice. He thought they would go easier on him if he told the whole truth. He thought wrong.'

'What happened next?'

'You know what happened next.'

'Please, I need someone to say it.'

'Next, they questioned your mother. You know that because you were there when they came to take her away. It was the same day they took Frank and . . .'

'Go on.'

'They were both accused of breaking the rules of the ship. Stealing is taken seriously. It's an enormous job to ration the food for so many people. They were used, I think, as an example to others. To show what happens if you break the rules. They were both ejected the next day.

'I've been looking into getting you moved,' Mrs Beecham continued, 'either into a single room or in with another family. Do you have any preference?'

‘Can’t I stay where I am?’ Matthew’s voice wavered.

‘For now maybe, we’ll see how things go.’ She removed a hanky from her sleeve and dabbed her sweaty forehead. ‘Is there anything else I can do for you? You look a little pale.’

Matthew felt like his head would explode at any moment. ‘No, thank you, I’ve taken up too much of your time already. It’s getting late and I’m supposed to be meeting someone.’ He needed to get away.

‘Oh my, is that the time?’ Mrs Beecham said, glancing at her watch. ‘I should be at work by now. It’s been lovely to see you. Do feel free to pop round whenever you want.’ And suddenly, Matthew found himself out in the corridor.

Ten minutes later and Matthew was retelling the whole story to Pete.

‘I don’t believe it!’ Pete exclaimed. ‘Your mother…and Frank! What was she thinking?’

Matthew sat silently, staring into space. ‘She doesn’t think, she never has . . . and now she never will.’

Pete put his arm round Matthew’s shoulders. ‘Are you okay?’

‘It’s taken me two days to notice that she’s missing!’ he sighed, ‘to be honest, I don’t think her not being here will really make that much difference to my life, and right now, we have much more important things to do.’

Ludo had been waiting impatiently by the stream. ‘I thought you’d got lost,’ he grumbled.

‘Sorry,’ Matthew shook his head, ‘I’ve had things to sort out. So, what do we do now?’

‘I’ve got instructions to take you both up to the flight deck.’

Pete sighed. ‘We’ve been there before, it was a nightmare trying to get in, even with Frank’s key card. How are we supposed to get through the door now?’

Ludo smiled. 'The room you managed to sneak into was the control room. I'm taking you to the real flight deck, the one which controls the whole ship, the one that *we* control, not your Captain.'

'But we've searched nearly every floor and then mapped out the whole ship. Where exactly is the *real* flight deck?'

'Top of the ship,' Ludo replied. 'Floor 200. You were close before. The staircase from the Captains control room took you up to floor 199. That is where we live, but it's floor 200 where we work to keep the ship and its residents safe.'

Pete looked puzzled. 'But the lifts only go up to floor 198.'

'Of course,' Ludo laughed. 'We're supposed to be kept secret, remember? No one is supposed to see us. Your Captain told us that people would be frightened if they knew the truth, that the ship is under the control of aliens, but *you're* not frightened. We think that if he was wrong about this, he could be wrong about other things too. All we want is to help the people of Earth in the best way we can, but we don't trust your Captain.'

'We don't think much of him either,' Pete shook his head.

'Okay, we're ready. What's the plan?' Matthew asked.

'I'll let Mah-jong explain, it's his idea.' Ludo led the boys to a panel in the wall at the back of the garden and slid it open to reveal a small lift, similar to the one they'd escaped in after their visit to the changelings. It obviously hadn't been designed with humans in mind. Matthew had to bow his head to fit in. Pete crouched on the floor at the back and tried to make room for Ludo to get in. Once the door slid closed, Ludo pressed a green button, marked with the number 200. A few cramped seconds later and they stepped out into a room so spacious that you could hardly see one end from the other.

A multi-coloured mosaic of brightly flashing lights covered one wall. The other three were made of glass. Several rows of monitors divided the room into equal sections, and half a dozen brown hairless creatures worked tirelessly at vast banks of controls.

Mah-jong glanced up as the children approached. He appeared to be having a conversation with a purple blob on the screen in front of him. The blob changed shape continually and vibrated as it spoke. Mah-jong instructed it to monitor humidity levels on floor 120, before joining the small group.

'I'll get straight to the point; we'd like to get you prepared for your first mission. Are you okay with that?'

Pete nodded. 'When can we start?'

'We'll begin by filling you in on everything we know so far, as well as our plan and a little basic training. Are you free all day?'

'Nothing to do; nowhere to go. We're all yours.' Matthew said enthusiastically, though it was a statement he would soon come to regret.

'If all goes well, there's no reason we can't try for our first mission tomorrow.'

If Mah-jong hadn't ordered them into the next room, Pete might have danced round the flight deck in delight.

As they entered a long, narrow chamber Matthew tried to focus on his surroundings. A single table stretched from one end of the room to the other, and had been pushed up against the back wall. Spread across it, were detailed drawings, maps and lists of instructions. Curious fabric pictures hung from the two shorter walls and what looked like a row of small, arched windows, were randomly positioned at varying heights on the wall opposite the table. The changeling sat down and indicated for the boys to do the same.

'There are two reasons we don't trust the captain,' Mah-jong began. 'Number one: Someone unloaded our escape pods. We had enough pods on the ship for all of us to leave once we felt you could manage without us. Some of us were supposed to stay for a year, others agreed to stay for two years. We never intended to stay permanently; we want to go home eventually, to see our families. We discovered recently that the pods were missing. The Captain denies having anything to do with this and has promised that if we continue to follow his orders he will take us home next year. We don't believe him. We loaded those pods ourselves. Someone must have unloaded them deliberately'

'Why can't you just take yourselves home? You're the ones controlling the ship.'

'Good question. We control everything from heating, oxygen production, gravity, temperature and lighting control, take off from Earth, weather in the garden and engine maintenance to thrusters, lasers and everything electrical. We do all these things from floor 200. The only things we've handed over to your people so far are very basic. Unfortunately for us, this includes the navigation — which they only just manage from their control room — and the communications system. Without control of the navigation system, we have to go wherever he takes us. Without communications we can't contact any of the other ships, or perhaps more importantly to us, our families at home. Blackstone is refusing to let us into the control room in case we're seen. Won't even let us in there at night.'

'Why do you think they did it?' Pete asked. 'I mean why would they get rid of your pods when you've already agreed to stay for so long?'

'They know of our powers and think that whatever goes wrong in the future, if they have us with them, they can always go back and put things right.'

'What's the second thing?' Matthew asked. 'You said two reasons you don't trust him.'

Mah-jong's face was deadly serious. 'Let's just say your Captain doesn't seem quite as keen to rescue the survivors on your planet as he makes out. I don't think he ever intends for anyone to go back. England's second ship, Freedom 2, is still awaiting orders to land. Your Captain controls both ships and he's told the Captain of Freedom 2 that there's a problem and he's not to land.'

‘England should have had a second ship?’ Matthew couldn’t believe his ears.

‘Every country on Earth was provided with two ships by our people. The Earth people only had to decide who should come aboard. Captain Blackstone delayed things and now he says it’s too late.’

‘But you don’t agree. You think we can change things and maybe save more people?’ Matthew needed to know.

‘We’ll do whatever we can. We have plans.’ Mah-jong pointed towards the mountains of papers on the table. ‘We’ve been working on this for quite some time. We just didn’t have a human to take back.’

Mah-jong and Ludo took it in turns to explain various drawings, maps and details of what they would have to do. This time, it seemed, nothing would be left to chance.

21

Matthew's head hurt. He and Pete had spent the last four hours listening to the plan, and being tested on their knowledge of the ship's layout. Mah-jong was relentless. He insisted they make detailed notes to take with them, *and* learn everything by heart in case they lost them.

'This is worse than school!' Pete whispered while Matthew recited a list of times and the relevant information to go with them.

'Now, for some really important details,' Mah-jong continued.

'I thought we were done.' Pete looked at Matthew in dismay, 'I can't take any more; my brain's frazzled!'

'I know.' Matthew shook his head. 'Me too.' For the next five minutes, he tried to get Mah-jong's attention, but the changeling, who was in mid-flow, refused to make eye contact and wouldn't stop. He only raised his voice and began moving furniture back to make a space for a practical demonstration.

The boys gave up. They watched Mah-jong measuring the longest wall in the room using his arms.

'This,' Mah-jong announced, as he stretched his arms wide and wiggled his fingers, 'is a wayoo. All fully grown changelings, no matter how tall, have exactly the same arm span.

'One wayoo.

'We use wayoos to measure everything. Anything smaller than a wayoo, is measured in wegs, but that's a lesson for another day.

'The distance from the south east corner of Capital Tower, to your entry point into the building, is exactly eighty-four wayoos along the south wall. Now, as I'm sure you have noticed, your arm span is considerably longer than ours and therefore useless when it comes to using wayoos. What I want to establish now, is exactly how many of your feet there are in eighty-four wayoos. The wall behind me is thirty wayoos. Pete, I want you to measure the same wall using your feet.'

'Can't I just pace it out?' Pete asked.

'No, it's important to be precise. The entry point is incredibly well hidden. If you don't have the exact location, you don't stand a chance.'

Pete carefully measured the wall with his feet. 'Sixty-eight and a half.'

Mah-jong looked to Matthew, clearly disappointed with Pete's results. 'Now you try.'

One foot, then the other; heel to toe, Matthew slowly made his way along the wall. 'I make it seventy exactly.' He said.

Mah-jong smiled for the first time since they had been trapped in this room together. 'Then we go with you. Eighty-four wayoos are equal to one hundred and ninety-six of your funny little feet.'

'You think *his* feet are funny?' Pete laughed.

'Seriously though, Mah-jong,' Matthew had the alien's attention now and decided to use the opportunity to their advantage. 'We really need a break. It would give us a chance to let all this new information sink in.'

'It's half past six. You can have ten minutes, but don't go anywhere. We still have positions of security cameras and hiding places to discuss. *And*, I want to go over the timings again.' Mah-jong closed the door as he left.

'What do you think?' Matthew whispered.

'I can't think anymore. I need to eat. Let's slip out before Mah-jong gets back. If we stay much longer we'll miss dinner again.'

'I don't think we should go until we're finished.'

'You stay if you want, but I'm off. I'll be able to think much more clearly after I've refuelled.'

Pete peered round the door, checking left and right, before tiptoeing away.

Matthew groaned. 'Wait up!' he shouted, but Pete had disappeared from view. Matthew grabbed a pen and scribbled a brief note, saying they'd be back in half an hour, and then sprinted to catch up with Pete.

The boys only just got to the hall in time for dinner. They ate quickly and without talking. Then they raced back up to the top of the ship. Matthew hoped Mah-jong wouldn't be too cross with them.

***

As it turned out, he hadn't even noticed their absence. He entered the room only seconds after the boys returned and apologised for keeping them. Matthew slowly slid the note he'd written towards him and carefully pocketed it, then glanced at Pete and tried not to giggle.

Mah-jong managed to wrap things up in a little over an hour, so Matthew suggested they both went home and got an early night. Tomorrow would be a busy and exciting day.

Matthew pulled the covers over his head and snuggled down for the night. Timings and measurements drifted through his mind until his breathing slowed. The weight of his eyelids became too much and slowly, he surrendered to sleep.

The metallic grind of the alarm burst into a dream in which Matthew had been drowning in a swimming pool full of coloured discs.

'You've got to be kidding me,' he said before dragging himself out of bed. His first thought was that it would be another drill, and he silently cursed the Captain for putting them through this so late. Matthew sat in the nearest yellow chair and angrily fastened the straps.

His mood changed however as the monitor came on. Nothing could have prepared him for this. The recording had no sound. The camera panned across a barren wasteland showing grainy images. The message that accompanied this shocking footage apologised for the poor quality and explained how these images had been collected by the ship's long distance recording equipment on full zoom. A thermometer reading showed that the temperature on Earth had reached over 80 degrees Celsius. Everything was a light brown colour. No grass, no trees, no people, no animals. Even the buildings had a thick coating of dust. An uninhabited urban desert. Every few seconds, the message changed, giving only the name of the town or village in the pictures. After twenty minutes of devastating evidence, a new message filled the screen. It said:

'There are no survivors.'

Matthew never felt so alone.

Then, another apology. He read that even those named on the list had perished as the temperature soared much higher and faster than they had expected. A tear ran down Matthew's cheek as he thought of his brother. *Is this really true? Just when we're about to save him*. The images burned his eyes, but he forced himself to watch.

And finally, the torturous thing came to an end with:

May we keep our loving sisters and brothers,
Fathers and mothers,
Friends and lovers,
Forever in our hearts.

Followed by the list of names.

It scrolled across the screen.

The same list.

The list of survivors was now a list of victims. Victims of the war on Earth. Victims of chance. Victims of difficult choices. And worst of all, victims of each other.

Some people had sacrificed themselves for the people they loved. Others selfishly chose to sacrifice members of their family in exchange for their own lives.

Matthew blamed his mother for allowing it to come to this; for the death of his brother . . . her son. She made him so cross. How dare she put herself first and leave Steve to die like that? Matthew's fists clenched so tightly, his finger nails hurt his palms. He didn't wait for permission to get up. He didn't want to see Steve's name on that list. He didn't want to accept it. He ran his hand over the edges of the screen, searching frantically for a switch, but couldn't find one. The screen couldn't be turned off. He gave up, stormed back to his room and cried.

On Sunday morning Matthew woke early, despite having only managed a couple of hours sleep. He showered and dressed, but before leaving the apartment, a strange desire to look into his mother's room came over him. He opened the door and peered inside. The room looked exactly as it had on the day they arrived, except for the unmade bed. It reminded him of a hospital side room. She hadn't even changed the crumpled white sheets for the brown set he'd collected weeks ago.

Matthew had thought that the sight of the room might bring back memories and emotions, but he felt nothing. He didn't love his mother; he didn't hate her either, though he had more than enough reason to. He felt that his life had been largely unaffected by her until recently. True, things could have been better if she'd been more maternal, enthusiastic or even slightly interested in her family. In the last few weeks, Pete had been more like family to him than she had ever been. He closed the door. Today would be easy for him. He had nothing to lose.

After school, the boys raced to the garden. They'd discussed the previous evening's announcement at lunchtime and were keen to get answers. They quickly found Ludo, who greeted them politely and took them straight to level 200. Mah-jong smiled briefly when they entered the room. His fingers drummed the table and appeared to be talking to himself. He even shook his head from time to time as though disagreeing with himself.

'Is it true?' Matthew demanded.

Mah-jong looked up. 'Is what true?'

‘That they’re all dead. They’re saying it’s too late to rescue anyone else because they all died sooner than expected.’

‘It’s difficult to know for sure. If the captain’s telling the truth it’s a bit of a nuisance after all the planning we’ve done.’

‘A bit of a nuisance! My brother’s probably dead and that’s a bit of a nuisance!’

‘You misunderstand,’ Mah-jong shuffled towards the boys. ‘It will force us to change things, but that is what we’re good at, remember. Don’t give up hope. Stage one of the plan will continue as intended. Stage two . . . well . . . we won’t worry about that yet. Let’s get down to business.’

Another changeling entered the room. She had much darker skin than any of the changelings they had met so far. Her eyes were coal black and shone warmly as she greeted them.

Mah-jong stood to introduce them. ‘This is Jummie,’ he said to the boys, though his eyes barely strayed from the clipboard he clutched with both hands. ‘Jummie, this is Matthew and that’s Pete, I know you’ve heard all about them. Why don’t you get to know each other while I deal with this?’ He tapped the paper on the clipboard with one of his spindly fingers and shuffled out of the room.

‘Hello,’ Matthew smiled as Jummie leaned forward to take his hand.

She spoke softly. ‘Pleased to meet you at last.’ Her hand was warm and Matthew liked her instantly.

Pete took her hand next. ‘Pleased to meet you too Jummie. I hope you don’t mind me asking, but how come you aren’t named after a game like the others?’

Jummie released Pete’s hand and drew up a chair beside him.

‘Jummie is a traditional card game on Thorlox 4. My great grandfather was Thorlox Champion in the game three years running. It’s rarely played these days as it’s so complicated to learn. Personally, I prefer some of your simple Earth games like Chess.

Once, I even held a Snakes and Ladders competition and it really took off. We had to adapt it a little, we called it Steps and Adders, but we kept its simplicity. We said from the start that we'd have no more than a hundred and twenty rules.'

Pete snorted, then covered his mouth to stifle a giggle. Matthew smiled and dug him in the ribs as Mah-jong entered the room, coughing loudly to get their attention.

'Fascinating as this all is, I would prefer it if we kept to the plan.' He looked from Pete to Matthew. 'Jummie here is our most talented and experienced Past Traveller. Her travels have reported much greater accuracy than any other changeling has achieved. Accuracy will be more important today than anything else, so Jummie has agreed to help us.'

Mah-jong continued by going over the plan three more times, until even Pete lost interest. Then, he clapped loudly, three times, obviously aware he was losing Pete, and wanting to regain attention for an important bit.

'When you are ready to come back, when you have either accomplished your mission or are in some sort of life threatening danger, you will need to ask Jummie to bring you back. The problem we have is similar to your last time travelling adventure. If you change anything, we may not be in this situation. So, this is an explorative mission only. We want you to find out exactly what happened without changing anything. How were the pods removed from the ship and who is responsible. Oh and try not to get into trouble. It's going to be difficult, but please try to stay out of sight as much as you can and we'll see you soon. Do you want to go through it one more time?'

'No, I think we're ready,' said Pete seriously.

'Are you sure you want to go through with it? We'll do our best to keep you safe, but it's mostly up to yourselves. As long as you don't change anything it should be ok. Once we know what we're dealing with we can start to make a few minor changes, but *not* today'

Matthew and Pete nodded eagerly and followed Jummie to the middle of the floor. Matthew noticed Ludo sitting quietly, a concerned expression on his little brown face. Jummie took their hands firmly. Matthew tried to relax. He could hear Pete's breathing quicken in anticipation, and then he heard only the humming. It was a softer sound than either Ludo or Yahtzee had made, but it filled his head completely. Concentrating on his bedroom on Earth, Matthew felt himself falling. Falling down, falling up, falling sideways, then he sensed it. The familiar aroma of home.

A few seconds passed before he dared open his eyes. The colours had already returned. And here he was, in his old bed, from where he recognised at once the whimpering sound coming from under Steve's covers. Matthew leapt out of bed and raced downstairs, suddenly aware of the tag that rubbed against his ankle as he moved. He found his mother making porridge, their last meal together on Earth. He looked at the clock and realised he'd have to hurry. He had things to do this morning and needed to be back by lunchtime to get ready to leave. As he put his empty bowl in the sink, he decided. Without his mother seeing him, he picked up the second tag and slipped it into his pocket. Somehow, when he came back, he'd give the tag to Steve.

'I'll be back by eleven.' He shouted as he left. He saw his mother turn towards him, mouth open, but the door closed before she had a chance to speak.

The streets were much quieter than Matthew remembered, but it was much earlier in the day. He jogged down the high street and didn't slow until he came to a crossroads. He turned right and followed this narrower road to the end, passing shops and businesses, all of which had been closed for some weeks. At the end of the road he saw the children's playground. He sat on the closest swing and waited. He amused himself by watching the clouds and tried to ignore the desperate pleadings that were beginning in the street behind him.

Pete jumped over the fence and took the swing on Matthew's left.

'You're late,' Matthew grumbled. 'We were supposed to meet ten minutes ago.'

Pete avoided eye contact with his friend and pushed his swing backwards, lifting his feet. 'It's just like before,' he whispered, hunching his shoulders and dropping his feet, so they dragged through the dirt.

'It *is* before. Of course it's the same. What did you expect?'

'I hadn't really thought about seeing her again.' Pete stared into the distance. 'My mum, I mean. I couldn't just run away. You know…I haven't seen her for so long, and now, we're going to miss all the time we had to say goodbye.'

'I know,' Matthew softened his voice. 'But we've done it already. This isn't more time. It's the same time.

'All the same, it would have been nice…to have it again.'

Matthew's breath caught in his chest. This is what it should be like to lose your mother, and here he was, plotting to leave his behind on purpose.

'And then,' Pete continued. 'I had a little trouble getting out of the house. Arthur saw me leaving and told Mum. She was worried and made me promise to stay. I had to climb out of my bedroom window and jump off the front porch. I twisted my ankle a bit, made it difficult to run.'

Matthew let go of the chains and jumped off his swing. Since being on Freedom 1, he'd forgotten how warm it had become on Earth. He saw the sweat running down Pete's face and realised that his own clothes were feeling a little sticky.

'We ought to get going. Have you still got the maps?'

'I know the way to the back of the building.' Pete patted his pocket, 'We'll leave the map hidden until we need it.'

They set off at a brisk walk, avoiding the main road and trying not to draw attention to themselves. When they reached the Capital Tower, they saw dozens of volunteers, setting up the fenced area. They managed to slip around the back unseen. Matthew quickly checked the area for security staff. Surprisingly, none were visible at all. They reached a large arched doorway, stopped and sat on the steps. Pete pulled out his maps; the first of which confirmed that they were indeed in the right place. The second was more like a drawing of the building from different angles. They found the back view and could see where Mah-jong had marked out the distance in wayoos and feet.

Pete pulled a thin piece of fabric from his pocket. 'This shouldn't take long,' he said. Then, he shinned up a tree and pulled himself along a thick bough towards a silver security camera.

As soon as the black material was safely fastened around the camera, Matthew raced to the corner of the building and began counting footsteps. At one hundred and ninety-six he stopped.

Pete, having returned from the tree, produced a small white stick of chalk and drew a line from the front of Matthew's shoe, straight up the wall to the top of the fourth brick. 'This should be the one.'

'I don't see anything.' Matthew said nervously. 'Maybe I counted it wrong.'

'Try feeling the grout. It's supposed to be difficult to see. It's camouflaged.'

Matthew ran his hand around the edge of the brick. 'It's here!' he said, relief washing over him. 'I can feel the release mechanism.' He pushed the tiny stone coloured switch which, according to Mah-jong, reversed the magnetism in the lock. A miniature door sprang open with a pop, revealing a silver lever the size of a small child's finger nail.

Matthew slid his own finger nail behind the lever, and then checked no one was close enough to see anything before pulling it.

‘Wow!’ Pete’s mouth fell open and he stumbled back to get a better look at the wall. ‘How does it do that?’

A rectangular section of the wall, the size of a washing machine, shimmered and the grout between the bricks glowed, golden and bright. Slowly, something silver, like liquid mercury, seemed to pour between the bricks, from the top right hand corner. As each brick in turn became surrounded, it shone brighter for a second, before solidifying and becoming part of one solid silver mass. When the whole area had joined, it glowed, fiery red, then slowly dissolved to reveal a lift, which looked identical to the one at the back of the park.

‘Another good reason for sending two kids,’ Pete laughed. ‘Anyone much bigger than us would never fit in there.’

The boys squeezed in. Though the top of the lift forced them to sit, it was deep enough to stretch out their legs.

‘I bet you could get at least twenty changelings in here!’ Pete exclaimed.

Matthew looked at the array of buttons on one side and pressed 3. He was surprised at how long it took to reach such a low floor. It gave Pete time to get out his notes, and a third map. This one showed the inside of the ship in detail and included three-dimensional photographs. It was far superior to the map of the ship Matthew and Pete had put together several weeks ago. Mah-jong had talked them through all the possible hiding places, whilst Ludo marked them on the map.

Level 3 was primarily used for storage. The boys hurried across the enormous room, impressed and sometimes surprised at some of the things that had been packed. About half way across they reached a locked cage, the size of a small bungalow, marked ‘UNIT 6’. The lights in the storage room were tinged with blue and hardly penetrated the cage at all. The boys recognised the shape of the escape pods from a drawing they’d been shown.

Matthew checked his watch.

‘According to my notes, Ludo and his team have only just finished locking up the pods, and left a few minutes ago to help prepare for the launch. They’ll be on their way to the top of the ship.’

‘So now we just wait, and hope that we have enough time to get back home.’

The boys settled themselves down in a small cupboard opposite Unit 6. The cramped cupboard offered limited hiding space. Matthew knew if they were caught now everything would be over, including their lives. They would have to forfeit their places and be left behind to die. Matthew shuddered and tried to focus on unit 6.

22

They waited almost an hour for something to happen. Pins and needles in his foot forced Matthew to change position for the fourth time in the last twenty minutes. Even though the back of cupboard had enough space for two to sit comfortably, neither boy was willing to surrender their view of the pods, so one knelt, while the other stooped behind at an awkward angle. In this way, two pairs of eyes could stare into the dimly lit storage area through a tiny crack in the cupboard door.

Pete broke first. 'What do you think this is?' he whispered.

Matthew glanced back to look at the strange metal gadget in Pete's hand, which resembled a tightly curled snail shell.

'Listen,' Pete thrust it towards Matthew's ear. 'It's ticking!'

'Maybe it's some sort of watch?'

'Maybe… But how would you tell the time? There are no numbers.'

Mathew shrugged and turned back to the pods. A rummaging noise soon caught his attention. 'What are you doing?'

'You should see some of the stuff in here! It's like Aladdin's cave.'

'Keep your voice down. We're supposed to be watching the pods.'

'I know,' Pete whispered, 'but it doesn't take two of us. Look at this.'

'Is that a compass?'

'I don't know. It spins round.'

'It's pointing to that box there,' Matthew indicated a cardboard box on the highest shelf.

'Do you think it's a sign?'

'A sign that you're mad!'

‘If we don’t look we’ll regret it.’

Matthew sighed, ‘Okay, but be careful. I’ll keep watch.’ He said and returned to his position by the door.

‘It’s…It’s…’

‘What? What is it?’

Pete sighed deeply.

Matthew turned from the door and pulled the box from Pete’s trembling hands.

‘What…?’

A vibrant yellow, silky material covered in forget-me-nots and lily of the valley — he wasn’t a plant nerd, he recognised them from his Nan’s garden — had been folded neatly in the box. Matthew pulled it out, looking underneath it for the cause of Pete’s distress.

One beautifully decorated fabric after another filled the box.

The expression on Matthew’s face changed from one of confusion, to concern for his friend, who had gone from laughing and joking to a gibbering mess in a matter of seconds.

‘I don’t understand.’

‘It’s my Mum,’ Pete cried, between short sharp breaths. ‘I haven’t really thought about her for a while. I guess today’s brought it all back. It was so real. And today, when I left, she was wearing this dress…Yellow…’ his voice became squeaky and high pitched. ‘…with blue and white flowers. Exactly like this.’ He lifted the end of the yellow material and shook his head.

Not knowing what to say, Matthew remained silent, and waited for Pete to continue.

After a few minutes, Pete’s ragged breathing subsided. ‘I don’t know if I can do it.’

‘Do what?’

‘When I go back for Arthur. I don’t know if I can go through leaving her again. At least with Steve you know he gets to the caves. But Mum…’ he trailed off.

‘I’m sorry.’ Matthew offered.

And of course, that's when things started to happen. You waste an hour in a cupboard, and just when you get to the point where best friend needs your support more than anything in the world, you have to tell them to be quiet and stop whimpering.

Matthew didn't hear the approaching footsteps until they were right outside the door. He shushed Pete as sympathetically as he could and edged closer to the door to listen. The footsteps faded and then an engine burst into life. Matthew opened the door a little wider and strained his eyes to see.

From the gloom of the passageway next to unit 6, he saw a tall man, in a maroon uniform, like Franks, sitting behind the wheel of a small tractor. The tractor pulled behind it a long, empty trailer which noisily jolted about. A second man, older and heavier set than the first, wearing a black suit, and with his grey hair greased back into a slick ponytail, walked alongside the tractor. He couldn't see the man's face from the shadows, but still recognised him instantly. He used what looked like bolt cutters to break the chain which secured the door to unit 6. Between them, and with the aid of the tractor, the men managed to load up all six pods onto the trailer.

The man in uniform stretched his back and asked, 'Where do you want me to put them?'

'Take them off the ship completely,' the older man replied.

'Are you sure? They're definitely on my list of things to be loaded.'

'Then the list must be wrong; they need to be removed. Now, are you going to get on with it or do I have to do it myself?'

'No Captain Blackstone, I'll take them now.' The man scurried around the back of the trailer, out of the Captain's sight, and saluted sarcastically as he climbed aboard.

The tractor disappeared from view and Matthew let out a breath that he hadn't even realised he'd been holding in.

Blackstone pulled out a phone from his trouser pocked and pressed speed dial. He waited to be connected and then spoke sharply.

'Where are you man? And what's all that noise? You should be on board by now . . . You're wasting precious time . . . I'm sorry about your wife and daughter, truly I am. If there was anything I could do then I would . . . Trust me John, even a blue token would make no difference, the other ship isn't coming, no one's coming back . . . I know what we discussed, I was there, but it's been decided, I decided. It's the only way. You might not like it now, but you'll thank me for it in the future. The more people we can leave behind, the longer our resources will last and the better our chances of building future elsewhere . . . I don't care what anyone else says. Okay, calm down . . . I see your point. Well in a couple of months' time, we'll just have to make people believe that everyone here is dead. Just hurry up and get back. I need you here.'

He pocketed the phone and turned away from the cupboard where the boys were still hidden.

'What a piece of work,' Pete said under his breath, his eyes still red and puffy. Then chuckled to himself. 'Well, that was easy! I don't know what the changelings made so much fuss about,' he sniffed, then stepped out of the store room and held the door open for Matthew. 'We know who unloaded the pods, all we have to do now is get ourselves home and make sure Arthur and your mother get to the ship the same as last time.' They crossed the room towards the lift. 'It should be simple enough,' he took a deep breath and tried to pull himself together. 'Like you said, we've done it all before.'

'Where's the map?' Matthew asked.

Pete checked his pockets. 'I think I left it on a box in there.' He pointed towards the storeroom.

'We'd better get it. We don't want to leave any evidence that we were here.'

As they headed back across the room, a sneeze startled them. Matthew glanced round, but saw nothing.

'Hurry,' he said, 'I think someone's coming back.'

Pete reached inside the cupboard and grabbed the map. As he pulled it towards him, a small silver box, that had been balancing precariously, came crashing down.

'Who's there?' a voice shouted from the other side of level three.

Matthew looked at Pete and whispered, 'Run!'

Pete shoved the map into his pocket as he raced across the metal floor.

'Hey you, Stop!' Matthew recognised Captain Blackstone's voice and realised the distance between them had closed to only a few metres. 'Come here at once!'

The boys skidded around a ninety degree corner and ran between two rows of shelves, straight towards a dead end.

'There's nowhere to go!' Pete stopped so suddenly that Matthew only narrowly avoided crashing into him. 'We're dead.' He whimpered. 'Let's go back now before he catches us.'

'We can't,' Matthew patted his pocket, 'I haven't given the tag to Mum.'

'You idiot! Why didn't you leave it there?'

'Mistake,' Matthew panted as he searched the shelving unit for ideas.

They both breathed heavily. 'Through here!' Matthew pulled Pete towards a gap on the left. They scrambled up and over, knocking boxes onto the floor as they went, then jumped clear just as Blackstone stomped down the aisle towards them. As Matthew glanced behind him, he saw Blackstone turn back. Within seconds he'd closed the gap to only a few metres and Matthew could almost feel him by the time they reached the small lift. They threw themselves inside, sliding on their bellies, and Pete hammered at the button marked ground floor, willing the doors to close faster. They saw Blackstone grinning wickedly as he got nearer, the gap between him and the boys disappearing rapidly. He ducked awkwardly and thrust an arm wildly towards the boys, only to have it blocked suddenly as the lift doors closed, grazing his knuckles as it went.

'That was far too close,' Pete laughed nervously.

'I don't think he'll give up. We need to get out of here fast.'

The lift doors opened onto the small car park behind the building. The boys scrambled out, looked both ways and ran towards the main road, hoping to get lost in the crowds. Turning right, onto the high street, Matthew saw Mr Harper and his daughter only a short way ahead of them.

'We saw them last time, me and my mum.' Matthew noticed the fear in Jess's eyes as her father dragged her first one way, then the other. 'Only . . . we weren't this close to the building. That means we're behind schedule. I think we should run.'

Before they had a chance to move, they heard a shout from behind.

'Stop those boys!' Blackstone's voice thundered from behind them. Just as they had suspected, he wasn't the type to give up easily.

Dozens of people turned in their direction. Strangers heard Blackstone's cries and echoed them. They joined in the hunt like wild animals chasing a scent and rushed towards the boys.

Matthew and Pete ran.

The noise grew as the chasing rabble drew nearer.

Matthew ploughed through a group of young men, sending one tumbling to the ground. 'Sorry!' he called over his shoulder, though he doubted they would hear him over the bellowing crowd.

He sprinted on without looking back. A few metres ahead, a wall of people blocked his path. He slowed, and then swerved suddenly to avoid a toddler that stepped out in front of him.

'Muuuummeeeeeeey!' she screamed. Her fists were balled tightly at her sides and tears streamed down her blotchy, red face.

Mathew frantically turned one way, then the other, studying the many faces in search of the child's mother.

All at once he realised two things: One — Blackstone was gaining on him, and two — He'd lost Pete.

'Pete!' he shouted, feeling as desperate as the young girl who now clung to his leg. She tugged at his trousers grizzling and sniffing. 'Okay,' He said to the girl, we'll find her.' He'd give it one more try. He searched more faces, noticing at least a dozen women in distress. Any one of them could be the child's mother, or indeed none of them.

'Stop that boy!' Blackstone, now only a few metres away, waved wildly in Matthew's direction.

Decision made.

Matthew pulled the child off him. 'I can't help you,' he cried. He dragged the girl towards the calmest lady he could see. She was plump, with a kindly face and a swaddled baby in her arms.

'Please,' he begged her as he pushed the girl away, 'Help her find her mum. I have to go!'

The startled woman's protests came too late.

Matthew slipped into the crowd and was moving forward again. He weaved in and out of the people, calling for Pete all the time. Pete didn't answer. When he thought he was clear of Blackstone, Matthew stopped, glanced back and saw dozens of people, but no Pete. He shouted again. 'Pete…Pete…' *What do I do?*

The post box behind him looked easy to climb. Matthew vaulted on and swung one leg to straddle the thing, before pushing himself up and standing on the top. He strained his eyes, desperately searching for his friend. Then, from behind a group of rioting teens, Pete appeared, obviously struggling with his injured ankle. Matthew changed direction, and in his hurry to help Pete, crashed into Mr Harper, almost knocking him off his feet.

‘Where do you think you’re going?’ Mr Harper grabbed Matthew’s sleeve and pulled him close. ‘Wherever you go trouble is never far behind.’ He sneered.

This is the last thing we need. Matthew scolded himself for not looking where he was going, then checked his watch. Fifteen minutes. Barely enough time to get Steve.

Then, noticing Pete, Harper said, ‘And who might this be? Your accomplice in whatever mischief you‘ve gotten into this time, no doubt.’ He turned towards the chasing Captain, whose sweaty face shone like a beacon, giving away his lack of fitness.

Matthew looked at Pete. ‘Go and get Arthur,’ he pleaded.

‘I’m not leaving you behind. I think we should go back. They said if we got into trouble—’

‘No! Get Arthur! I’ve got a plan.’

Pete glanced up at Blackstone and then back to Mathew, undecided.

Blackstone had closed about half the distance between them by now.

‘Hurry!’ Matthew urged.

Pete ran.

Matthew threw himself backwards, trying, and failing, to jerk his arm free from Mr Harper’s grip. Sighing, he turned to Harper, then looked at the ever growing crowds. If he didn’t get on that ship then so much would be changed, he didn’t know what would happen. Everything rested on his young shoulders now. So many lives depended on him getting back safely and without changing anything. Now he had to decide. Stay behind or make a change? What would Pete do if Matthew got caught? A dozen thoughts flew through his mind, but he could only think of one way out, one way back. He made up his mind and hoped it would work.

‘Can I ask you a question sir?’

‘Shut up, Jones.’

‘Is that your daughter?’

'None of your business! You know you could lose your place, even for committing a minor offence. You'll be left behind to rot, probably what you deserve.'

'Like Jess, you mean?'

'What? How do you know Jess? What's it to you anyway?'

'I've got a spare tag Sir. If you help me get away, Jess can have it. I'll take her with me on the ship. She'll be safe.'

'That's a low stunt to pull even by your standards Jones. You can't lie your way out of it this time.'

Matthew put his hand in his pocket and pulled out the tag, which should by now, have been secured to his mother's ankle. He threw it towards Jess, who caught it. She looked at her father as if asking for permission, but his attention had now been averted by the arrival of Blackstone.

'Where's the other one?' Blackstone panted as he made a grab at Matthew.

Matthew held his breath.

Mr Harper stepped in front of Matthew and spoke with authority.

'May I ask what your business is with this boy?'

'I caught him and another boy snooping on floor 3. Who knows what he was up to, or how he got in?'

'When was this?'

'Just now, I followed them.'

'There must be some mistake Captain, Master Jones here has been with my family all morning, Isn't that right Jess?'

'Yes father.' She replied.

Matthew couldn't believe his on ears — Mr Harper had just lied to save his skin. He couldn't wait to tell Pete about this.

'Are you sure?' Blackstone eyed the small group suspiciously. He looks exactly like the boy I saw inside.'

For the first time, Mrs Harper spoke. 'Do you doubt my husband, your son-in-law? For goodness sake Dad, do you really think a couple of kids could get through such tight security?'

Matthew did a double take — *Dad?* He looked from Jess, to Mrs Harper and then to Blackstone and saw for the first time, the striking family resemblance.

'No of course not,' Blackstone replied, looking slightly embarrassed and still out of breath. 'My mistake. I'll let you get on. Busy day for everyone.' He sped off back towards Capital Tower.

Mr Harper released his grip on Matthew's sleeve and helped Jess fasten her tag. Matthew stood watching, not sure how to proceed.

'Thank you, Sir.'

'Don't think for one minute that I did it for you,' he spat.

'John!' Mrs Harper pleaded. 'Let him be.'

Matthew caught the look Mr Harper gave his wife, and saw relief flood both their faces. Jealousy flared for an instant, but faded just as quickly when his teacher spoke.

'I should . . . what you did . . . I mean . . . one good turn deserves another, so now we're square, agreed?'

Matthew nodded curtly.

'And don't think I'll go easy on you in the future.'

This was as close as he would ever get to a thank you.

'I think we should get moving. There's more fighting the closer you get,' said Matthew remembering his previous journey with a pang of guilt. He wondered how his mother would react when he didn't come back and he hoped that she wouldn't take it out on Steve.

As they headed towards the corral, Matthew struggled to think of anything to say to Jess. He knew he'd made the right decision. In fact, this way could work out better for his mother too. If she could get to the caves with Steve she may get another chance. Matthew told himself off for daydreaming and made himself concentrate on weaving safely through the crowds. With Jess and her parents, his passage proved uneventful. For once, being with Mr Harper was an advantage. Matthew searched the corralled area for Pete. He had no idea of the time since his watch had been damaged in the chase and had stopped.

Slowly they moved closer to the doors, Matthew saw Pete's head, jumping up and down like a puppy lost in a corn field. Matthew's shouts were lost amongst the noise of the ever increasing crowd, so he waved his arms furiously, trying to get Pete's attention. Before long, Pete had been dragged through the doors and disappeared out of sight.

After listening to the monitor woman, Matthew directed Jess towards the staircase he had used before. Her parents followed them. Eventually, they reached the top of the stairs and once again Frank greeted them. Matthew wondered if being ejected was still Frank's future, or would this be changed now that his mother was gone. Matthew remembered the waiting room. He told Jess and the Harpers that he would see them later. Mrs Harper surprised him by pulling him into a hug and kissing him on the forehead.

'Thank you.' She whispered. 'I'll never forget what you did.'

As they left with Frank, Matthew asked another uniformed man to take him to the waiting room. Both Pete and Arthur were waiting for him. Arthur looked confused as Pete leaped out of his chair and bounded across the room to give Matthew a hug. Pete was so excited he could barely contain himself. 'How did you get away?' he demanded. 'I thought you were a gonner for sure.'

'I'll explain later. I think we're done for now.'

'But shouldn't we wait for your mother? She won't know where you are.'

'She's not coming. I had to leave her behind. I know we're not supposed to change anything but somehow I knew it was the right thing to do.'

'But she's your mother! I know she's not been the best lately, but still, that's a bit harsh isn't it?'

'She's never been like a real mother, not really.'

'If I didn't know better I'd say you planned this.'

‘How could I *possibly* have planned this? I had no idea Harper would get in the way!’

‘Sorry,’ Pete whispered, remembering Arthur and their guide were well within ear shot. ‘I guess I’m just annoyed that if you really weren’t that bothered about your mum, I could have brought mine instead.

‘I didn’t plan it like this, honestly,’ Matthew insisted, which technically was true, though he couldn’t help feeling a little guilty when he remembered his original plan. And Steve. Again he hadn’t managed to save his brother. He sighed. Pete was right to be angry. He didn’t dare tell him about Jess yet. ‘Anyway,’ he snapped, ‘it’s too late now, it’s done. We need to get back.’

‘Not in front of Arthur, let him walk ahead of us and we’ll go when he’s not looking.’

They soon found someone to take them to their rooms. They waited until their guide and Arthur disappeared around a corner before saying in unison, ‘We’re ready Jummie.’

23

Matthew's feet touched the floor of the flight deck and he stumbled forward, grabbing the back of a chair to prevent himself from falling. Pete appeared on his left and grabbed an unbalanced Matthew's arm to steady himself. It didn't work. The fine line between stability and instability had well and truly been crossed meaning both boys landed in a rather ungainly heap.

First to his feet, Matthew immediately wanted to check if anything had changed. Mah-jong, Ludo and Jummie all stood exactly as they had before, as if no time had passed at all. Mah-jong and Ludo hurried forwards, keen for news. Jummie, however, stayed back, a concerned expression on her wrinkled face.

'Well?' Ludo prompted, 'Did you see what happened?'

'It *was* Captain Blackstone,' Matthew began, but Pete jumped in and took over the story, explaining how Blackstone had ordered the removal of the pods. He went on to tell them what he'd said about the Blues, and how they would never be saved.

Mah-jong listened attentively as the boys filled in the details. When they were finished he leaned forwards in his chair and rested his head in his hands. He eventually spoke with a calm, but determined voice.

'Sadly, this only confirms our suspicions. This is not what we agreed to. The changelings are a loyal and honourable race who *voluntarily* tried to save the humans from an unimaginable disaster. We have been tricked and misled right from the beginning. The captain is a heartless monster who thinks only of himself, and I, for one, will not stand back and let this happen. I had hoped that keeping us here for his own purposes would be the worst of his crimes, but to hear how easily he's allowed so many of his own race to die, I cannot comprehend it. Thank you Matthew and Pete for helping us find out the truth. I'm afraid I may have to call on you for help at least once more to put things right.'

Pete looked worried. 'We want to help, but that last trip was a bit more complicated than we thought. It was close back there. I wasn't sure if we would make it back, at least not without problems here.'

Matthew looked at Pete. 'What choice do we have? We can't let him get away with it. My brother's down there somewhere and I don't know if he's dead or alive. We know he made it to the caves before, and assuming he still did, I need to try to change things. Also I'm not sure about that video they showed us before. You heard what Blackstone said. It could have been a fake just to make us give up hope, to stop us from wanting to go back, so he could just leave them behind without any objections from the people.'

'Okay,' Pete nodded and then turned to Mah-jong. 'What do you want us to do?'

'I'm afraid that this time, you'll have to change something.'

Jummie rose from her chair. Matthew had almost forgotten about her, she'd sat so quietly, listening to the conversation.

'They already have,' she said so softly they hardly heard her.

'What do you mean?' Mah-jong snapped.

'I can sense a change, although I'm not sure exactly what.'

Mah-jong's facial expression turned to one of surprise as he looked from one boy to the other.

'It's true,' Matthew confessed. 'I had no choice. We were caught.'

'Why didn't you mention this before?'

'It's not important.'

'After all we've said to you, and all that's happened recently, I'm sure you realise there could be consequences. What did you change?'

'I had to give away my second tag in exchange for my freedom. It means that a girl came on board the ship instead of my mother.' Matthew said, his voice showing no emotion or regret. 'It's only a small change. I'm sure it won't make a difference. The important thing is, we know about Blackstone and we both got back safely.'

'What about your Mum?' asked Ludo.

'Why would you care about her after what she did to you?'

'But she's your Mum. You sacrificed your Mum so that you could complete your mission. Most people couldn't do that.'

'Most people don't have a mother like mine. Anyway, she threw it all away when she had her chance. I lose her either way.' Matthew stared at his leg and thought of the child who'd clung to him only an hour ago. The child he'd left behind, screaming for her mother. Was he any better than his own mother? 'I don't want to talk about it anymore, okay?' his voice wavered slightly. 'Is everything the same here or not?' he asked, changing the subject.

'I haven't checked yet,' said Mah-jong before turning to Jummie. 'Go and speak with the others, see if anything obvious has changed. We may be okay, but I daren't go any further with our plans until we know where we are.'

Mah-jong instructed the boys to go and get some sleep.

After saying goodbye, Matthew walked back to his room. Their adventure had drained him and he desperately needed some sleep. When he reached his room, he was surprised to find his key card wouldn't open the door. He thought he must have made a mistake through tiredness so re-checked the room number. 23,777. He tried again, but the door stayed locked. Matthew inspected the card. Curiously, he ran his finger across the raised number — The *wrong* number. It was Pete's card! They must have been switched at some point during the day. Matthew followed the corridor to Pete's room and banged on the door.

Pete looked at the card, but didn't seem surprised. He led Matthew in and showed him into the second bedroom. Matthew had been inside several times, but there had never been two beds in there before.

'Your things are here too.' He said.

‘Matthew blinked, ‘Do you think I live here now?’

‘Well your Mum’s not here and I can’t imagine they’d make you share with a girl. My guess is that Jess is probably in a room with her parents. You must have come to stay with me and Arthur. It makes sense, don’t you think?’

‘I suppose.’

‘I wonder who’s in your room.’ Pete pondered that evening as they ate dinner.

Matthew wasn’t really listening. He was glad to be in a room with Pete. It meant he didn’t have so much time to think about his mum or Steve and what they were going to do about any of it. For a while, he just wanted to be an ordinary boy.

That night he dreamed of insects trapped in a burning building.

***

Monday morning, the boys bunked school and went straight to floor 200 — some things are more important than science and history. Jummie seemed more relaxed. Apparently there were no major effects from the change. The changelings had already been up for hours, working on new plans. It seemed that they couldn’t agree on the best line of action.

‘I say we get rid of Blackstone,’ said Ludo. ‘Somehow we could stop him coming aboard the ship.’

‘Too risky.’ Jummie shook her head. ‘There are infinite possibilities. Anything could go wrong. We’d lose control of the situation for sure.’

Mah-jong agreed. ‘There has to be another way.’

‘What if we could stop the escape pods from being unloaded?’ Matthew suggested. ‘You’d have more power over Blackstone if you could leave at any time. You could tell him that if he doesn’t let us go back for the Blues, then you’ll leave and he’ll have to fly the ship by himself — he is Captain after all.’

‘It’s a good idea Matthew, but it’s flawed on two levels. One: you can’t go back to the same place twice, and two: even if you could, you'd come back to now, and were not really sure if anyone is still alive now. It would be better if we could have done this sooner, we need more time.'

'But it's worth a try, you have to admit that.'

'But you can't go back, not to the same time.'

'Okay, in theory then. If we could go back, would it work?'

Mah-jong considered this. 'It's possible.' He agreed.

'Then all we need,' continued Matthew, 'is someone else to help us.'

'I take it you have someone in mind,' Ludo guessed.

'Who?' Pete asked.

'Jess of course. She owes us.'

Pete shook his head. 'You can't be serious! She's Harper's daughter and she doesn't even know us…'

Matthew decided now was not the time to reveal his recent discovery, that Jess was in fact Blackstone's granddaughter.

'At least let me talk to her.'

Pete shook his head. 'She'll think you're crazy. You are crazy!'

'I saved her life! She owes it to us to at least listen. If I explain things, I'm sure she'll help us. Like I said, she owes us.'

'Even if she agrees, which she won't, how would she get into the store room? It would have to be after Blackstone ordered the removal of the pods, and by then she's with her family on her way to the ship. How's she supposed to sneak away and get back in time for you to give her the tag?'

'It would be tight, I know. Does anyone have any better ideas?'

No one had, and Mah-jong agreed that although the timeline restricted them greatly, in theory he had enough to work with. Matthew would talk to Jess and then they would all meet tomorrow. In the meantime, everyone would try to think of alternatives. On the way back the boys stopped at the manager's office. Matthew wondered which manager it would be this time. Mrs Beecham opened the door, looking considerably more presentable then the last time Matthew had seen her. After a few minutes of pleasantries, she happily told them where Jess lived. As they suspected, she lived with her parents not far from Matthew's old room.

When Jess answered the door herself, Matthew sighed with relief. He didn't want to have to explain himself to Mr Harper. Jess looked surprised to see him, but agreed to accompany him for a walk in the gardens.

It was difficult to know where to start. Should he begin with the aliens, the time traveling adventures or the fact that all the people on Earth would all die because of her evil grandfather, if she didn't agree to help them.

'Can you keep a secret?' he asked, after several minutes of awkward silence.

'Sure, I've nobody to tell anyway. My mother works all day, every day sewing clothes in a factory that I'm not allowed to visit. As for my father, he's too busy bossing everyone around and pretending he's important.'

'You have to promise you won't tell another soul or everyone here will be in danger.'

'You've been watching too much television.' She giggled.

'Actually, I've not been to the TV room since we've been on the ship. This is no joke. I'm serious. You have to promise!'

'Okay, you saved my life, so the least I can do is listen. You can trust me, I won't tell.'

'What would you think if I told you this ship, with all its remarkable technology, is not the work of any government on Earth, but that of aliens?'

'That's crazy!'

'But true.'

'My Grandfather's team spent months developing his ideas at the Space Agency.'

‘Maybe, but I know for a fact that a group of aliens designed and built this ship, among many others, to the specifications set by your grandfather’s team.’

Jess tilted her head to one side and frowned. ‘Let’s say I believe you. Why are you telling me all this now?’

‘Like I said, the aliens built many ships, but they didn’t all land. With your help we could land another ship and save hundreds of thousands of people.’

‘But they all died. I wish it were possible, but there’s no one to save. I heard about your brother…I’m sorry for your loss, but you shouldn’t feel guilty just for being alive—’

‘This isn’t guilt! You don’t understand. I think it would be easier if I just show you.’

Matthew led the way to the lift at the back of the garden. ‘Tomorrow, I’m going to introduce you to the captain of the ship.’

Jess laughed out loud. ‘But I know the captain really well, he’s my grandfather, remember.’

Matthew had been about to open the lift door, but stopped short, ‘About that…What I don’t understand is, if you’re his granddaughter, why didn’t you get a place on the ship automatically.’

‘My grandfather doesn’t really like us - me and my mother.’

‘What? Why?’

‘He thinks we are a distraction to my father and have stopped him from achieving great things.’

‘What sort of man leaves his own family behind when surely he is in a position to do whatever he wants?’

‘An ambitious one! He thinks there is more to life than friends and family. His work is what makes him happy. I haven’t seen much of him for the last five years, but I hear about him from my parents. They’re always arguing about him.’

‘So you don’t really know him well.’

‘I know I hate him, and the way he treats my mother like she’s dirt. My dad still respects him, says he’s a genius that's been misunderstood.’

‘Your grandfather is a bad man.’

‘Oh I can believe that, but what reason do you have for thinking this?’

Matthew showed Jess the small lift door. ‘I think I’ll need a little help from my friends, and the real captain of this ship, to explain. Meet me here tomorrow after school and tell no one.’

‘Who’d believe me anyway? Ok, Matthew Jones. I’ll meet you and your captain tomorrow. It sounds like fun!’

***

Surprisingly, on Tuesday morning, no one questioned the mysterious absence of both Matthew and Pete from school the previous day. Perhaps because neither boy had truanted before, but more likely because Matthew and Pete were considered goody-goodies and quite frankly, most people assumed they wouldn’t have the guts.

Jess leaned patiently against the wall beside the lift and smiled as the boys approached.

‘You’re keen,’ Pete remarked, with perhaps a hint of jealousy in his voice.’

‘I guess I’m intrigued.’

Matthew opened the door to the secret lift and they all bundled inside. ‘Don’t be scared,’ he said as the lift started to climb.

‘I’m not.’ A curious expression crossed her face.

When the lift arrived on the 200th floor, Jess stepped out beside Matthew. Pete pushed past and made himself at home. Mah-jong sat behind his desk, his hat pulled low enough to mask his eyes. Ludo saw the children and rushed to greet them. If Jess was surprised, she hid it well. Matthew made the introductions. Then, with the help of Pete and the changelings, he tried to explain everything about Captain Blackstone, and the way he had manipulated things, and sentenced hundreds of thousands of people to death.

Jess listened patiently to their plan. She was curious more than surprised about their claims to be able to change the past. Jess seemed to be one step ahead of the changelings, because as they were explaining the rules of time travel, she realised why she was there.

'You want me to go back?' she whispered.

'We can't think of another way,' Mah-jong admitted. 'We have to stop Blackstone and we need to do it soon.'

'What do I have to do?'

Matthew had to give her credit for the way she had completely accepted the situation, and had given herself, wholeheartedly to their cause.

Mah-jong explained. 'All you have to do is get the pods back on the ship.'

'We know that after he saw us, Blackstone chased us for at least twenty minutes,' Pete continued. 'You could get in through the back exit, the same as we did. We'll be hiding in the room opposite unit 6. Wait till we're gone and then find the driver of the tractor. Tell him he was right, that the Captain made a mistake, but he's busy and sent you to ask him to put the pods back into unit 6. They are on the list after all. As soon as you're done you'll have to hurry because we bump in to your father — and you have to be there so that I can give you a tag. It's a really tight time frame and I'm not sure it's possible, but we can't think of another way.'

'And if I don't . . . what happens to the others?'

'The people who drew a red token in the lottery, probably can't be helped either way, but those who drew a blue . . . they're in a cave somewhere, deep underground. We think they can be saved.'

'But the list of people who died . . . It was the people who drew blue.'

'You're grandfather wants everyone to believe that they all died. To put a stop to any future rescue plans.'

'Why? Why would he do that? It doesn't make sense.'

'Like I said before, he's a bad man. And selfish too. He's keeping all the resources meant for the blues for himself.'

'So how does this change things?'

Mah-jong looked grave. 'If we have our pods on board, we can force your grandfather to stick to the original plan by threatening to leave. I'm pretty sure he wouldn't want to risk that just yet as he is a long way away from being able to control this ship without us.

'One thing that's for certain — if we don't change this, then the Blues will die. I wish I could go back myself but it doesn't work like that. We hate to put you in danger and will accept whatever decision you make.'

'I'll do it. If you all agree it's possible then I'll give it a shot. Where do we start?'

Pete grinned, 'Well, for a start, if you've got any plans for the next . . .' he checked his watch, '. . . say, eight to ten hours, I'd cancel them.'

***

Wednesday and Thursday evenings involved more planning and revising, mostly involving only the changelings. Mah-jong insisted on silence while he worked, so the recent excitement soon gave way to boredom.

By Friday, a preliminary plan had been drawn up. Mah-jong assured them everything was almost perfect. Jess sat, swinging her legs in the corner. She'd tried, on several occasions, to take a peek at Mah-jong's calculations, only to be sent away with her tail between her legs and given something new to memorise.

Before he sent the boys home, Mah-jong showed Jess an accurate timeline for the morning of the launch. From time to time he checked with the boys on one detail or another.

'You'll need to reset your watch so that you know how much time you have. We know the boys waited for an hour in the cupboard so we have a good idea of when to send you in. You'll be with your parents so you'll have to slip away. It shouldn't be too difficult; the streets are packed with people. The most important thing is that you get back to them before Blackstone catches up with Matthew. I hope you're a fast runner.'

'When do we do this?'

'Do you need some more time to think about it?'

'No, the sooner we go the better, while it's fresh in my mind.'

Mah-jong looked from one face to the next. Jummie had joined them by now and was busy going over the timings.

'Is everyone in agreement?' Mah-jong asked.

Everyone nodded.

'You two go get some rest,' he nodded at Matthew and Pete. 'While we get on with it.' he shuffled towards Jess. I'll talk you through the timings now. I have a few more checks to make, but if all goes well, we'll aim to go first thing in the morning.'

'Hang on!' Pete protested. 'How come she's only got to go through the plan once and is ready to go? We had to do a whole day of learning stuff!'

'She's ready,' Mah-jong assured Pete. 'I can sense it. Some people pick things up quicker than others. It's a human thing.'

'Are you saying we're slow?'

'No . . . I'm saying she's quicker.' Mah-jong reached up a wrinkly brown arm and patted Pete affectionately on the head, before turning back to Jess and his clipboard full of notes.

24

Jess pushed her cereal around the bowl and stared at the water dripping from the ends of her hair onto the table. Usually she ran on the treadmill for her prescribed weekly exercise, but as the gym didn't open until eight on Saturdays, and she was keen to get today under way, Jess had joined the boys at the pool.

Jummie had explained to her how things worked yesterday and the boys did their best to describe what it felt like. Pete made her go through the timings twice more to be sure she'd got it. Jess had refused to recite them a third time.

'You really should eat something. You've got a long and important day ahead of you.' Matthew slid into the seat opposite Jess.

Jess grinned. 'I hardly slept a wink last night. Tell me again, what does it feel like?'

'Amazing! I wish we were going with you,' Matthew sighed. 'Hey Pete!' he called, as he noticed his friend. Pete looked round from where he stood at the breakfast counter. 'Hurry up! We've nearly finished.'

'A man's got to eat well before he takes on a day like today.' Pete said as he joined them with a large plate full of fried food.

'How did you manage to get all that?' Jess asked.

'I told the girl on the till that I had to work late yesterday and missed my dinner.'

'And she believed you're old enough to go to work?' Matthew raised an eyebrow.

'I think she fancies me.' A faraway look crossed Pete's face.

'Get real.' Matthew shook his head in disbelief. 'She's got to be at least nineteen. You haven't got a chance.'

'Her name's Madonna.'

'She's winding you up!'

'Boys! Boys, please!' Jess interrupted. 'If you're really going to eat all that then do it quickly, I want to get going.' She swiped a sausage from Pete's plate and took a bite.

'Oi! That's mine!' Pete lunged for it.

Jess snatched it out of his reach, looked him square in the eyes and took a slow deliberate bite.

'I worked hard for that!' Pete moaned.

'You'd better eat faster, or I'll have the other one!' Jess joked. 'Or perhaps you're not as *quick* as me in more ways than one!'

Pete ate the rest of his breakfast with one arm protectively around his plate and they were soon on their way to meet Mah-jong.

The mood on the top floor was sombre. The children, who had been giggling as they entered the room now stood silent and expectant, looking at Mah-jong. The Changeling rubbed his eyes as he sat in a high backed chair behind a desk. His purple hat hung on the back of the chair.

'What's wrong?' Matthew asked

'Maybe something, maybe nothing; Jummie isn't happy. She's had a vision. Sometimes they come true and other times they're more like warnings. She can't be sure. She's refusing to continue with the plan.'

'Maybe we should talk to her; make her see sense.' Pete said.

'You don't understand. There's a significantly high probability that what she saw could come true if we carry on.'

'And what exactly did she see?' Matthew asked.

Mah-jong fiddled with some papers. 'She won't say exactly,' he said without making eye contact, 'only that too many things would go wrong and she doesn't want to be held responsible.'

The door behind them flew open with a bang.

Ludo marched into the centre of the room and bowed majestically. 'I'll do it!' he announced as if he were saving the day and with more attitude than could be expected from an eighteen inch tall individual.

'I can't let you Ludo. I wish it were that simple.' Mah-jong smiled kindly then shook his head.

'Why not. I know I'm not as experienced as Jummie but I have had some success in the past. Please give me a chance to prove it to you.'

'You're a brave changeling and I don't doubt your ability,' Mah-jong said sincerely.

'Then why? Why won't you let me?'

'I was anxious about the whole thing yesterday, but you all convinced me to go ahead. I take Jummie's opinion seriously. She's worried, and that makes me nervous. With her on board I was willing to take a small risk. Now, it seems, the odds of success are not in our favour. You're a young changeling—'

'I'll be 97 next birthday!'

'As I said, you're a youngster. Something like this, if it goes wrong, could affect you for the rest of your life. Jummie feels that she couldn't live with the burden of being responsible if her vision comes true.'

'*If* it goes wrong. She doesn't know for sure. If we do nothing there are terrible consequences for thousands of people on Earth.'

'If we do *something* it could be worse.' Mah-jong stood up and grabbed his hat.

Matthew had heard enough. 'Have you got a better plan? Time is running out. You said so yesterday. Whatever the outcome, it can't be worse than leaving all those people to die.'

'There is always a worse possible future. Ludo, if, and I mean *if*, I let you do this, it's important that you understand how terrible you will feel if we make things worse.'

'I feel terrible now. I want to do this.'

Jess stepped up to Ludo's side. 'We all want to do this.'

'We have to do this,' Matthew agreed.

Mah-jong cast his eyes across he small company. 'Even if it works, if Jess manages to get the pods back, everything changes again. I've been thinking about it all night and to be honest the more I think, the more confusing it gets. With enough changelings present I can try to stabilise things here a little, make sure that we all remember afterwards, but there are some things that are beyond my control. Without Jummie, I have less power and that worries me.

'After careful consideration . . .' he sighed, 'I still think it's worth the risk.'

***

Jess needed to think back to that terrible day and concentrate on the journey she'd made with her parents to Capital Tower, but being so excited made it difficult to think.

Ludo took to the centre of the floor, gestured for her to stand next to him, and then slipped his hand into hers.

Focus.

All the planning in the world wouldn't have been enough to prepare Jess for the sudden weightlessness she experienced. Everything the boys had said sounded to incredible to be true, but remarkably, as she plunged backwards, Jess felt they'd been unbelievably accurate, only no words could describe the feeling strongly enough.

Matthew and Pete, having never experienced the whole thing from the changeling's point of view were equally unprepared for the way in which Jess departed. Matthew had expected her to fade away or lose her colours, but she stayed, eyes still open, in front of them. A golden radiance emanated from her body which moved as if submerged in water. Ludo continued to hold Jess's hand, and hummed without pausing to take breath.

'What's wrong?' Pete asked, 'Why isn't it working? Usually we go really quickly. Is she alright?'

Ludo's humming persisted.

‘Be patient,’ Mah-jong insisted quietly, ‘She’s fine.’

Matthew and Pete stood silently, staring at Jess’s body. The fact that the changelings weren’t remotely worried reassured Matthew slightly.

After what seemed like hours, but in reality was only a few minutes, they heard a faint voice. Gradually it got louder, repeating like an echo from the past. As it got louder, it got clearer, until they could easily make out the words ‘I’m ready Ludo, I’m ready Ludo, I’m ready.

Ludo stopped humming and let go of Jess’s hand. Mah-jong let out a long breath and smiled.

25

A few minutes earlier

It was so dark that Jess didn't know which way was up! Her chest felt tight and, as panic gripped her, she struggled to breath. Pete had described the journey, so she knew it would be over quickly. As the light filtered in, colour by colour, a frighteningly familiar scene greeted her. Her father darted from one stranger to another, pleading for help. Her mother, having given up hope already, followed him, her sobs drowned out by the persistent din of the crowds.

With both her parents distracted Jess glanced at her watch and then ran, without stopping, until she reached the car park behind Capital Tower. She hurdled a small fence and began to search for the way in to the building. Using Mah-jong's diagram, she located the south–east corner and looked up. She noticed the already covered CCTV camera and breathed a sigh of relief, before measuring the wall. You might say it was unfortunate for Jess that her feet didn't easily convert to wayoos. Or, you may think her way of measuring the wall was easier. Mah-jong had carefully marked one wayoo on the side of Jess's map, which she could now use to measure the south wall of Capital Tower. Jess proved herself to be quicker than the boys by locating the lift instantly. She squeezed herself in and found a moment to get her breath back as she rode up to the third floor. After checking the coast was clear, she crawled out and skirted the outer wall, staying low, until she reached a stack of wooden crates. There, she crouched in the shadows and cast her eyes over the room.

Jess checked her watch; she had less than a minute to spare, assuming that Mah-jong had set it correctly. A sudden noise startled her and she jumped back further behind the crates, knocking them enough to dislodge a thin layer of dust. She sneezed.

'Who's there?' a man's voice called out.

Jess's heart sank at the thought of being discovered so soon. Had she ruined things for everyone? Before she could make up her mind what to do, Matthew and Pete hurtled past her then turned to run between two rows of shelves and disappeared from view. She shrank back into a gap between two piles of crates before her Grandfather rounded the corner. He followed the boys for a few seconds, and then turned back. Jess caught a glimpse of the boys across the room before they threw themselves into the lift. Not far behind them, her grandfather, tall and menacing, closed the distance between them. Jess held her breath, and then relaxed. She already knew the outcome of the chase although she hadn't realised how close the boys were to capture.

Her grandfather turned away from the lift and left the room through a pair of large metal doors. Jess made her move. She could hear the distant rumble of the tractor engine fading away and raced towards the sound. She soon found it, stopped in a short corridor off the main room. The driver got out of his cab to open a set of gates.

'Wait! Please stop!' Jess shouted.

He couldn't hear her over the sound of the engine. Jess used every last ounce of energy to sprint towards him. The gates swung open under their own weight, so the man turned and hauled himself back up into the driver's seat. He leaned out to grab the door.

'Wait!' Jess panted, reaching the door before he could pull it closed.

'What are you doing down here?' the man asked.

'The Captain sent me.' she lied. 'He made a mistake. You were right. These things were supposed to stay on board.'

'You've *got* to be kidding me!' The man slapped the steering wheel with both palms. 'So why couldn't he tell me that himself? Why'd he send a little kid?'

‘Something came up upstairs; he was needed in a hurry. Actually I don’t think he wanted to admit he was wrong.’ Jess bluffed.

‘Yeah, that sounds about right. I suppose I ought to ring him just to make sure.’

Jess crossed her finger behind her back.

‘You can if you want, but he doesn’t take to kindly to people reminding him of his mistakes, It’s probably best not to make a fuss and get these back into Unit 6 before anyone notices they’ve been moved, but it’s up to you. If you want to check, he went up to the control room.’

‘Too many Chiefs and not enough Indians, that’s the problem. The right hand doesn’t know what the left is doing, but never mind, there’s always muggins here to do the fetching and carrying at only a moment’s notice. Nobody thinks that I might have a family that needs looking after and other things to do besides running around fixing other peoples mistakes. I don’t get paid enough for this . . .’

He continued grumbling as he reversed the tractor towards Unit 6, but Jess was long gone. She squeezed into the lift, hoping that this way would be shorter than the route taken by her grandfather. Jess checked her watch. There were six minutes left to get to the other end of the high street and hopefully find her parents. Again, she ran as fast as her legs would carry her.

‘Stop those boys!’ Blackstone cried from only a few paces ahead of her.

Jess ran faster. She went wide so as to remain unnoticed and get ahead of her tiring grandfather. She saw her father, about fifty metres ahead, grab Matthew. The sight of her mother, clearly distraught, would have brought tears to her eyes, had she the time to cry them. A short sprint reunited them. They clung to each other like long lost relatives at a reunion. Jess explained how she became lost among the crowds and had been searching for her parents for half an hour. A promise to stay close reassured her mother enough to relax her grip. Jess needed to get into position. She remembered where she had been standing last time and moved closer just as Matthew looked at her and threw his second tag in her direction. She caught it and glanced at her father, who looked shocked and confused.

Jess found no opportunity to travel back unnoticed until she reached the ship. Once in her apartment which she shared with her parents, she sat on her bed, relieved to have pulled it off and exhausted after all the running. She shut her eyes.

'I'm ready Ludo,' she called out, 'I'm ready Ludo. I'm ready!'

Jess felt herself pulled back into the darkness, through which she travelled until she felt Ludo's hand holding her own. Her breathing settled as the colours came back to reveal five concerned faces. Mah-jong spoke first.

'Well, what happened?'

Jess talked non-stop for the next five minutes to bring them all up to speed. Mah-jong then gave some hushed instructions to Ludo, who left. Jummie, who had re-entered the room only a moment ago, listened nervously as the boys bombarded Jess with questions.

An excited Ludo returned several minutes later and confirmed that the changeling's escape pods were all present and correct. Other changelings entered periodically with various reports for Mah-jong. Matthew only caught a few words here and there, but felt that on the whole, things had gone well. After the sixth unfamiliar changeling had been and gone, Mah-jong relaxed and called the boys and Jess over to him.

'It seems,' He began, 'That between you, you've done rather well. I don't mind admitting, I was a little nervous, what with Jummie's vision and all, but nobody has reported any changes here other than the presence of the pods. I don't think the Captain is aware of their return. As Captain, he ought to know everything about the ship and it is our duty to inform him. I think I'm going to enjoy this!'

26

Instead of using the lift, Mah-jong led the small party down the staircase that Matthew and Pete had used the first time they'd been here. They descended two flights and emerged in the middle of the control room. Captain Blackstone sat in a tall, black, leather chair, with his feet raised and the back slightly reclined. As the group of six, half children and half changelings, closed the gap towards him, crew members stopped and stared. Nobody challenged them. The room grew quieter as the party continued. They came to a halt in a small semi-circle around the back of the Captain's chair.

Mah-jong coughed twice. 'Captain Blackstone,' he said confidently from the centre of the group. The chair spun around and Blackstone used a remote control to raise the back. On seeing the unusual gathering before him, he sat forward.

'What's going on here?' he demanded. 'Jess, what are you doing with them?'

Jess smiled.

'We have things to discuss,' Mah-jong replied.

'Are you aware that between you, you must have broken at least a dozen rules?'

'Your rules, not ours,' Ludo said through clenched teeth.

'They are the rules of this ship!'

Which I still control,' Mah-jong reminded him. We have only done what is necessary to get your attention.'

'You have my full attention.' Blackstone glared at Jess. 'You wait 'til your father hears about this,' he hissed before turning back to Mah-jong. 'You have two minutes to explain yourselves before I have you all removed. You're lucky I don't have you ejected!'

'What for?' Jess asked angrily.

'You, you and you . . .' Blackstone pointed to each child in turn, '. . . for entering a clearly marked restricted area without proper clearance. 'And the rest of you,' he indicated Mah-jong, Ludo and Jummie with a wide sweep of his arm, 'for allowing yourselves to be seen; for bringing a bunch of children in here *and* for the lack of respect you show towards your captain. What did you think—?'

'I don't think you're in any position to threaten us and I'm sure ejecting us won't be necessary.' Mah-jong interrupted.

'I'll be the judge of what's necessary on my own ship. You have ninety seconds remaining.'

'Yes, you'd like that wouldn't you, judging us and deciding our fate, as you decided the fate of the rest of the Earth people weeks ago, by choosing not to go back for them.'

'We could never have saved all of them; there wasn't enough room. You know that.'

'I know exactly how much room there is.' Mah-jong continued edgily. 'I helped design this ship. Every country on planet Earth saved two ship loads of people. Every country except one! Yours! You chose to only save half as many people as we originally planned. Well, I'm giving you the chance to change things.'

'Never!'

'You know you really should reconsider,' Mah-jong persisted.

'Or what? What are a bunch of miniature aliens and three good for nothing children going to do about it?'

'We might just choose to have *you* ejected.' Matthew shouted angrily.

Blackstone sat back and roared with laughter. 'You? That's a joke. How are you going to get rid of me?'

'We won't have to if you agree to go back for the others,' Mah-jong said calmly. 'This is your last chance.'

'Why would I want to change my mind? Things have worked out rather well. Anyway, it's too late. You saw what happened to the Earth. Nobody survived.'

‘That’s what you want everyone to believe,’ said Pete. We know that the Blues made it and were alive only a few days ago in the caves.’

Blackstone stopped laughing. ‘Now how exactly could you know that?’ he demanded.

Matthew smiled. ‘You thought that if everyone believed there were no survivors, that it would be easier to leave them behind. But we know they’re still alive.’

Blackstone took a deep breath and sighed. ‘Why couldn’t you all have just kept your noses out? Everyone’s a do-gooder these days. How much good do you think you’ll do a few years down the line if we run into problems here. Like engine failure, or food shortages. Say in five years’ time, after all your little alien friends have deserted you, we run into some disaster or other. You know how to fix a Freedom engine, I presume. You know how to trade with other alien species out there. This is our only hope. You should be thanking me for having the foresight to plan for such eventualities. When something happens, and I don’t doubt it will, sooner or later, I will personally ensure the safety of my passengers. Freedom 2 is our back up plan. Our life line. People will love me. I’ll be a hero.’

Mah-jong pulled himself up to his full height and straightened his hat. ‘You’re a fool! These ships are so much more advanced than any technology you’ve ever dreamed of. They are self-fixing. This ship could last in excess of fifteen thousand years without a single faulty light. We more than fulfilled our promise. Your people are safe and secure and set up for life. A new life. A different life, but a fully sustainable one.’

‘Science fiction! We’re living on borrowed time and you know it!’

‘Enough!’ Matthew shouted. ‘It doesn’t matter what you think. We’re saving the others and there’s nothing you can do about it.’

‘If it wasn’t for the fact that she’s my granddaughter,’ he nodded towards Jess, ‘I’d have you all ejected right now.’

'She's your what?' Pete looked from Blackstone to Jess, whose expression had changed to resemble that of a wild animal, about to pounce. He turned to Matthew. 'They're family! She's in on it too — a spy or something.'

'Don't be ridiculous. She's on our side. She knows better than anyone what he's like.'

'You knew?' Pete eyes widened. 'Why didn't you tell me? Don't you trust me or something? I thought we were friends!'

Ignoring Pete's outburst, the captain continued. 'As a sign of good will, I'll let you leave unharmed this time. But, be warned. Come back here and the only way out will be through a little trap door into space!'

'You'd have your own granddaughter ejected for trying to help save thousands of lives!' Mah-jong stated in utter disbelief. 'What kind of monster are you?'

'I'm the one saving lives here. How long do you think we can manage here with the resources we have. If we double the number of people we half our chances of survival long term. More mouths to feed, clothe and keep healthy. It won't work!'

'Talking of managing Captain,' Mah-jong said, 'how long do *you* think you can manage this ship if the changelings were to leave tomorrow?'

'Now we've had this conversation already, Mah-jong and you know that's not possible. Somehow, your pods got left behind so you are stuck here until I choose to take you home, *if* I choose to take you home. Now,' he tapped his watch, 'I believe your time is up.'

'We know it was you who ordered their removal,' Mah-jong continued calmly. 'But all is not lost, we changed it, that's what we do best, change things.'

Blackstone jumped up and lunged at Mah-jong, but Jess forced herself between the two of them and shoved her grandfather backwards with as much strength as she could muster. The captain grabbed her arm as he faltered then cast her roughly aside, a look of pure resentment on his face as he watched her fall to her knees.

Without hesitation, Jess flew to her feet, grabbed his coat and spun him to face her.

'That was a wicked thing to do. You went back on your word after all the changelings have done for you, for all of us. That's why I had one of your men bring all of the pods back.'

Blackstone looked confused. 'I don't understand.'

'When you were chasing after intruders, I followed your man in the store room and had him bring them all back.'

'That's not possible. He wouldn't do that without orders from me.'

'I told him I was passing on a message from you and he believed me. I got the impression he didn't like you much. He was cross that you'd wasted his time.'

Mah-jong jumped in. 'If you don't believe your own granddaughter, you can check for yourself, only I wouldn't get too near, we have them under close guard. We wouldn't want any harm coming to them after all the trouble we've had getting them back.

'Now, let's get down to business. We agreed to save a second group of people. Our ship, Freedom 2 is waiting. I want you to take us to it, today, and allow a team of six of my crew to board it. They will take it to the caves and attempt to collect the second group. We will also require two dozen or so of your staff to organise the passengers as they arrive. The ship won't be as luxurious as this one as the Earth is too hot for us to stay there long enough to prepare it, not that there's much left on the surface that's worth taking now.

'You will give the order for Freedom 2 to land. You will allow us to save them. The alternative is that we will all leave and you will have to fly this ship yourself, Captain!'

For the first time, Blackstone looked uncomfortable. He sighed and shook his head in defeat.

'Where do you want to start?'

Mah-jong rose up to his full 18 inches in height. 'I suggest we begin by plotting a new course.'

'When that's done,' interrupted Matthew, 'I, for one, would like to see the CCTV footage you have from the caves.'

Mah-jong agreed that this would be a good place to start, however his reasons were different from Matthew's.

'I'd like to work out the best place to position Freedom 2 so that there is minimal exposure to the sun, and so allowing your people the best possible chance of boarding.'

The Captain relented and barked a few, short commands at anyone who got too close.

The small party looked on in wonder at the scene unfolding before them.

Except one.

Pete skulked miserably at the back. 'I thought we were friends,' he grumbled to himself. 'Best friends. And best friends tell each other everything.'

A hand, placed gently on his shoulder, turned him around.

'I'm sorry,' Matthew began. 'You're right . . . I should have told you about Jess.'

'Then why—?

'I guess, because I knew you weren't keen on the whole idea of involving Jess in the first place. I thought that if you knew, you wouldn't . . . you know . . . trust her. And I had a feeling about her . . . I just knew we were doing the right thing.'

'You should have told me.'

'I know that now. I wanted to, but I felt bad because I didn't think of your mum. I was so focused on my own miserable life on Earth that I didn't stop to consider how you might be feeling. As soon as I realised I didn't need my mum I should have thought of yours. Then, the longer I left it, the harder it was to find the right time.' Matthew held out his hand. 'Friends?'

Pete pulled a strange pouty face, while considering his options. 'No, I don't think so…' He turned slowly away. Then, he spun round and grinned. 'Gotcha,' he slapped Matthew on the shoulder. 'Just don't do it again,' he said in mock seriousness. Then, 'I guess you must have had Steve on your mind too. Did you ever think about bringing him instead of your mum?'

'I…' Matthew knew it was time to come clean. 'Remember I accidentally picked up my mum's tag…'

'It's ok. I kind of figured it out. I don't blame you.'

After a brief friendly hug, the boys returned their attention to the screen which now flickered to life.

A desperate scene met their eyes.

Jess cried out, breaking the silence that had crept up on them.

Matthew shivered.

At the back of the room, Jummie shuffled silently.

***

It was dark and difficult to make out at first. There were hundreds of people crammed in to a narrow tunnel. The picture changed every few seconds to reveal different images from within the caves. Matthew soon realised that rather than several large caves that he'd imagined, this underground hell was made up of one enormous cave surrounded by dozens of narrow tunnels and lots of small, low ceilinged caves, each one overpopulated with motionless, filthy human beings. Matthew felt their despair and shuddered.

Mah-jong took over the control room which was suddenly overrun with changelings. Matthew hadn't realised how many there were. He tried to count them, but they moved so quickly that he soon gave up and guessed that there must be at least fifty.

In the centre of the room, Blackstone stood hunched over the main control panel. On his right, a tall chair, resembling a baby's highchair on wheels moved from one end of the panel to the other. Perched on top, Mah-jong leaned forward, inspecting various readings, while continuously mumbling to himself.

Once satisfied, Mah-jong parked his chair as close to the Captain as possible. 'I think we're ready now. Captain . . . if you would be so kind as to instruct your crew to give up their seats.'

Blackstone closed his eyes and flipped a switch on his head set. 'This is your captain speaking. All crew members, I repeat, *all* crew members, you are to stop whatever you are doing immediately and move to the back of the room.'

The changelings gathered around the surprised and somewhat suspicious crew members, pestering them for their head sets, keys and various other technical equipment.

Mah-jong adjusted Blackstone's head piece as much as possible, removed his hat, and did his best to balance the communication device on his head.

He cleared his throat loudly before organising the changelings. 'Ludo, Jummie, Pogo, Kalookie . . . I want you here with me. See if you can get the radio working. I want communication with Zelda Twelve established as soon as possible. Then get a message to Freedom 2, inform them of the plan, the itinerary, operational statistics and all the data we have.

'Yahtzee, Jenga, Scrabble and Solitaire . . . I want you on the quegger. Check it's fully operational and calibrated.

'Chess, Mhing, Tiddlywinks and Blackjack...I want you to take over control panel two. You'll be in charge of getting this ship aligned with freedom 2 for the link up.

'Senet, Twister, Cludo and Domino . . . Take panel three. Keep an eye on our surroundings. Report back on anything out there that moves, within one million wayoos of either us, or Freedom 2.

'Rubik, Uno, Zippler and Choupat . . . you're operating the force field. I only want it shut down for the minimum amount of time needed to get this done.

'Da Bai Fen . . . I want you to take Mancala, Bridge, Tantrix, Buckeroo, and Tarot. Board Freedom 2. Go straight to their control room and await further instruction.

'Chaturanga, get us some refreshments. And everyone else…please, get some rest, you'll be taking the next shift!'

Approximately half the changelings left the room. The children hovered at the back, wanting to help, but not daring to get in the way.

'It's like an episode of Milky Way Races,' Pete said, clearly impressed.

'They all just fell into place,' Jess remarked. 'They really look at home here.'

Matthew moved closer to the controls. 'It is their ship, remember. They built it. It makes perfect sense that they can control it with ease,' he said with awe.

'What do you think will happen next?' Pete asked.

'They'll follow the plan of course,' Jess laughed. 'Keep up!'

'Remind me. So much has happened; I think I've lost the plot.'

Jess took a deep breath. 'First, we connect the two ships, so some of the changelings can go aboard Freedom 2. Then, they go to the caves to rescue the survivors. And in a few weeks' time, maybe a month, we join up and greet the Blues.'

'I'll see my brother again,' Matthew whispered.

The buzz of the control room increased exciting the children further.

Matthew approached Mah-jong. 'What's happening?' he asked.

'Nearly there now. A few minor adjustments . . . and that's it. We're connected. Time to send in the team.' Mah-jong flicked a switch on his head-piece. 'Da Bai Fen, do you hear me? It's time. Yes . . . yes . . . all good to go. Wonderful . . . see you soon.'

After Da Bai Fen's departure, things calmed down. One by one, the changelings, having completed their individual tasks, gave up their seats and left the room. Mah-jong exchanged a few words with each one as they passed, often nodding to show his approval. When finished, only Blackstone, Mah-jong, Ludo and the children remained in the room.

Matthew turned to Mah-jong. 'Well, can you do it?' he asked, 'Can you save them?'

'We're going to give it our best shot. Freedom 2 will enter the Earth's orbit in a little over 24 hours, but we'll wait until early Monday morning, when it's a little cooler, to land. It has enough food and basics for a while. If we can get the people on safely they'll have enough to survive. It won't be as organised as this ship but once they are settled we'll link the two ships and share everything.'

'When . . . how soon will it be?'

'Getting Freedom 2 to Earth is the easy part. We have enough queggers up here to send it pretty quickly. We'll have to reposition a few ships here to bring it back, and even then it'll be much slower to return. Probably a few days. Then we'll let them settle in for a few weeks. We'll need to work out some sort of system for reuniting people with their loved ones.'

Matthew felt excited. He had hoped and prayed for Steve to be saved but until today he'd never considered that he might actually get to see him again, and so soon. Butterflies tickled his stomach. He closed his eyes and imagined having Steve here with him. Would they be allowed to stay in the same room? Could he share his time traveling secrets? Would his brother forgive him for leaving him behind? Only time would tell.

'Ludo!' Mah-jong called, bringing Matthew back to the present with a start. 'Ah, Ludo. There you are. I need you to get a team together to work on this through the night. Jummie, if you can find her, and yourself of course. You can help me with the timings as you already have a good idea of what's going on. Then, in the morning, I want a fresh team at the controls. Can you organise that? I'll need four at each control panel, four on the quegger, and send two to the flight deck to initiate tomorrow's launch from Earth'

Ludo nodded, thoughtfully, and left the room, in search, no doubt, of enough changelings to complete the next day's task.

Mah-jong finally turned to the children. 'Sorry that took so long. You're probably all bored senseless.'

'Bored! Pete exclaimed, 'That was amazing! Like being on T.V.'

'Well, if you want, you can come back tomorrow, as long as you keep out of the way. We'll have the screen set up and you might get a peek at what's happening on Freedom 2.'

Jess nodded enthusiastically.

'We'll be here!' said Pete.

Matthew grinned. 'Oh. And one more thing,' he asked, his curiosity getting the better of him. 'What's a quegger?'

'A quegger . . .' Mah-jong began, '. . . is a quegger. Don't you have them in Earth?'

'I've never heard of one,' said Matthew. 'What's it do?'

'What does it do?' Mah-jong echoed in surprise. 'It's the most important device any space craft ever had. No wonder you Earth people never got out of your own galaxy. Now, how can I explain it in simple terms?' Mah-jong picked up a collection of random objects, none of which looked familiar to the children, and cleared a space on a small occasional table. 'This,' he plonked a bright blue stone in the centre of the table, is our quegger, and these,' a green metal ring, a heavy silver ball, a five legged model animal of some kind, and a dirty brown, three sided box, took up positions surrounding the blue stone, 'Are queggers on other nearby ships.' Mah-jong paused to check everyone was still with him. 'To move this ship here,' he pointed at the silver ball, 'you would need these two queggers on and the others off. See?'

The children exchanged puzzled looks and shook their heads.

'Not really,' Matthew stared at the objects.

'It's a bit like magnetism, but much more powerful, only the quegger is not magnetic. In fact, it's the opposite of magnetic. Two or three well directed queggers can force a ship to move at great speed with zero fuel. Mah-jong proceeded to whizz the random items round the table giving various examples at lightning speed.

'I think we've got it now,' Pete lied. 'Thanks.'

Mah-jong nodded to the children, seemingly pleased with himself, and waved goodbye.

The children, now equal parts confused and utterly excited, went home to get something to eat and some rest, leaving Mah-jong and the changelings to work through the night.

***

Jummie sat in the dark and rocked silently in her chair.

***

Matthew checked the clock. 3:46 am. Three minutes since he'd last checked. Crazy ideas raced through his head. He wished that he could have seen his brother on the screen, but the inky blackness made it impossible to make out any of the sad, individuals that littered the cave floors.

The next morning, the boys went to the dining hall to meet Jess. She wasn't there, so they ate slowly, waiting. After a breakfast of both porridge and toast, she still hadn't arrived, so they made their way up to level 200, thinking she must have got up early and gone on ahead of them, impatient to find out what was happening.

She wasn't there.

The boys ran back to her room and knocked loudly. Mrs Harper opened the door, and tried to hide her tear stained face.

'Where's Jess?' Pete demanded.

'She's gone out,' Mrs Harper sniffed.

'Did she say where she was going?' Matthew asked.

'She didn't say anything. My husband wanted to show her something. They left together.'

Matthew glanced at Pete and then back to Mrs Harper. 'What did he want to show her?'

'I don't know. He wouldn't tell me. They left half an hour ago. Do you want to leave a message?'

The boys didn’t respond; they were already half way to the lift.

‘It could be a coincidence,’ said Pete.

‘I don’t believe in coincidences. Blackstone’s got something to do with this and we need to find him fast.’ Matthew paced up and down as they waited. A green light announced the arrival of the lift. The door slid open and the boys rushed through, only to run straight into Mr Harper, who immediately reprimanded them for their rough behaviour.

‘Where’s Jess?’ Matthew asked, ignoring the man’s outburst.

‘Spending some quality time with her grandfather. She won’t be back until this evening, so I suggest you run along and leave me in peace.’

‘But she was supposed to meet us this morning.’ Matthew said.

‘We were going to the library to research our history project.’ Pete continued, ignoring Matthew’s perplexed face. ‘Didn’t she say?’

‘Trust me, even if I believed you, which I don’t, she’ll learn a whole lot more from her grandfather than she could ever get from a day in the library. The man’s a genius and I think he plans to teach her a thing or two today.’

‘You don’t understand. Blackstone's a dangerous man. He threatened her yesterday; he threatened all of us actually.’

‘What do you know about the Captain? He can be a difficult man, but he’s sorry for upsetting Jess yesterday. He told her he didn’t mean it and he wants to make it up to her. Anyway, it’s getting late. Surely you two should be at the library yourselves by now.’

‘He said he’d have her ejected,’ Matthew persisted, ‘and I’m pretty sure he meant it.’

A flicker of worry crossed Harper’s face. ‘Don’t be ridiculous. He was just trying to scare you off.’

'Please, Mr Harper, you have to at least check that she's okay. What have you got to lose? If we're wrong, all you've lost is a little time. If we're right, you could lose Jess forever.'

Mr Harper sighed and looked thoughtful. 'She's his own flesh and blood. He's my father-in-law and I know him better than you ever will.' And with that, he pushed passed them and stormed away.

Pete turned to follow, but Matthew grabbed his arm and pulled him back.

'There's no point. He won't change his mind, you know what he's like! We'll have to find her ourselves.

The boys took the lift back to the top floor and looked for Mah-jong. A changeling they hadn't met before, waved them towards the control room stairs. They descended, taking two or three steps at a time, and emerged into a quieter than usual control room. Blackstone stood in the middle of the floor, his back towards the staircase as the boys entered the room. Mah-jong stood atop a wheeled chair facing him, head held high and shoulders thrust back. Their faces, only inches apart, showed no sign of either one backing down.

'I'm warning you Captain, this is your last chance. Give the order to land, or we're leaving today.'

'No, Mah-jong. I'm warning you! Back off now. Forget going back, because it's never going to happen. Leave if you want to, I'll eject the girl the second you leave.'

As the boys reached Mah-jong's side, Matthew's hopes for a resolution to this unbearable standoff began to fade.

'She's innocent in all this!' he cried. 'She's your family.'

'The girl means nothing to me. She's a useful bargaining tool . . . nothing more.'

Matthew pulled Mah-jong into the stairwell and whispered, 'He means it you know, he's got Jess.'

'I know he has.'

'What are we going to do?'

'We have to carry on with our plan.'

'But Jess will die!'

'Thousands will die if we don't go back.'

'Please, give me an hour to find Jess before you do anything.'

'Sorry Matthew, there just isn't enough time. We may already be too late.'

'No deal!' Mah-jong shouted as he re-entered the control room. 'We do this today. No more stalling. I'll give the order to land myself, right now!'

Blackstone stepped away from the controls.

'Bring her up,' he growled, at the same time signalling to one of his team, who promptly scuttled out of the door.

***

Mah-jong seemed to be holding his own, so the boys charged after the Captain's crewman. They followed him from the main corridor into a smaller passage, then, through a door and down four flights of stairs. A silver door, with "floor 194" printed across it in large red numerals, slid open to reveal another long corridor. Although similar in layout to the floor where they lived, this place oozed grandeur. Thick, luxurious carpets moulded to the shape of their feet, and grand, gold-framed pictures hung on the walls. They watched the man enter a room and waited. A minute later and he reappeared looking confused. He took out a mobile phone and held it to his ear.

'Captain Blackstone, It's me . . . Billy. I'm outside your room now. I've been inside and she's not there.' He looked both ways down the corridor and, seeing the boys watching him, he turned his back and spoke more quietly. 'Of course I'm sure. Either you didn't lock it, or someone's let her out.'

Even from their position down the corridor, the boys could hear Blackstone raging down the phone. Billy held it away from his ear and waited for the noise to stop.

'How'd she get out?' Pete looked confused.

'No idea. Let's go back.'

The boys turned, raced up the stairs, and barged through the doorway almost crashing head long into a furious Captain Blackstone.

'Who do you two think you are barging in here like animals? Get out! Get out now and stay out!' Blackstone waved his arms wildly and herded them back into the corridor. 'You don't have the authority to be here and I'm fed up with your attitude. Just because you *think* you know the aliens, doesn't give you the right to treat the place as if you own it!'

'Something happen to upset you Captain?' Matthew stood his ground.

'It was you, wasn't it? You let Jess out of my room. How dare you? Coming in here is one thing, but breaking in to my personal suit is definitely an offence punishable by ejection.'

Telling Blackstone they had nothing to do with Jess's escape seemed pointless, so Mathew went with it. 'How dare *we*? How dare *you* lock her in there in the first place?'

'I am the Captain! You will not question my decisions or my authority.'

Mah-jong chose this moment to step out of the control room to join his friends in the corridor.

'Maybe not on my own,' Matthew began, his confidence growing as Pete and Mah-jong drew closer, 'but together . . .' Pete moved to stand behind Matthew's right shoulder and Mah-jong positioned himself in front of the boys. 'Together, I think you'll find we've made quite a few decisions of our own.'

'I don't know how you did it, you meddling fools!' He lowered his voice, 'but I'll get you. I'll get all of you! You've ruined everything.'

Matthew stepped into the doorway, blocking Blackstone's path. 'We've helped the changelings create a better future.' He glared at the captain, 'A future you seemed intent on destroying for thousands of people. You're the most selfish, evil man I've ever known. You're no better than a murderer. You will let us save the others, and if you try anything else, you'll regret it!'

'I'll never forget this,' Blackstone roared and shook his fist. 'You mark my words!'

As if on cue, Jess rounded the corner and flew towards the captain. She shoved Matthew out of the way and stood right up in Blackstone's personal space. 'No Granddad,' she whispered. Then, she leaned in close so that only he could hear her.

If it were possible, Blackstone's expression darkened further before he scuttled away silently fuming.

Before Mathew could question Jess, Mr Harper appeared. He ran wildly towards his daughter, picked her up and swung her around in a circle. 'Don't you ever run away from me like that again,' he scolded, though his words held no anger. He let her find her feet, before dragging her away.

'What about Freedom 2?' Pete called after her. 'Don't you want to see?'

Jess, looked helplessly over her shoulder. 'I'm sure nothing important's happening today. Mah-jong said they can't land 'till tomorrow morning.'

'We'll meet you at breakfast.'

'See you tomorrow,' she called. Then, on noticing the boys' worried expressions, she smiled and waved.

27

One Hour Earlier

He said he'd have her ejected and I'm pretty sure he meant it.

What have you got to lose? If we're wrong, all you've lost is a little time. If we're right . . . you could lose Jess forever . . .

Mr Harper stood in the corridor deep in thought. Jess really hadn't wanted to go. She'd ranted and stubbornly dragged her heels.

Guilt crept in.

Why hadn't she wanted to go? He'd been so caught up in his own world he hadn't paid her any attention.

Mr Harper massaged his chin as he weighed up his options.

They'd had a silly argument the day before. It was something and nothing. Her grandfather had apologised to her.

On the other hand . . . he'd almost lost her once before and wouldn't risk it again.

He'd just check.

The corridor stretched out endlessly in front of him. He broke into a run. Getting faster as he passed door after door. As luck would have it, the lift arrived just at the right moment. Mr Harper flew through the doors and punched in the number for his father-in-law's floor, 194.

The doors sprang open. Immediately he sensed something was wrong.

Then, he heard her scream.

Bang . . . Bang . . . Bang . . . The sound of a heavy object being rammed into something solid. As he drew nearer, Mr Harper could see the vibrations coming from his father-in-law's door. Then, came another scream, louder this time.

‘Heeeeeelp meeeeeeeee!’ Jess wailed. ‘Somebody pleeeeease,’ she sobbed.

Mr Harper reached the door. ‘I’m here! Jessie, I’m here!’ he cried. ‘I’ll get you out!’ He fumbled through his pockets, desperately throwing things out onto the floor. Eventually, his fingers found what they were searching for. A master key.

Blink, blink, blink…The LED on the lock flashed red. Mr Harper swiped the card again. Blink, blink, blink…same thing. He threw the key to the floor. ‘I’ll be right back!’ he shouted as he ran down the corridor.

The floor manager’s office was located in exactly the same place on every level, staff quarters included. Mr Harper had been in enough of them to know that their layouts were also identical. He hoped the master key card for this floor would also be kept on a little hook behind the desk.

The maroon uniform didn’t look quite right on the man, who sat deep in concentration at said desk. He had long braids cascading down his back and facial hair winning the fight for space in a war where ‘designer’ had fled some time ago. He yawned, and leaned back, just as Mr Harper dashed through the door.

Mr Harper remained focused on one thing alone. Getting Jessie out. *No time to explain.* He roughly shoved the floor manager’s chair sideways into a spin and fumbled under the desk for the key. Seizing it, he ducked out of the way of the maroon arm trying to grab him, and fled back to his father-in-law’s room, leaving the man from the office leaning against the door frame, looking on in disbelief.

In a flash, the door slid open and Jess collapsed into her father’s arms.

Mr Harper stroked his daughter’s hair. ‘Come on. I’ll take you home.

Jess started to follow then pulled back. ‘Wait!’ she cried. ‘The boys!’

‘What’s wrong?’

‘Grandfather kidnapped me! Who knows what he could do to the boys!’ She turned to run, but his hand grasped her shoulder.

‘No!’ he protested. Not now! I saw the boys only a short time ago. They’re fine. They told me to look for you. Right now I want to get you home, where you’ll be safe.’

‘I’m sorry, Dad…There’s no time. I’ll explain later!

Jess wrenched herself out of his grasp and made a run for it. She covered the length of the corridor way ahead of her father and bolted through a door next to the lift. The stairs to the right led up. There were four flights. *A private staircase for crew? Does it lead directly to the control room?* Before she could decide, footsteps rang out as a man descended the metal staircase. He muttered to himself, an unmistakable voice which filled her heart with dread. The man her grandfather called Billy. The man who’d forced her into the room and locked the door. Jess fled as fast as her feet would carry her to the left, down two flights of stairs and cowered in the shadows of the stairwell. The clattering from above suggested several people were getting closer. Soon they’d know she’d gone and would be after her.

She needed to get up, but her legs wouldn’t move. Jess peered up the stairs, but pulled back sharply when she saw the silhouette of a man cast onto the wall opposite the door upstairs.

‘Jess?’ Her father’s voice filled her with relief and she started to get up. She wanted to answer, but something stopped her and she watched silently as her father’s shadow grew smaller and the door closed. If she ran to her father now, the boys could still be in danger.

Again, Jess allowed indecision to hamper her progress. Again, the door at the top of the stairs opened. Jess could see the outline of two people as they burst through the door and sprinted up the stairs, further away from her.

She needed to get back to the control room, so she took a chance and ran. Up the two flights to where she’d started, keeping an eye out for her father all the time, then round a corner to where a further four flights led upwards. Half way up and her chest felt tight from exertion. The sound of the door closing from two flights below suggested her father was still searching for her.

The door at the top opened onto the short, unfamiliar passage. *Which way*?

Then, shouting from the right, 'I don't know how you did it you meddling fools!'

Grandad!

Jess couldn't make out the replying voice, but she had her suspicions.

As she neared the corner she recognised two things: One, the corridor leading off this one — it definitely led to the control room. And two, Matthew's voice calling her grandfather all sorts of names.

'I'll never forget this,' her grandfather roared.

As she rounded the corner, she saw the boys. Matthew stood confidently in front of the captain, who looked positively ill. *This is better than good. The boys are both fine and it looks like we're winning*.

'You mark my words!' Her grandfather shook his fist.

She shoved Matthew out of the way and stood in front of him, hands trembling with a mixture of anger and fear.

'No Granddad,' she whispered, suddenly feeling light headed. Then, she leaned in close so that only he could hear her. '*I'll* never forget this. And remember . . . the boys and I . . . we can change anything we like. And we have. More than once. So, *you* mark my words. Watch. Your. Back.'

28

Things were well under way when the children entered the control room on Monday morning. All three were happy to accept any consequences given for missing school.

Ludo filled them in. ‘We landed Freedom 2 at 1:36 am. A small human crew of six boarded the ship within the first half hour, for a short briefing. The rest of the staff, more than two thousand, I believe, boarded an hour ago.’ Ludo rubbed his bony hands together with glee. ‘And you, my friends, are here just in time because we’re ready to start loading the passengers.’

The children looked on in excited anticipation. A large screen had indeed been erected to show the survivors, as they climbed through a temporary, alien made, jet bridge. The jet bridge had been joined, at one end, to the solid rock at the mouth of the cave. At the other end, it connected neatly to Freedom 2, creating a perfect seal. Dozens of flights of steps led from the caves, directly into the ship. At first, Matthew’s heart leapt with the expectation of seeing the survivors. After the first few people, though, the rest became a blur. Partly because the camera only showed the top of people’s heads from its position in the roof, and partly due to the ferocious blast of cooled air being sent through to maintain the temperature inside

By lunchtime, Pete had had enough. ‘This is giving me a headache,’ he complained. ‘I need to get out of here.’

Jess waved Ludo over. ‘How much longer?’ she asked.

‘We’re nearly half way now. Probably another three or four hours, give or take.’

‘What time will Freedom 2 launch?’ Matthew asked. ‘We don’t want to miss it.’

Mah-jong joined them. A large elastic band secured the captain’s head-set to his ears. ‘Are you going somewhere?’ he inquired.

‘Only for some lunch and maybe a bit of fresh air.’

‘Take-off is scheduled for seven thirty. Be back here by seven and I’ll take you up onto the flight deck. We won’t be controlling the launch from there, Freedom 2 can manage that by themselves now. We will, however, have a fantastic view from there if I synchronise our visuals with theirs.’

‘We’ll be here,’ Mathew said.

‘Wouldn’t miss it,’ Jess agreed.

‘Now let’s eat!’ Pete reached for the door.

‘One last thing . . .’ Mah-jong stopped them. ‘It might be a good idea for you three to stick together until this is done. I don’t want to give Blackstone the opportunity to try anything risky.’

Once all three had agreed to stay together, Mah-jong let them past. ‘Seven o’clock then,’ he called after them. ‘Don’t be late!’

***

Stomachs satisfied, after managing both lunch and a speedy dinner in one day, the children hurried into a bustling control room ten minutes early.

‘Follow me!’ Mah-jong shouted, to be heard above the hubbub. He led the small group up the spiral staircase, through the changeling’s quarters and up again onto the flight deck.

Vast sheets of glass stretched from floor to ceiling on three sides of the room allowing the most spectacular view of a dense band of pale pink stars. In the distance, Matthew could just about make out the writing on two colossal Ships: Liberté 1 and Kalayaan 2. The fourth wall housed the control panel. An assortment of buttons and dials covered every inch of space, though on this occasion there were no lights.

Mah-jong indicated seats in the middle of the room and the children obediently sat.

‘Where is everyone?’ Matthew asked.

‘Ludo’s busy downstairs. I left him in charge. The rest of us are either working in the control room or sleeping. Many worked through the night you see.’

‘I mean, why is it empty in here?’

‘We’ve switched everything to automatic, just for an hour. I wanted you to see this in all its glory, without distractions.

Mah-jong casually made his way along the vast bank of controls, stopping intermittently to turn dials, flip switches and enter strange symbols into a golden keyboard.

Several beeps of random pitch sounded, followed by a computerised voice: ‘Visuals synchronising.’

‘What was that?’ Jess jumped out of her seat and pointed to the window on the right. ‘The stars just changed. Are we moving?’

‘No,’ Mah-jong chuckled. ‘Don’t panic. We are now looking at exactly the same view as Freedom 2. Doesn’t it look familiar?’ he continued. ‘It should. It’s the night sky as seen from Earth.’

‘Amazing!’ Pete exclaimed.

‘I see Orion,’ Jess gasped.

‘Oh, you know Orion — I have a second cousin who lives on a small planet in the orbit of Betelgeuse.’ Mah-jong mused as he sat down and patted the seat next to him. ‘Five minutes and counting; make yourselves comfortable.’

‘What about Blackstone?’ Matthew asked. ‘Where’s he in all this.’

‘We’ve decided he needs some help. Two vice captains to support him in his role as captain, at least one of whom must agree every decision that he makes from now on. One man should never have been given so much power. Tonight, he has the night off.’

They sat in silence, watching a large green count down display. With thirty seconds to go, the timer became red, and flashed in warning.

Matthew gripped the edge of his seat and stared, unblinking, at the stars.

Five . . . four . . . three . . . two . . . one . . .

The stars became streaks of light as Freedom 2 launched into space. Matthew leaned back and tried to take it all in.

'This is incredible!' Jess breathed.

Matthew opened his mouth, but couldn't find the words.

'I feel sick!' Pete covered his eyes, and then peeped through his fingers.

They sat there, immobilised by the spectacle before them. Three children and one small alien, together, allowing themselves to be hurled through the universe with the survivors on Freedom 2.

***

Over the next few weeks, there were many changes. Mah-jong forced the captain to make a public announcement during which he admitted making a terrible mistake in thinking everyone was dead. He explained his plan to save the survivors and surprisingly, instead of everyone loathing him for leaving the others behind for so long, the people thought of Blackstone as a hero. They shook his hand and congratulated him wherever he went.

One man, who wasn't fooled this time, was Mr Harper. After the dramatic rescue of his daughter, he'd taken time off work to spend with his family and hardly let Jess out of his sight since.

One Friday lunchtime, in June, Freedom 2 was successfully connected to Freedom 1. All passengers on board both ships were strapped into their harnesses. Captain Blackstone himself gave a speech welcoming the new passengers and inviting them to share everything. It was a wonderful speech that made Blackstone out to be a saint. It was a speech cleverly written by Mah-jong and his team and it ensured that Blackstone could never go back to his original plan.

Today, a day where families would be reunited and many more people celebrated being saved, Matthew felt truly happy. Things were finally working out well and he realised for the first time he'd found his place and been accepted by the people, and changelings, that mattered to him.

The human crew now worked alongside the changelings to create the chance of a future for many, many people. Matthew hoped that one day it would be possible to introduce the changelings to the entire population of the ship. They had considered doing this as part of Blackstone's speech, but then decided that there had been enough excitement for one day.

The Captain followed Mah-jong's orders to the letter for fear of losing the changelings' support before he was ready to fly the ship without them. He also insisted his crew worked with the changelings, to learn as much as possible about the ship as they could. Even Mr Harper treated Matthew differently since he and Pete had helped him save his daughter.

When they were finally allowed to remove their harnesses, Matthew left Pete to go in search of Steve. Everyone had been given the day off from work and school. A party had been promised, to celebrate the success of the mission. The passengers from both ships would come together on level 125. Matthew had only been there once, when they were putting together the map. It was an enormous banqueting hall, the size of Wembley stadium. When the halls from both ships were connected, there would be room for 50 thousand people, so the party would take place in shifts.

Finding lost relatives among so many people called for some serious organisation. Over the last few days, passengers on Freedom 2 had submitted the names of relatives they believed to have escaped all those months ago and those on Freedom one hoped and prayed for happy reunions.

The changelings gave everyone on both ships a coloured ticket. A meeting place had been set up, in the hope of reconnecting people with their loved ones before the party got started.

Food had been brought up from the kitchens and tables had been set around the edges of the hall, which was already crowded when the doors opened and the passengers from Freedom 2 spilled out into the room. Matthew searched for Steve in the crowds, but there were so many people that it was impossible to find him. He picked up a drink from the nearest table and waited.

People came and went all afternoon. Some blissfully happy, others disappointed. At three o'clock, purple tickets were called through. Matthew dug his out of his pocket and raced inside.

It took a long time for everyone to filter into the room. Matthew decided to wait somewhere near the door. That way, Steve would have to pass him there at some point, to enter the room. His stomach grumbled as he noticed that the tables in this room too, dipped under the weight of so much food.

It was getting difficult to move through so many people. Matthew still hadn't found Steve and wondered if maybe his brother was one of the first people to enter, before he had taken up his position by the door. He must have missed him.

Matthew made his way across the room towards one of the long tables to get some something to eat. As he leaned across the table to reach for a sausage roll, he felt a tap on his shoulder. Excitedly he turned, desperate to see his brother after such a long time and after so many adventures.

A smiling face greeted him.

'Matthew, how lovely to see you again,' said his mother, 'I thought something must have happened to you when you didn't come back to the house.'